In the
Shadow of Stone

A Novel

Rob Kaufman

For Those Who Believed in Me...
Way Before I Believed in Myself.

IN THE SHADOW OF STONE

1

When Jack Fontaine's sister asked him to fulfill her dying wish, he agreed without a moment's hesitation. It was a simple mission; one he thought would cost him nothing.

"I know we haven't been close, Jack," she said, looking so deeply into his eyes he felt she was grabbing his thoughts. "But I also know that you're the one person who can do this for me."

Except for the dim light above her head, the hospital room was cast in silhouette, a pervading darkness swallowing the numerous get well cards taped to the wall. Jack studied her face, trying to remember how she'd looked before. Over the past year her eyes had fallen deep into their sockets, creating a skeleton-like shadow above her cheeks. The skin of her face was stretched thin, the outline of her cheekbones deforming her face. Her mouth, where there'd once been voluptuous lips, was now a thin slit; when trying to smile, she looked more like a corpse than a living being.

Jack touched the back of his hand to her forehead, wiping away the mist of perspiration. "Of course, Dana," he said, his voice tight with emotion, "anything."

She turned her head away from him and looked to the door. A tear slid down the side of her face into the deep wrinkles lining her neck. She turned back to her brother. "You're very successful." She licked her dehydrated lips and tried to swallow. "And so organized. That's why I'm asking you to do this for me."

"Organized?" Jack forced a smile. "I think you mean obsessive compulsive, don't you?"

Her lips tightened into a faint smirk. "You're not compulsive," she whispered, turning away slightly.

Just obsessive, Jack thought, fighting himself not to read too deeply into her omission of words.

As though she sensed his struggle, Dana lifted her hand from the soaked bed sheet and let it fall on his arm. "You're great at everything you do, Jack. You know how to take control over any situation. That's why I know you'll be able to do what I need you to."

This was the first time in recent memory he'd received a compliment from her. For as long as he could remember she'd been so judgmental, so high and mighty, that he didn't realize she noticed his positive traits, let alone his success. He wanted to take hold of her thinning hair and pull it hard. "Why couldn't you tell me this before?" he wanted to scream, "while there was still time to rebuild our relationship?" Instead he continued wiping her forehead.

Her tongue slowly edged through her teeth to try to moisten her lips. "I made a DVD for Jenna," she whispered, "and I want you to keep it safe until her eighteenth birthday. I'd give the DVD to her father, but I know he'd either lose it or forget about it." She held his eyes with hers. "You know I love Glen, but there are some things I can't trust him with. He'll be a good father to Jenna, I'm sure of that. But I can't expect him to hold onto a DVD for ten years … it just won't happen. And I don't know if Mom and Dad will even be around in ten years." She stopped talking and looked at the ceiling. The realization that she was going to die before their parents struck them both at the same time. Her eyelids swelled with tears. "I know you'll be able to do this for me."

She blinked away her tears and cleared her throat. "I hid the DVD in the piano bench a few days before I came to the hospital. No one looks in there. I don't even think anyone realizes the bench opens. No one except you." She struggled with her tongue to keep it from sticking to the roof of her mouth.

"I got it," Jack said, taking the small cup of water from the nightstand and bringing it to her mouth. Unable to swallow the tepid liquid, she swirled it around her mouth and spit into the cup with a look of embarrassment. "It's okay," he whispered, the emotion holding back his full voice. "And I'll take care of the DVD for you."

She let her head drop back onto the pillow and closed her eyes. "One last thing," she said, her eyes still closed. "The DVD is for Jenna's eyes only. No matter what, she should be the only one to see it – and preferably alone on her eighteenth birthday, okay?"

She took a long, heavy breath and within seconds was in a deep sleep – without warning or effort. Jack placed the cup of water back on the nightstand and glanced at the clock. It was 3:30 AM and he was starting to feel the hour. He strolled over to the window, opened the blinds, and pressed his forehead against the cool glass. Stars glittered in the black sky, reminding him of the nights he and Dana had camped out in their backyard as children. "Star light, star bright," they'd say in unison, "first star I see tonight. I wish I may, I wish I might, have the wish I wish tonight." Staring at the brightest star in the sky they'd make their wish. Back then, Jack would always wish for friends. Dana, he figured, probably wished for a new baseball bat or catcher's mitt.

As she lay in the cold hospital bed on the edge of death, Jack wondered what Dana had wished for as an adult. He was certain it wasn't this.

The lights of Boston's skyscrapers blurred through his tears. Jack closed his eyes to squeeze out the teardrops so he could feel them on his face. He needed to know he was crying, to recognize the emotions he'd hidden for so long. He wanted to let everything out, cry until his eyes swelled, wiping the tears on his sleeve until the white cotton fabric was soaked. But only a single tear fell, the room so deathly quiet, he heard it hit the floor.

He picked the brightest star in the sky and made his wish, painfully aware he was already too late.

The sharp smell of hospital antiseptic pushed Jack's thoughts back twenty years to the nurse's office at Whitmore Junior High.

"Hop up on the table," Nurse Ann instructed, rubbing her hands together as if she were about to pluck a chicken. "Let's take a look."

Jack studied the gray hair piled on her head, the wrinkles around her eyes that made her look both happy and sad at the same time. She was Jack's picture of the perfect grandmother: a face filled with kindness and caring, misshapen fingers always fiddling with something and a rail thin body, slightly hunched over from years of catering to others. Jack wondered why she wasn't at home, rocking in a chair, knitting socks for the hoards of grandchildren he imagined visited her every Sunday.

"Up! Up!" she said again, patting the table behind him.

Trying not to crinkle the tissue paper covering the soft cushions,

Jack jumped onto the table, his feet dangling more than three feet from the floor. He watched the nurse carefully, noticing the precision with which she poured the clear liquid from the large brown bottle onto a cotton ball, squeezing the excess into the sink. By the way she slowed her pace as she walked toward him, he knew it was going to sting. Frantically, he tried flattening the tissue paper that crumpled on each side of him.

"Don't concern yourself with that ,Jack," she said, using her index finger to gently lift his head. "I need to make sure this doesn't get in your eye."

Before the cotton ball touched his broken skin, Jack flinched.

"Please, Jack. I need you to sit still." Her voice was stern, but still held the same warmth Jack had come to know all too well. "This cut is very close to your eye and we need to be very careful."

Jack clasped his hands and closed his eyes. Visions of the brawl he'd just escaped swarmed his thoughts as Nurse Ann softly dabbed the cotton ball on the cut. It didn't hurt as much as he thought it would.

"How did this happen?" she asked, grabbing a fresh cotton ball from the square glass container.

Jack opened his eyes and turned toward Dana who stood in the corner of the room, covering her left eye, then her right eye, trying to read the eye chart on the wall behind him. She gave him her typical I'll take care of this expression.

"He ran into a door again just as someone was opening it. He's such a nerd sometimes," Dana said, making faces behind the nurse's back.

Jack nodded his head. "A door," he mimicked.

But the lie didn't make him feel any better. He'd been humiliated again, the same way he'd been humiliated since school had started four months ago. The two most well-known bullies of the ninth grade had labeled him a nerd from the first day of school. It didn't matter that he was two years their junior; they'd pegged him the perfect target and let him know it: constantly surprising him from behind and pulling the pens and pencils from his shirt pocket or dumping his books as he walked home from school, making sure to leave a trail of crumpled notebook paper for him to pick up. The torment had become so routine Jack was astounded if a day went by without incident. He'd built his hurt into an invisible wall, resolving himself to the fact that he'd been chosen to bear the brunt of other people's anger.

But today's events had been different. There was pushing and shoving, cursing and pulling hair. When it started, Jack remembered thinking they must've had a bad morning and wondered if there was any way to soothe their souls before things got out of hand. He quickly found out there wasn't.

As he walked through the school cafeteria from recess, clipping his favorite pen to his shirt pocket, he suddenly heard snickering behind him. Before he could turn around, Jack and his books were sprawled out on the floor.

"Look," said Albert, the chubbier of the two, "his shirt's all dirty! Mr. Clean is dirty!"

His laughter cut through Jack like a sheet of ice. He darted his eyes around the room, searching desperately for a teacher, but it was just the three of them. Somehow he'd been left alone without adult supervision. At that moment he vowed never to forgive them, or himself, for allowing this to happen.

"Oh my," Frank said, using his tall, lanky form to pretend to dance, "and his pen fell out of his shirt. What's he gonna do? How's he gonna write?"

As Jack tried to grab the pen from the floor, a giant sneaker landed on his hand. He studied the sneaker, noticing ripped pieces of rubber swinging down its sides, deformed pendulums wiping against years of caked mud hiding in the crevasses. That's when he felt the tug on his hair, shocked into the realization that obsessing over a dirty sneaker shouldn't be his top priority.

He was facing the tile floor as the fingers gathered his hair and pulled his head so far back he could see the fluorescent lights flickering in the ceiling. About to scream, he heard a door slam. Albert released his hair so quickly Jack's head shot forward and hit the floor right below his right eye.

"You fat hunk of crap!" Jack heard Dana's voice coming from a place somewhere miles and miles away. "Why don't you pick on someone your own size?" There was no response. "If you can find someone your own size!"

The silence spilled through the room. Jack rolled onto his back to see Albert and Frank backing up into the exit doors with each deliberate step Dana took toward them.

"We were just kidding around," Albert said, sounding like an injured kitten.

They all knew who was in charge of the situation. Dana was the most popular girl in school, and the strongest. She'd taken karate for almost three years and was nimble and smart enough to make these boys suffer. And they knew it.

"If I ever see you doing this again, you'll regret it more than your parents regret having you as kids."

Seconds later, they were gone. Dana ran to Jack and examined the cut below his eye. She sighed as Jack tried desperately to smack the dirt from his pants.

"Will you not worry about that now, please! C'mon, I'll bring you to Nurse Ann. She's probably wondering why you haven't shown up for your daily visit."

Jack stamped his foot. "I don't go there every day! Take it back, Dana!" he screamed.

Placing her arm around Jack's shoulder, she helped him pick up his books and all his pens and his pencils.

"I take it back," Dana said, gently pulling him toward the nurse's office. "You're so much younger than they are. That's why they pick on you, you know." Jack nodded, the embarrassment too thick on his tongue to utter a sound. Dana squeezed his shoulder. "C'mon. Nurse Ann's probably worried by now."

Jack jumped off the table and ran his finger lightly against the band-aid. He turned around and smoothed the tissue paper that still held his indentation.

"Why are you doing that?" Nurse Ann asked, rubbing the top of his head.

Dana ran across the room and grabbed Jack's hand.

"He worries about those things," Dana sighed, "always does. I heard my parents say he has control issues."

Nurse Ann tilted her head and grimaced. "What do you mean?"

"Yeah," Jack questioned, "what do you mean?" It never occurred to him that he had an issue, not to mention his family had been talking about him behind his back.

"I'm not sure," Dana said to Nurse Ann, using her hands to iron out the air in front of her. "I do know that when everything's clean and neat and in its place, Jack's a lot happier. You should see how mad he gets when he comes into my messy room." She giggled, looked down at Jack and tousled his hair. "But I did hear my parents say that he'll grow out of it. I'm hoping it's sooner than later!"

Jack felt the last of his energy drain from his body and was unsure if he could make it through the rest of the day. He'd not only been beaten up by bullies and saved by his sister, of all people, but now he discovered he had an issue. His head started to hurt and all he wanted to do was go home. But he had no choice in the matter. Dana had already grabbed his hand and was pulling him out the door.

"Wait!" Nurse Ann yelled, grabbing the pen from behind her ear. "I'll write you a late pass so your teachers will know where you've been."

Jack and Dana were half way down the hall when Dana turned her head around and yelled, "I got it covered!"

And she did – Jack knew that better than anyone else. He tightened his grip on her hand and tried with all his might to hold back his tears. She rubbed her thumb against his sweaty palm, making Jack painfully aware of her special gift, something he'd searched for within himself but could never find. Dana had a way of knowing what a person was thinking and the ability to soothe their soul with a simple look or tender touch. It was a gift she'd share with all the people who came into her life. A gift she had so often shared with Jack, until the day she took it back and left him with empty hands and an aching heart.

Bars of light from the hospital parking lot crept through the vertical blinds along the ceiling above Dana's head. Jack watched the thin, white cotton sheet on her chest rise and fall with each shallow breath. Although she was only thirty-one years old, her illness made her look fifty; an appearance caused by the rampant white blood cells that had turned against her and run amok, killing her with every breath she took.

He'd tried to reconnect with her over the past year, asking for private meetings, opening dialogs to clear the air and cushion the blow of this very day. They'd met a few times and tried talking through their issues, but the meetings never worked out as planned. The hugs he'd imagined didn't come; the kisses and cries of forgiveness never materialized. Her belief that he betrayed her ran too deep, and she couldn't let it go.

The previous winter, in celebration of Jenna's eighth birthday, Dana and Glen threw a party complete with disc jockey, an orange-haired clown whose afro was three times too big for its head, and twenty-three screaming children. Although it was only the fifth of November, the New England chill brought with it sporadic bursts of snow showers. The small amounts of precipitation created more excitement for the guests than the clown's red, honking nose or the limitless supply of balloon-twisted animals.

When everyone was gone, and the house quieted, Jenna sat on Jack's lap in the living room, begging him to read to her. Dana and Glen were sneaking some wine and cleaning the kitchen. Jack snatched up the book she received as a gift from her grandparents: A Big Girl Now. As he read to Jenna, she picked at her toes through her sheer, white cotton socks and played with the buttons on his yellow Polo shirt. After reading a few pages, it was obvious the book didn't interest either of them and he closed it with a snap.

"You don't like this book, do you?" he asked.

"Nope," she quickly responded, still twirling the buttons on his shirt.

Her shiny blond hair was messy from a day of cake, play and constant motion. Her bangs fell over her eyes and she swept them away with the back of her hand. He looked at her face and caught her big blue eyes staring at his nose. "Go ahead," he said with a smile. She pinched the tip of his nose. "Honk… Honk." He made the sound of a car's horn. She squeezed it again. "Honk… Honk." She squeezed it again. "Okay, I think that's enough," he said, wanting to make her happy but not willing to jeopardize his appearance.

"How old are you?" she asked, in her 'too smart for her own good' tone.

"Twenty-eight. That's old, right?"

"Yeah." She started picking at her toes again. "Why don't you have a wife? Why won't you get married?"

Jack felt his heart skip a beat, the same skip he felt when his parents had asked him a similar question two years before. He wasn't sure if Jenna would be able to absorb what he had to say and also knew Dana had wanted to explain the situation to her only daughter when the time was right. A time Jack was convinced would be too late. By then, Jenna would already have her prejudices ingrained and he wouldn't stand a chance.

Laughter and clanking dishes from the kitchen told him Dana and

Glen were enjoying their wine and putting the plates into the dishwasher. He felt the sudden urge to tell Jenna who he was, allowing her to learn to love him regardless.

"Why won't I get married?" he repeated her question, thinking the answer through as he spoke. "Well, I might get married one day, Jenna. But it probably won't be to a wife."

She squinted her eyes, now playing with her fingers to make the church, the steeple and all the people. "What do you mean? Don't you HAVE to marry a wife?"

His heart fluttered. This was it. Spill it or get off the pot, he thought.

"Well, sometimes, men marry men." Her fingers stopped moving and she dropped her hands to her side. She looked up at him with bewilderment. "What do you mean?"

"I mean," he cleared his throat and wrapped his arm around her tiny waist, "there are some men who would rather marry men than woman. There are also some women who would rather marry women instead of men. It's a little complicated and you might be a little young to understand, but one day you will. And I want you to know that no matter who I decide to marry, I will always love you the most."

Jenna wrapped her arms around his neck and kissed his cheek. She didn't say a word or make a sound. He felt she already knew who he was and loved him anyway. As he hugged her, he caught a glimpse of Dana standing in the doorway with her arms folded. Every muscle in Jack's body tensed. He instinctively tightened his grip on Jenna when Dana unhooked her arms and clapped her hands.

"Come on, Jen," she said softly, "time to clean up."

Jenna kissed his cheek and hopped off his lap. Too frightened to say anything, Jack stood up and grabbed his parka from the piano bench, an inner uneasiness telling him it was time to go.

"Jack, no, stay," Dana said. The words resonated like a command to a dog: Sit. Stay. Fetch. "I want to talk to you."

Jack threw his coat on top of the piano and fell onto the bench. The riot act was about to be read – he heard it in her voice; saw it in her face; felt it in the space between them.

Glen appeared behind Dana, holding an empty wine glass.

"Dana," he said, "let it go, please."

Dana shot Glen a look. She didn't need to say a word to be understood.

He offered Jack a look of apology on behalf of his wife, put the wine glass beside Jack's coat, and took Jenna's hand. Although he knew Glen wouldn't stand up to Dana, Jack didn't want him to leave, fearful of being left alone with her wrath. "C'mon, Jenna," he said, his voice barely audible. "Time to take your bath."

For a moment, Jenna studied the floor and then looked into Jack's eyes. She waved her hand and said, "Bye-bye, Uncle Jack," Jack smiled at her and watched them walk up the stairs.

Dana plopped down into the brown suede, high-back chair. Looking like a queen on her throne, she crossed her legs and glared at Jack. "What were you doing just now?"

"What are you talking about?"

"I leave you alone with her for five minutes and you're talking about… about your lifestyle. I told you a thousand times I'll take care of that. She's too young to understand these things." The shrillness in her voice sent a shiver up his back. "When the time is right, I'll talk to her about it. I want her to know what's right and what's wrong about it."

The empty feeling in Jack's stomach spread to his chest and he took a deep breath. He wiped his hands on his khakis and gave a slight cough to fill the silence. At that moment he decided that all the years of self-loathing where his sister was concerned were going to end. For once, speaking his mind was more important than keeping the peace.

"What's right about it and what's wrong about it... are you kidding me? Are you out of your mind?" By her growing expression of anger, he knew he had chosen the wrong words. "You tell me, Dana, what's wrong with it? What's wrong with who I am?"

Dana uncrossed her legs and folded her arms again – her defensive posture at its best. He'd seen it before and he could feel the hair on the back of his neck slowly rising. "I didn't say anything's wrong with who you are, Jack. But it's up to me to explain these things to Jenna. I asked you not to talk to her about it, ever. You betrayed my trust. It's a very sensitive matter and..." She repeated herself, "You betrayed my trust, Jack. She's my daughter and I don't want her getting the wrong ideas about these things."

Jack slid his coat off the piano and stood. She'd finally verbalized what she'd been thinking since the day she discovered the truth about him and he wasn't about to let it go.

"Too late, Dana. It's out. You already said it – there's something wrong with the way I live, with who I am. Not who I've chosen to be, mind you, but who I am. You've always said it was fine, acting as though it didn't bother you. But you know, I'm a little more perceptive than that. I can see it in your face when I talk about a man I've met or the way your head jerks when I mention I'm going away for the weekend with someone. I can even hear it in your voice when I try to talk to you about my heartbreaks. And now, it finally comes out. You think there's something wrong with me and you don't want Jenna to have any part of it."

Jack was almost at the front door when he paused, hoping she'd call him back and apologize. But she hadn't moved since he had started to speak, didn't argue with a word he said. She was using her typical strategy and he'd stepped into her trap, saying aloud what she'd always wanted to tell him but never had the guts to. With every word he spoke, she nodded in agreement without making a sound.

He touched the doorknob and paused again, hearing the familiar rationalization inside his head: She likes me as a person, she just disapproves of my lifestyle… sure, that has to be it. Two separate things… person, lifestyle. Yeah, that's it. She loves me, but hates who I am. I can live with that.

He knew that walking out the door would cut his ties with Jenna, the one pure thing he'd ever let into his heart. He was in the midst of making the decision when Dana finally spoke.

"Yes, there's something wrong with it, okay?" She rose from the chair. "But you're still my brother."

"I'm still your brother?" He echoed her tone. "What the hell does that mean?" He lowered his voice to keep it from reaching Jenna's room on the second floor. "I would think you'd say, 'That doesn't mean I don't love you', or 'That doesn't mean I think you're a bad person.' Wouldn't that make more sense?" Finally it hit him. To Dana, their relationship was obligatory. Family is family. Even if you don't like or respect each other, you should still stick together. Not out of love, compassion, or decades of sharing lives. No. It was all about familial relationship – she would tolerate him because he was her brother, but that's where it ended. He put his hands on his hips, waiting for a response. There wasn't one.

He was still in her trap, spilling her thoughts for her, exposing the truth behind the emotional distance she'd exhibited since he came out of the closet. Instinctively, he lifted his foot, stepping out of the steel trap she'd set. He opened the door and felt the November wind slash his face, a sharp frostiness that hurt and comforted him at the same time.

"I got it, Dana," Jack said. "It all makes sense now." He searched her face, still hoping she'd cross the distance between them, wrap her arms around him and apologize. Maybe she'd weep on his shoulder and tell him she loved him, no matter who he was or what he did. But all he could see were the dark circles beneath her eyes. "Yeah, it all makes sense now."

Jack walked out onto the front porch and slammed the door behind him. His eyes filled with tears and he could feel the warm drops falling down his cheeks. He lowered his head and walked down the steps, the frigid night air feeling warmer against his skin than the biting wind inside the house.

A gentle tapping sound stirred Jack from his thoughts. Turning away from the window, he saw his mother peering through the narrow opening of the hospital room door. Her hand was cupped over her eyes, trying to make sense of the shadows. Jack smiled, waved, and tiptoed around Dana's bed to join her in the hallway.

The bright lights overpowered his sense of sight and he squinted to adjust his eyes. He felt the warmth of his mother's hand on his cheek and let his face fall into it. With her other hand, she pulled the back of his head onto her shoulder, neither of them making a sound. He suddenly felt like a child again, holding onto his mother after his latest confrontation at school, feeling her affection protecting him against all that was evil and hurtful in the world. He started to give in to the emotion and quickly pulled back with the realization he was now an adult and should be taking care of her.

"Where's Dad?" he asked, wiping the tears from her face.

"He's with Glen, getting some coffee." Her eyes seemed bleary, distant, the thready veins reddening the whites of her eyes. "How did things go?"

"Fine. Everything's fine," he replied.

"That makes me happy," she whispered, wiping her nose with a shredded tissue. "Very happy."

Since his last argument with Dana, his parents had attempted to help patch the rift. Playing both sides of the fence was difficult, but they'd attempted to repair the foundation of their family without walking over the fine line of intrusion. With subtle comments and frequent recommendations, they tried to strengthen the bond that Dana and Jack had once had – or, as Jack often thought – the bond he thought they had.

"I need to turn her now," the nurse said, slipping between them and pushing her back against the door. "I'll let you know as soon as I'm done." She offered a compassionate smile and disappeared into the room. Jack put his arm around his mother and gently led her down the empty hallway.

Jack sat with his parents and Glen in one corner of the waiting room, about forty feet from Dana's room. Glen worked on his latest proposal, his leather-bound pad on his lap, his pen in his mouth. His parents, Lisa and John, whispered to one another about nothing, trying to fill the empty moments. Jack watched the scene from a great distance, an inner chill creating a warm, clammy mist over his entire body that stuck his shirt to his skin.

Fanning himself with the Boston Globe's business section, Jack focused in on the pocket protector clipped to his father's shirt. It held three pencils with full, clean erasers and three identical pens that glimmered with the fluorescence from above. Jack felt a jolt in the pit of his stomach and threw out the words, ignoring the voice inside that tried to stop him.

"Why are you wearing that?" he said, pointing to the pocket protector.

John moved his hand up his shirt to the protector, eventually massaging the tip of each pen.

"What? This?" he asked, patting the hard plastic.

"Yes. That." Jack's voice was mechanical, like a frustrated robot.

"In case I need to write something." He looked beside him at Lisa and shrugged his shoulders.

Jack rolled his eyes. "Dad, you've been retired for ten years. What the hell do you need to write? A shopping list? The title of the next matinee you're going to see? I mean why do you need that thing?"

"Jack!" Lisa tried to keep her voice below a whisper. "This is neither the time nor the place! Leave your father alone."

Jack leaned back in his chair, fanning himself with more zest than it required. He looked at Glen. When their eyes met, Glen looked away and started to write on his pad.

"God! You wonder why I'm so neurotic – why I always need to be prepared, why everything has to be in its place. Look at his pocket! That's where it all started."

Lisa glanced around the room and angled herself away from the other visitors.

"Jack! Keep your voice down." She turned to John. His arms were crossed against his chest, hiding his pocket protector. "You're twenty-eight years old. You're a big time advertising executive. You have a very good life. Start enjoying what you have! And don't you dare blame your father or me for your issues. You're old enough to make your own decisions and change the things you're not happy with. Leave us out of your personal problems." She looked down the hall towards Dana's room. "Especially now."

John leaned forward and placed his hand on Jack's knee. "Where is this coming from?"

Jack didn't have a response and was not about to use the remaining strength he had left to figure it out. What he did know was that the urge to lash out at someone pulled at him from somewhere deep inside, a dark place filled with winged phantoms. He looked to the floor and studied the crumbs caught between the tile cracks. The walls were closing in; the smells were too sterile. He needed to escape but couldn't. Like everyone else in the room, he was waiting for something – perhaps the morning light to awaken the sleepless souls; maybe an angel to break the chains that restrained him to the chair, holding him captive in a building bleached of both color and hope.

When he looked up, the nurse who they'd left only minutes before stood behind Glen. From the look on her face, Jack knew the angel had arrived and his inner screaming begged her to disappear.

"She's gone," the nurse said, looking down at Glen with a sad smile. "I'm sorry."

"She's gone?" Jack said aloud, testing the words. She's gone? His thoughts were a blur and he couldn't latch onto one in particular. Where did she go? he almost shouted. China? Illinois? Back home? Where did she go? How did she get there? Did she take a bus? A train? Did she fly? What do you mean she's GONE?

He looked at the others: his parents who'd just lost their first born child; Glen, whose lover and best friend of ten years had just surrendered her soul. Their expressions told Jack exactly what the nurse meant.

Two doctors in stark white coats passed by, arguing about last night's Patriots game; a lab tech hurried past with a rolling basket of tubes filled with blood and other mysterious liquids; a Pink Lady delivered the morning newspaper to the nurse's station. Jack watched the morning begin, as it did every day, except this time they would pass by Dana's room as they delivered their goods to the living – patients who would one day leave the hospital and continue on with their lives. And then there were the others, the patients who lay waiting until their turn came to take the same journey as Dana – to China or Illinois, or maybe, back home.

2

Wearing a pair of skimpy Calvin Klein briefs, Jack pressed his arm against the floor-to-ceiling window and rested his head against the back of his hand. A hint of sunlight brought a soothing glow to the Charles River below, thin ridges of liquid rippling across the surface of the water.

It was almost 6:30 in the morning and Jack could hear the faint hum of the ferry motors from Long Wharf Harbor preparing for the mindless trek across the river to Hingham, Provincetown, and Deer Island. Passengers would sip their morning coffee, reading the Boston Globe or reviewing notes they'd use as cue cards for their first meeting of the day. Others would carry picnic baskets and binoculars, looking forward to a day filled with whale watching and New England history.

Gazing over the water, Jack considered these travelers lucky. Although it was mid-September, the temperature wasn't expected to fall below seventy-five and the calm water meant a fast, even ride for both commuters and sightseers. But that was only a small piece of their luck. Today they'd breathe the fresh, crisp New England air. It was a day some of the passengers would recall with great fondness, while others wouldn't be able to set it apart from any other day in their lives. Unfortunately, Jack knew he'd remember this day forever – a day of sadness and remorse filled with events and people he wanted no part of.

"Hey," he heard the half-whisper from the bed, "why you up so early?"

Jack jumped away from the window, startled from his thoughts. He turned toward the bed, stretching both arms above his head. "I couldn't sleep." He shuffled back to bed and crawled beneath the goose down comforter. "Too many thoughts."

A deep orange glow from the rising sun entered the bedroom and he could see the soft outline of Marc's face. Even at this early hour, Marc's eyes were wide and bright, his preppy haircut still perfectly groomed. Jack reached across the feather pillows and touched Marc's cheek, slowly moving his fingers across his nose, down his chin and along the jaw line. Marc's features were flawless: Patrician nose, high cheekbones, the sharp curve of his upper lip. He had the look of a New England Wasp, someone who should sleep until noon, with servants at his beck and call, horses being groomed for a day of polo. But that wasn't Marc Whittaker at all. He didn't have the wealth or the personality to match his looks. In fact, it was not only Marc's striking looks, but also his ability to raise himself up from the lowest rung of society that had Jack yearning for him from the moment he walked in his office six months earlier.

It was Jack's fourth interview of the day and he was growing weary. Although each copywriter candidate had provided top-rate samples, Jack had concerns about their ability to fit in with his team. They had all been talented enough, but each had an air of competitiveness about them, an attitude he was certain would not work with his current group of writers and designers.

As VP of Creative Services at the second largest advertising agency in Boston, Johnson and Macrae, Jack knew his duties consisted of more than simply producing the best direct-marketing campaigns. He was also responsible for forty employees, a team of creative people who needed to be content, excited and driven every single day. He'd created a dynamic, cohesive force that would only accept others like themselves and they counted on Jack to keep the flow of energy in a positive direction.

"Are you competitive?" Jack asked Marc. He placed the resume on the neatly stacked pile of papers and used his desk to push back his chair.

Marc closed his eyes as though he was preparing to recite poetry. When he opened them, he looked directly into Jack's stare. "Yes and no," he said, and left it at that, still looking into Jack's eyes.

Jack stared back, unsure how to respond. "Can you expand on that a little?"

"I'm competitive with myself, I guess," Marc said. "I need to know that I've done my best possible work before I submit it. I'd be competitive with other ad agencies that were going after the same account as J&M, but I wouldn't be competitive with the people I work with. I'd count on them to help me do the best job possible."

This is too good to be true, Jack thought. He rolled his chair back toward his desk, pulled Marc's resume from the stack and studied it closer.

"I don't see any agency experience here. If you haven't worked in the advertising arena, where did these writing samples come from?"

"I made them up," Marc said. He shifted positions a few times and Jack felt his self-consciousness. "Some I wrote at the university, others I created while pretending to work at an agency." He again squeezed his eyes closed, oddly longer, Jack thought, than the typical blink. "I know it sounds weird, but I haven't had the opportunity to get actual agency experience because people don't want to give someone without experience a chance. It's a catch twenty-two."

Jack nodded, his mind wandering to places he typically never allowed it go during the work day – Marc's smooth skin, his dark brown eyes, his subtle self-conscious demeanor. This would definitely be too dangerous, Jack thought to himself. He felt a peculiar yearning, something much stronger than what he'd felt during the three one-night stands he'd had over the past year – the two-hour relationships that allowed him the physical contact he needed while keeping his emotions surfing above the sheets. Life had been working out well for him this way – using ninety-eight percent of his energy trying to make J&M the number-one agency. But there was something going on in the space between him and Marc and as hard as he tried, Jack couldn't let it go.

As if he were reading his thoughts, Marc widened his eyes and smiled. Jack returned his focus to the interview, glancing back down to Marc's resume.

"I see you live in Little Italy, one of my favorite parts of town. And not too far from here."

"Yes," Marc sighed.

It was obvious Marc didn't want to discuss his living arrangements. Jack continued to scan his resume. He noticed the residence listed under "previous address" showed Chelsea, a city considered one of the poorest in Massachusetts.

"Did you grow up in Chelsea?" he said, immediately aware he'd asked the wrong question. Marc turned away and looked out the giant window. Jack waited a few more seconds for a response. The silence continued. "It has nothing to do with your qualifications, Marc. Your writing is outstanding and your education just as impressive. It was a harmless question." Jack straightened the papers on his desk. "Or at least I thought it was harmless."

"I'm sorry," he said, turning back toward Jack. "It's just something I'm not very proud of. I shouldn't have even put it on my resume."

His cheeks held a slight blush and his eyes shone with a hint of sadness, pulling on a heartstring Jack hadn't known existed. In an instant of weakness, tired of pushing away anything that might make him feel good, he decided to give Marc Whittaker a try. He'd wait a week before delivering the good news, needing the time to set the boundaries and build the invisible wall to separate his work life from his personal life. A wall that would crumble within a month after Marc started working for him.

"Are you sure I can't go with you today?" Marc wiped his eyes with the palms of his hands. "It's your sister's funeral, for God's sake. I want to go. I want to be there for you."

Jack propped his pillows against the headboard and caught sight of his reflection in the mirror above the bureau. He tried pushing down the tuft of hair standing straight up from the back of his head, but it was useless. It seemed to have a life of its own. With both hands, he touched the skin beneath his eyes; the dark brown irises melted into the shadowy semi-circles, making it appear as though he had nothing but sockets.

"I look like shit," he whispered, rubbing his eyes with the palm of his hand. "I have bags under my eyes, I look like Alfalfa, my skin is—

"

"You're gorgeous," Marc interrupted, sliding his hand down Jack's cheek. "You're always gorgeous. Look at that thick black hair. Those long lashes. Those beautiful lips." He slid his palm onto Jack's chest and sighed. "And these muscles are rock solid. Your skin's so soft, your arms are—"

Jack grabbed Marc's hand and laughed. "Okay, I got it. I'm beautiful. Let it go."

"Great. Now can I go with you today?"

He'd like nothing more than to have Marc attend the funeral – someone to lock eyes with when the going got tough, a life raft to climb into when his emotions ran too high. But he knew it wasn't possible, too much was at stake. His relationship with Marc was pushing the line of corporate ethics and they could both suffer heavy consequences should their relationship become public.

"Marc, I told you already that it's too dangerous, especially because David Macrae will be there. He might be my friend, but he's also the CEO. If he thinks something's up, I'm screwed."

Marc scrunched his pillow, bringing his head closer to Jack's. "Jack, you're a VP with a staff of forty. I would think you'd be allowed to do what you want. You've earned it."

"That's the point, Marc. I busted my ass to get where I am. I might have everyone's respect now, but in the end, it really doesn't matter. J&M is a rumor mill and people will grab onto anything they can and turn it into a sordid mess. I've already been there and I don't want it to happen again."

Jack grimaced, remembering two years earlier when he'd gotten the promotion to vice president. His colleagues knew this was a huge responsibility for someone so young, but the Board of Directors was convinced that Jack could handle the position. Within a few months of acquiring his new title, he felt comfortable enough to restructure the entire Marketing Services Division and hire the talent he knew J&M required for success. After the restructuring, productivity increased three-fold and new client acquisition was at an all-time high. Word spread throughout the advertising community that Jack was the hot ticket and art directors, copywriters and even administrative assistants from all over the New England area were vying for the opportunity to work for the man who'd helped make J&M the number-two agency in Boston.

He'd proven himself, day after day, month after month, and it was apparent to most that his promotion was well deserved – except for a few employees who steamed with jealousy as he'd passed them on his way up the ladder. They spread rumors about Jack and David – fictitious stories about a personal relationship and seedy sexual encounters. Unable to believe that he reached his VP status on merit alone, the envious few passed along their gossip with such fervor and veracity that Jack and David were forced to hold strategy meetings, hoping to stop the rumors before they reached the Boston Globe or Advertising Age. It didn't matter that David was a fifty-four-year-old man, married for over two decades, with two grown children and a beautiful home in the suburbs of Scituate. Or that Jack was considered a great catch among the legions of single women (and some men) at J&M. The rumors spread like wild fire and the two men knew they had to take action.

"At this point we have two options," David said, slapping his palms on the mahogany boardroom table, "We can react with honey or vinegar. It's our choice."

"Honey or vinegar? You mean, we can promote the assholes to shut them up or fire them and sue them for libel and slander?"

David nodded, his full head of silver-gray hair bouncing with the motion.

"I choose vinegar!" Jack shouted. "These people suck. They're liars. They're making up stories because they're envious. We have to teach them a lesson!"

"It's your age." David laughed, "When you're in your twenties, it's all about vinegar. Trust me, honey works a lot better."

"But, David, it'll be like we're giving in to blackmail. We're telling them they're right when they're not. We're letting them win when there's no basis to their accusations. They have no right doing what they're doing and I want them to pay."

David nodded in agreement, all the while sketching out the new organizational chart on a legal pad. "I know, Jack," he said, his expression, as always, exuding self- control and limitless patience, "but we have a business to run and profits to make. We can't have a scandal here and let the envious few jeopardize what we've worked so hard for. Justice will come in time. For now, we have to give them what they want."

Jack slammed his fist on the table and forced a breath through his tightened lips. His eyes burned as he watched David draft the organizational chart, placing upward arrows beside the boxes that held the names of Jack's new enemies. "It's better this way," David said, "have patience. It will all work out."

David's plan worked like magic. Within a week after they announced the promotions, the rumor mill shut down as though someone flipped a switch and turned off the power. Chitchat at the water cooler returned to the mundane: pain-in-the-ass clients, the building's climate, and cafeteria menus. The honey had sweetened things up for the moment, and J&M returned to the business at hand. But, at times, Jack's resentment nearly overwhelmed him and it took a lot of self-control to stop it from eating him up inside.

With Jack's success also came constant recognition and pay raises. He used his new level of income to buy things he felt would make him happy and fill the nagging void within: a recently built loft in a trendy south-end neighborhood, a BMW Roadster, designer clothes, the latest in digital audio and computer equipment, high-tech kitchen appliances, and anything else that would fill his insatiable need. Within a few months of his promotion, Jack had every tangible item he'd ever wished for, everything money could buy, and yet he still felt emptiness, a longing for something he couldn't quite put his finger on – until the following spring when Marc arrived for his interview.

"I'm really sorry, Marc, but you just can't show up with me today," Jack said, smoothing Marc's pencil-thin eyebrows. "I'd love you to be there, you know that. But if David sees you there, he'll get suspicious. We're doing something…" He closed his eyes. "I'm doing something I shouldn't be doing. If anyone finds out about us, it'll all be over." Beneath the blanket, Jack crossed his arms and wrapped his hands around his finely-toned biceps. "Once this day is over, we're going to have to figure something out. I want you in my life more than anything, but I can't continue to risk losing my position at J&M. I've worked too hard."

Marc lifted the feather-filled covers and moved closer to Jack, laying his hand on Jack's chest and sharing his pillow. He closed his eyes and let his head rest on Jack's shoulder.

"I understand." Marc sighed, rubbing his lips against the curve of Jack's neck. "But I'll be thinking about you the whole day."

Jack laced his fingers within Marc's so their hands were entwined. It was all he could do not to ask Marc to move in with him, to share his life. But his compulsive logic seeped through, dictating that he'd have to wait until he developed a working plan.

Gently rubbing Marc's hand with his thumb, Jack thought how soft it was, how his fingers were so delicate, so thoughtful. It was no surprise to him that the fingers he caressed could not only write such intensely stirring copy for some of J&M's biggest clients, but could also compose the groin-tingling notes of passion Jack would find every so often in his desk drawer or the side pocket of his briefcase.

Slowly, Marc slid his hand down Jack's smooth, hard stomach and under the elastic waistband of his briefs. Jack closed his eyes and took a deep, quivering breath. This is the hand of a great writer.

For the first time in over a year, Jack sat in Jenna's bedroom. A swift pang of guilt ran through him. With Dana gone, he now had open access to Jenna, and yet he felt he was committing a crime.

He'd seen Jenna only twice during the year before Dana's death: at a family gathering his parents had assembled with the futile hope of repairing the familial tear and through a chance meeting at Fanueil Hall during Boston's July 4th celebration.

Through the mob of sightseers, Jack and Jenna were the first to see each other and instinctively ran to one another. Jack knelt down and Jenna threw her arms around his neck, not a word passing between them. They held onto each other tightly, both fearing Dana would physically pry them apart before they'd had the chance to connect. But Dana stood back, allowing them to swap stories and sorely missed kisses, while the throngs of people passed, shoving the newly reunited aside.

Moments later Jack felt a hand on his shoulder. He glanced up to see Marc standing above him, awaiting an introduction. With all the excitement of seeing Jenna, Jack had forgotten he'd been waiting for Marc to return from the bathroom. He stood up, his hand still on Jenna's head, his eyes darting to Dana's face, gauging her reaction. She gave Marc a polite smile, quickly looking away into the crowd. The introductions were hurried; few words passing between them as the level of discomfort increased with each passing moment. Dana offered a half-smile, nodded to Glen and grabbed Jenna's hand, leading them into the throng of passersby.

Still kneeling, Jack watched his family walk away and fought back his rising emotions. Jenna turned and waved to him. He waved back and through his watery eyes recognized the familiar smile that made its way into his dreams at least once a week. He felt Marc's fingers rubbing the top of his head and could do nothing but take a deep breath and slide his sunglasses up to hide the tears.

Now, sitting on Jenna's bed, Jack wondered if Dana could see them, if she now understood and approved of his life. He stroked a one-eared, stuffed bunny and scanned the Crayola sketches taped to the wall. "That's a nice one, Jenna," Jack said, pointing to a drawing above her mirror, a colorful sketch with three stick figures and a yellow-filled sun bleeding off the bottom of the page. Jack wondered if the sun was rising or setting. "Is that you with Mommy and Daddy?"

"Yup," she said, sitting on her pillow, playing with the pink ribbon tied to the end of her long braid. "That's heaven. And that's me and Daddy with Mommy. It's my favorite."

Jack swallowed, trying to push down the growing lump in his throat. "It's my favorite too." Unsure if he'd said the words aloud, he repeated himself. "It's my favorite too."

Sitting in the quiet of her room, the sound of hushed conversations drifted upstairs from the living room. The voices were a blur of noise, but Jack could pretty much figure out the main topic. He wanted to sit with Jenna all day, away from the mourners, separated from the blank faces of strangers, some marred with tracks of mascara running down their cheeks, others with nothing but expressions of pity. He didn't want Jenna exposed to such sadness, worried it would steal away the tiny bit of joy she had left.

A knock on the door broke the silence.

"Come in," Jack said. He and Jenna looked to the door.

"Hi," Glen said softly, his eyes swollen from sadness and insomnia. "Sorry to bother you, but David Macrae's downstairs."

Jack turned to Jenna and wrapped his hand around her thin ankle. "David's my boss, Jenna. It was very nice of him to come and I have to say hello. Would you like to come with me?"

Jenna shook her head and slid down the pillow. She took the bunny from Jack's hand and hugged it to her chest.

"It's okay," Glen whispered, taking Jack's place on the bed. "I'll stay with her awhile."

Jack placed his hand on Glen's shoulder and gently squeezed it.

"I'll be right back, Jenna," Jack whispered. He walked into the hall and was halfway down the stairs when he heard Glen call his name. Jack turned. Standing on the top step, Glen peered at Jack, his hand wrapped tightly around the wooden banister.

"Are you okay, Glen?" Jack asked, meeting him on the landing.

"Yes, I'm fine. I just wanted to say something." Glen looked to the floor and then the ceiling, fighting to hold back the tears. Jack rubbed Glen's arm.

"What is it, Glen? What's going on?"

Glen cleared his throat and looked Jack in the eyes.

"You know I loved Dana more than anything in this world," said Glen. Jack nodded, wondering where this was going. "But we had our disagreements like any married couple — especially when it came to you." Jack glanced over the landing at the crowd of mourners below and saw David standing against the living room wall. He turned back to Glen. "I just wanted you to know that I never felt anything was wrong with your lifestyle. You're a great person. You love Jenna to death and she loves you. That's all that matters."

Jack gave a hard swallow, trying to keep the growing lump in his throat as far down as possible. Glen continued, pulling Jack in with emotions Jack never knew Glen possessed. "I tried to talk to her about it, I can't tell you how many times. But she wouldn't budge. It's not that she didn't love you. She did. She told me that over and over again."

"It's okay, Glen. Don't worry —"

36

"No Jack, I want to say this. I actually think she acted like she did because she felt bad for you, knowing you'd never live the kind of life she – and you – had imagined. I don't think it was you she had the problem with, I think it was the injustice of the whole situation."

Jack stepped nearer to Glen and wrapped his arms around him. He felt Glen's hands on his back, squeezing him closer, as though trying to absorb the part of Jack that, as a brother, he'd shared with Dana. "I loved her," he whispered in Jack's ear.

"I know you did," Jack whispered back. "And thank you for telling me this. It means a lot to me."

Glen straightened his back and pulled away from Jack, wiping the tears from the lapel of his suit jacket.

"Okay," Glen shook his head, still weak with emotion, "I've got to get back to Jenna."

Jack smiled, letting his hand glide down Glen's arm. They walked to Jenna's room together and caught her humming a lullaby. When she looked up, she didn't smile or say a word. She just continued to hum as Glen pulled her into his chest and started to hum with her.

Jack closed the door and walked down the stairs, trying to gain some composure. At least fifty people milled around, filtering through the rooms. Many of the children were sitting in the family room watching a Disney movie play on the muted television. Jack caught sight of David's gray hair and slithered through the guests, receiving kisses and pats on the back as he made his way. David stood by himself and gave a relieved smile when he saw Jack heading towards him.

"Hey, David, thanks for coming." Jack snuck his hand behind the back of a man he thought was Glen's brother and grabbed David's hand. David took Jack's hand and pulled him close. With his other hand around Jack's shoulder, he gave him an awkward hug.

"I'm sorry, Jack," David whispered. When he released Jack, he took a sip of his water and cleared his throat. "I wanted to stop by and pay my respects."

Jack noticed a bead of sweat falling from the center of David's forehead to his furrowed brow, an expression Jack hadn't seen David wear in the three years they'd worked together. By the tone in his voice and the stiffness of his movements, Jack knew the current circumstance wasn't the only thing making David feel uncomfortable.

"What's up, Dave? What's going on?" Jack took David's elbow and steered him away from the crowd.

David's eyes darted around the room, another indication something was amiss. David was a person who looked everyone straight in the eyes and never broke away first. "What's wrong?"

"Jack, we're at your sister's funeral. Just let things be until you come back to work."

Like a shard of glass, the twinge in Jack's stomach almost made him yelp with pain. Something had happened – David's eyes and slumped posture gave it away. "Let's go outside."

Jack led his boss out the front door and into the brilliant sunshine spilling onto the porch. The day was warm and humid for September, just as the Weather Channel predicted, and Jack took a deep breath of fresh air. He walked David along the front porch to an unoccupied spot, stopping beside the two wicker chairs and bench swing. Neither of them sat down.

"What is it, David? What's up? Is it the Samson account?"

David shook his head and waved his hand for Jack to stop talking. Behind him, a group of new visitors poured out of an oversized SUV and streamed up the walk to the front door. David stared at the green boards of the porch floor.

"No, it's not Samson. They're under control." David carefully set his cup of water on the glass table beside them. "I really don't want to get into this now, Jack. It's not the time or the place."

Jack's temples were throbbing and he felt his neck muscles tighten. "C'mon, Dave, give it up. I'm not letting you go until you talk to me."

David combed his fingers through his hair, wiped his hand on his thigh, and sat down. "Mary Mulligan came by my office yesterday."

Jack's first impulse was to fold his arms and take on a defensive posture. He couldn't stand Mary, a middle-aged woman who ran the HR department with an iron fist. Concerned that his pose might convey guilt, he put his hands into his pockets and nodded. "Okay," he said, motioning for David to keep going.

"Well, she's concerned about you and an employee named Marc something-or-other."

The throbbing in Jack's temples pulsed harder and he had a quick vision of blood trying to force its way through the narrow blood vessels. He kept his eyes on David, nodding and making fists with his hands still hidden in his pants pockets. "That would be Marc Whittaker. He's one of my writers."

"Yes. Well, it appears… she said … Mary says you and Marc have a personal relationship outside of work." David clasped his hands together. "She was jabbering about sexual harassment, legal ramifications, staff morale and a whole lot of other clichéd crap." He looked up at Jack with an expression that longed for denial.

Jack folded his arms across his chest, trying to get control of his spinning thoughts. He leaned against the window and peered into the living room. Men in dark suits hugged other men they'd never met before; women flaunted their stylish funeral attire while clearing paper plates from coffee tables and the piano. He wished he could be somewhere else – anywhere but here.

David continued, "I hope you know that I consider your personal life just that – personal. But when it comes to mixing that personal life with your job, things get complicated." He stood and placed his hand on Jack's shoulder. "By the look on your face and the fact that you're not saying anything, I'm assuming Mary must be right."

Jack stepped back, letting David's hand fall from his shoulder. " David," he began, uncertain how he was going to finish his sentence, "I have to think about this. But there's one thing I want you to know: there's no sexual harassment involved. I'm not that kind of a person. I hope you know that."

"I know the kind of person you are, Jack. That's why I'm standing behind you on this." David reached into his pocket and jingled his keys. "I didn't want to talk about it today. You have enough on your plate right now and I know this only adds to your stress. I'm sorry for that." He pulled his car keys from his jacket pocket. "When you come back next week we'll start strategizing."

"I'll be in tomorrow. I need to take care of this right away, before it gets out of hand."

David put his arms around Jack, giving him a fatherly embrace. "Remember, honey, not vinegar," he whispered. "Especially now." He moved backward and held out his right hand. "I'm here for you."

Jack watched David walk to his car, the only Mercedes in the mass of cars parked along the street. He waved as David climbed inside the silver machine and started the engine.

The sudden feeling of emptiness hit him with such intensity that Jack had to hold on to the chair beside him. He felt as though the struggle he'd endured two years ago had been creeping up behind him finally finding just the right moment to attack. And to make matters worse, he could think of only one person who had knowledge about his relationship with Marc, and that was Marc himself.

He looked to the ground and shook his head. Just another chapter, he thought, in the wretched story of my life.

The house finally emptied out except for Jack's parents, who bustled around in the kitchen, placing the leftover food into Dana's vast collection of Tupperware. Water splashing in the upstairs bathroom told him Glen was helping Jenna with her bath. Jack was beyond tired, but he knew this might be his only chance to retrieve the DVD from the piano bench. He forced himself up and made his way over to it.

The rectangular pillow covering the bench was encased in beige linen, stained from years of use, frayed at the edges. Jack smoothed his hand along the fabric, wondering if he was standing in the same spot Dana stood when she hid the DVD. Moving his fingers along the inside of the seat, he found a small latch. He pushed it to the left, unclasping it, allowing the bench to open. He expected to see music books, papers, maybe old photographs Dana had thrown in – photos, perhaps, she'd hoped to forget about and enjoy sometime in the future.

But there was only a manila envelope with "Jack" written across the front.

He took the package, refastened the latch, and brought the envelope up to his nose, hoping to touch Dana one more time through a scent she might have left behind. He smelled nothing but the faded odor of cedar.

Jack sat down on the sofa and looked around for any potential witnesses. Glen and Jenna's voices came from upstairs; his parents were still in the kitchen. He peeled the tape from the back of the envelope and slid the DVD out into the open air. A folded piece of white printer paper fell onto his lap. When he unfolded it and read the words, he heard a moan, so loud and guttural it took Jack a few seconds to realize he'd made the sound himself. He looked at the paper again, trying to catch his breath and clear the water from his eyes. She'd left him with only two words:

I'm sorry.

3

Marc rubbed the towel over his wet hair and stepped out of the shower; a puddle of water formed around his feet, the imported Italian tiles trying to resist the moisture.

"Shit," he whispered, frantically sopping up the water. He could hear Jack's voice in the back of his head: "It's simple, Marc, just put the mat down when you get out of the shower." But he forgot, again, and was now kneeling naked on the cold floor, using the lip of his towel to dry the water-stained grout.

It had been almost three hours since he'd left a message on Jack's voice mail and paranoia started to sweep over him. It wasn't like Jack not to check in, let alone not return his call. He tried to shrug off his concern, let it slide down his sweaty, bare back. When he heard the ring of his cell phone coming from the bedroom, he almost slipped on the stone tile as he dove out the bathroom door to answer it. "Shit," he muttered again and grabbed the big toe he stubbed against the nightstand. He flipped open the phone.

"Hello?" he answered, holding his toe and trying to catch his breath.

"Hey, it's Cory. Just checking in. What's going on?"

Marc fell onto the bed and covered himself with a sheet. This was not the call he'd been hoping for. "Nothing," he sighed, "just waiting for Jack to get back."

"Has anything happened? What's the latest?" Cory asked, the music from his car radio blaring so loudly Marc could barely hear him.

Marc rolled his eyes. "Jack's at his sister's funeral, genius. What do you think the latest is?"

"Hey, don't get so snippy with me. I'm just calling to find out if anything's new and how our plan is working out."

Marc slid further under the sheet and rolled his eyes.

"Caramel Grande Latte, not too hot this time," he heard Cory say.

"Who are you talking to?" Marc lifted the sheet to check his throbbing toe for any sign of blood. There was no sign of injury, only a small chip in the nail where he'd banged it.

"Just ordering my Saturday morning wake-up call." Cory replied. "When can we get together? We have to catch up on things."

Marc leaned back on a pillow. "I'll get back to you, Cory. This isn't a good time."

"It's never a good time for you, Marc. C'mon, we need to –"

In the middle of Cory's sentence, Marc flipped closed the phone and threw it on the pillow beside him. He stared at the ceiling, wondering why he'd answered the phone in the first place and struggling to figure out how he was going to disentangle himself from Cory's clutches.

He'd met Cory during his last semester at Boston University while attending the Tremont Center's Career Placement Expo. Exhibitors from the world's largest companies crammed the oversized room, looking to recruit fresh blood. After hours of strolling the infinite rows of exhibits, the mindless chatter had dulled Marc's optimism. So many people, he thought. I'll be working in a convenience store forever. He was heading for the front doors, trying to escape the stuffy corporate atmosphere, when he heard Cory's voice call out to him over the crowd.

"Hey you!" Cory yelled, motioning for Marc to come nearer.

Marc strolled back to Cory's booth, straightening the nametag haphazardly pinned to his shirt. After a few minutes of conversation, he pegged Cory as a player – a smooth-tongued recruiter, bursting with grandiose promises. But, beyond Cory's boyish good looks and piercing blue eyes, Marc was intrigued with the way Cory so eloquently caressed his professional fantasies.

"I can only promise you the world, Marc." Cory offered Marc an embossed business card. "But it might not be right away. It's going to take careful planning to find you the right position, so just hang on. Do your graduation thing and keep working at the store 'til I call you. Trust me, I'll jump-start your career before the year is up."

Marc shoved the business card in his pocket, shook Cory's hand and headed toward the exit, wondering if Cory's promise was as bogus as his smile. As he walked through the crowd of Armani suits, Zegna ties and flawlessly manicured hairstyles, he felt the familiar ache in his chest. Years ago, he'd silently labeled it the ache of envy, a cutting pain that burned through his ribcage when he'd have to interact with people who were living the life he'd only been able to dream of. Hours afterwards the pain would become a dull ache, throbbing and pulsating until it gradually worked its way out of his system, leaving a residue of depression along its path.

This time, the pain was more intense than usual. Surrounded by the mass of wealth and success, Marc's paranoia grabbed him like a vise. They know where I'm from. They know I'm from Chelsea. They can smell it. They know who I am. Just wait… one day I'll be able to buy you and your family! They'll know who I really am then.

With his hand pressed hard against his chest, he dashed through the doors and into the blinding May sun. Trying to appear in control, he took a deep breath, slipped on his sunglasses and walked wearily down the path toward campus. His legs were still shaking, the voices in his head not yet settled. When he placed his hand back on his chest to help calm his thumping heart, he felt Cory's card in his shirt pocket. He rubbed it, over and over again, like a genie's bottle, wishing for his dream to come true.

After graduation, he'd stayed on at the Mini-Mart, waiting for the call from Cory that would deliver him from selling greasy hot dogs and stale donuts. He kept Cory's business card on him at all times, pulling it out every so often, wondering if he should call and check on his progress. But he always stopped himself, afraid Cory would get annoyed and he'd end up pushing away his only connection to an advertising career.

It was a couple of months after they'd met at the Expo when Marc's cell phone rang while doling out change to a woman who'd just purchased three hot dogs for herself.

"I found a job for you," Cory announced. "It's in the mailroom at Stetson Limited, that multi-billion dollar mortgage company on Beacon. It's right in the middle of the Financial District." Marc heard car horns sounding in the background. "Damn it! Get out of the way, you idiot!" Cory screamed. "Sorry dude, this traffic is killing me. Anyway, just so you know, I'm making like no commission on this placement, but you're a good kid and I like you. Remember me when you hit it big."

"Hit it big in the mailroom?" Marc asked. "Did you forget I have a college degree? I want to be a copywriter."

"I know, I know, but there's nothing else available right now and this job will get your foot in the door. Hang tough, kid, it'll be worth it. I promise."

Marc figured Cory couldn't be any more than two years his senior and the "kid" label made his stomach churn.

"When you're rich and famous, remember who got you your first gig. It's all about paybacks."

"I'll remember," Marc said, wondering if this new job would pay him more than his position as a convenience store clerk. "And you remember me when the real jobs come along."

Six months into the Stetson job, Marc was sick of the smell of bubble wrap and postage ink. The cramped quarters of his windowless office situated in the basement of the giant building reeked of dust, mildew and depressing isolation. He knew it was only his daily mail delivery excursions to the upper floors that kept him working there as long as he had. During these jaunts, he'd walk the plushly carpeted halls, handing envelopes and packages to the slick-haired executives who thanked him with a nod, or, if not on the phone, with a grunt of gratitude. Since it was now ever-present, he'd become accustomed to his ache of envy by forcing himself to look to the future and repeating his mantra: This is the first step... this is the first step.

With his ability to control the green-eyed monster came a new way of seeing the world around him. It wasn't so much the people that intrigued him as it was the actual scent of wealth – the wood paneled walls; the lacquered meeting room tables; the kitchens on each floor complete with ingredients for a three-course, gourmet meal. It was the yearning to smell mahogany instead of bubble wrap that grabbed hold of him every time he strolled through the massive structure, and kept him walking through the entrance doors each day.

It was almost 6:30 in the evening, and, unlike the convenience store, Stetson didn't pay overtime, so Marc wrapped the packing tape around the small, square box in his hand and tossed it into the OUT bin. He grabbed his coat and scarf off the hook behind the door, shut off the lights, and let out a huge sigh as he closed the door behind him.

He passed the line of conference rooms, each room filled with young executives, doodling on legal pads or typing notes on their laptops. The last room was empty and he reached inside, turning on the light switch. Catching sight of his reflection in the glass wall, he gasped. A young man with messy hair, wrinkled khakis, and eyes that looked as if they'd been swallowed up by his face stared back at him. The smooth, preppy-looking graduate from six months ago was now a scruffy mess. He started to panic.

What would happen if he showed up on his parents' doorstep? Would they allow him back into their lives, in spite of how they felt about his lifestyle? Could he even stomach the sight of the dilapidated shack he'd run from years ago? Leaning against the wall with his eyes closed, Marc pictured his father opening the screen door, pulling him inside with a hug so tight he had to catch his breath. He then pictured the same door slamming in his face – exactly as it did the night he'd come out to them.

Marc pushed the thoughts from his mind and stared harder at the reflection in the glass. Maybe he'd been spending too many hours in the windowless dungeon, packing boxes and sealing envelopes. He realized the sunlight and scant interaction he got while delivering mail twice a day wasn't enough to feed his soul. He was starving, physically and emotionally, and he had to take action. He rubbed Cory's business card, now crumpled in his back pocket, and made a decision: With or without Cory, he needed to find a job in advertising, before twenty years passed and he found himself at a Stetson employee dinner accepting the Mailroom Employee of the Year award.

With a wave to the security guard, Marc left the ten-story building and stepped into a wall of arctic air. The blustery December wind smelled of the approaching snow. He wrapped the blue knit scarf around his face, tucked the frayed edges into the collar of his coat, and started walking toward the T stop. He kept his head down to hide his face from the biting wind, only looking up now and then to make sure he was heading in the right direction. As he turned the corner onto Tremont, he spotted Cory across the street leaning against a silver Jaguar. The ends of his gray cashmere scarf, partially hidden by the thin lapels of his black wool, three quarter length overcoat, flapped eagerly in the wind. It was evident to Marc that the coat had been tailored to perfectly fit the shape of Cory's body – the narrow waist, broadening to wide shoulders, and opening up to a face that Marc thought should be plastered on the cover of GQ.

As he approached Cory, Marc scanned the Jaguar and smiled, thinking how perfectly the car matched its owner: a suave and sophisticated exterior hiding a sleek interior, an engine programmed with an unlimited set of calculated moves. Cory waved and opened the car door. "Get in! I'll drive you home."

Although Marc hadn't expected to see him, he didn't give Cory's kindness much thought. He had only one thing on his mind: A ride in a car – any car – beat the crowded subway during rush hour. He ran around the front of the vehicle, opened the passenger side door and hopped in. The seat was lower to the ground than he expected and he pressed the button beneath the seat to level his line of sight with the windshield.

"I've been thinking about you," Marc said, using his gloved hand to wipe fog off the window beside him.

"I kept the heat on for you." Cory edged the car into the crawling traffic on Tremont, barely missing a taxicab's rear bumper. "Now tell me where you live."

Marc directed him to the North End, describing his small studio apartment above Giuseppe's Ristorante, one of the more popular restaurants in Little Italy.

Turning onto Boylston Street, Cory cursed the traffic but made no attempt at conversation, forcing Marc to take the lead.

"So what's up, Cory? Why the limo treatment?"

"Not much." Cory whipped through a yellow light. "Although, I may have a copywriting job for you in Stetson's marketing department. And the best part is, it comes with a $5,000 bonus."

Marc sat straight up. "Finally! What's the job?"

"You'll be a junior copywriter, working on ads and some direct mail. It's a great place to start. I just want to make sure you're up for it."

"Oh, I'm up for it! It feels like I've been waiting for this forever. I'm going nuts in that mailroom."

"I can imagine." Cory laughed. "Now, if this goes through you'll be working for the VP of Marketing, Lance Talbot. Do you know him?"

"I know of him. I deliver his mail every day. I've only seen him a few times because he's never in his office, so I usually leave the mail on his desk. But I hear he's a really good guy to work for."

Cory reached over to the dash and switched on the seat warmers. "I've heard that too. That's why I thought you'd like this position." He thumbed in the direction of the back seat. "See that package back there? Can you grab it for me?"

Marc turned around and snatched the yellow envelope from the back seat. He held it up to the window using the streetlights to illuminate the address label. "This is for Talbot? There's no return address. Who's it from?"

"Actually, it's from my boss. He's friends with Talbot and asked me if I could get it to him. He told me it's a birthday surprise or something and he wants to hide it inside Talbot's office. When I told him I knew someone in the mailroom, he asked me to have you deliver it. Do you think you can do that for him?"

Marc removed his gloves and rubbed his fingers along the edges of the package, trying to feel its contents. Marc felt a wave of uneasiness. "It feels like a videotape or a book or something. You're sure they're friends?" A bead of sweat fell from his left temple. He looked at Cory who stared straight ahead, waiting for the traffic light to turn green.

"Definitely sure. Supposedly my boss and Talbot grew up together and that's a videotape of them as kids. I guess they're into the whole nostalgia thing." Cory pulled to the side of the street. "Is this your place?"

Marc looked out the window to see Giuseppe's red neon sign lighting up the wet cobblestone sidewalk. "Yeah, this is my place," he said. "Are you sure this is okay? This package I mean. I don't want to get in trouble."

Cory swiveled in the seat and rested his hand on Marc's knee. "There's absolutely nothing to worry about, Marc. I promise. Like I said, they're friends and it's going to be a great surprise. Just put it inside his file cabinet or something. On his birthday, my boss will call him and tell him where it is."

Marc looked into Cory's eyes and smiled. For a split second he thought about inviting him in for a drink. But with the crimson glow of the Giuseppe's sign on Cory's well groomed face, Marc knew the bare walls, unkempt bed and lack of furnishings would embarrass them both.

As if reading Marc's mind, Cory withdrew his hand. "I have to meet a client for dinner now. I'll keep you updated on the copywriter position. And let me know how you do with the package. I think his birthday's on Thursday, so if you can put it in his office tomorrow, that would be perfect."

"Consider it done!" Marc used the package to salute Cory and opened the door, wincing at the blast of frigid air. "And thanks for the ride."

He slammed the door and saw Cory wave back as he sped down the narrow side street and turned right onto Boylston.

As Marc walked toward the thin screen door leading up to his apartment, he thought about all the things five thousand dollars would buy. "Another first step," he said to himself.

He turned around and peered inside Giuseppe's front window where Maria, Giuseppe's wife, was setting tables for the evening rush.

With five grand coming in, Marc thought, I can at least afford a nice meal. He stepped inside the restaurant, unbuttoned his coat, and laid it on Maria's outstretched arms.

"Buon giorno, Marco," she said, a look of pity cutting across her face as she looked him up and down. "Look at choo, Marco, so skinny, so pale, you looka like a stringa bean from Giuseppe's antipast'. Come sit down. I'm gonna feed you sometin good."

Marc followed Maria's solid frame, staring at the circular bun cropped tightly to her skull – a secret hiding place for pins, barrettes and other small objects foreign to him. He wondered if she ever let her hair down and released the objects from their nest.

"I'm paying for dinner tonight, Maria," he said as he sat in the chair she pulled out for him.

"Oh no, Marco. We feed you tonight." She pushed the chair beneath the table and stuffed a napkin into the collar of Marc's shirt.

"No, Maria, I want to pay tonight. I'm getting a bonus at work. I want to pay."

Maria shook her head and stared down at him, holding his chin in her hand.

"When you getta rich, you canna pay. Tonight isa on the house."

Marc smiled and turned his head, waving at Giuseppe standing behind the stainless steel counter in a fog of smoke filling the room with the scent of roasted garlic. He knew how lucky he was to have found this tiny spot in the world – a small community of people with a friendliness and warmth that provided him with a connection to family he'd never experienced before. And with Maria and Giuseppe as his landlords, there was one thing he was sure of: He'd never starve.

Some nights he'd sneak up the stairs to his apartment in order to avoid their offerings of food. He didn't want to take advantage of their kindness, and although Giuseppe's cooking tasted much better than his Swanson frozen dinners, he also wanted to avoid Maria's interrogations. "Marco, where'sa your parents?" She'd ask at least once a week. "Why don't they come an visit you?" Most of the time, he'd shrug his shoulders and look to the floor. "Where'sa your family? Why don'ta they help you out? Such a sweet boy." By the end of Maria's tirade, she'd be rubbing the back of Marc's head like a tigress licking the neck of her cub, pushing a plate of pasta or meatballs in his face.

But tonight, after hearing Cory's news, Marc's sense of hope had skyrocketed and he wasn't about to take another free meal.

"No, Maria," he tucked the napkin further into his collar, "tonight I pay."

Maria widened her eyes and placed her hand over her mouth.

"Oh, Mr. Bigashot. Okay, that's a fine. Buta only a tip for Antonio." She pointed to the silver-haired waiter tying a soiled apron around his waist. "He's another one who needs a gooda family."

Marc smiled, realizing that fighting Maria would be a lost cause. "Okay, only a tip."

Marc watched her hobble away from the table toward the kitchen. She pushed one of the objects jutting out from her bun further into her head, making it disappear and causing Marc to wonder if she might be hiding some sort of treasure in there.

Rolling the mail cart down the narrow path of cubicles, Marc's hands were cold and clammy. He'd had a morning bout with paranoia, but felt determined to fulfill his task. He knew his future depended on it and was not about to let his fear stand in his way. He reached beneath the cart, grabbed Cory's package, and stacked it with the rest of Talbot's mail. Whistling under his breath, he strolled toward Talbot's door and stopped short when he saw Todd Lindsay, one of Stetson's many computer technicians, sitting behind Talbot's desk smiling at something on the computer screen. The thin, white stick of a lollipop protruded from his mouth, a direct contrast to the yellowed teeth filling his grin. Todd looked up and lost his smile when he saw Marc standing by the door. They stared at each other, speechless.

"Hey, Marc, what's up?" Todd asked, sliding a DVD into his shirt pocket. "I was just upgrading Lance's computer. Man, this drive hasn't been touched in years." He walked around the desk and headed toward Marc, using his tongue to push the round head of his lollipop into his cheek. "Dropping off some mail?"

Marc nodded, although he could barely understand Todd's question through the flood of sugar-induced saliva. He felt a cold drop of sweat crawl down his back. "Yeah," was the only reply Marc could muster.

"Well, gotta bag this joint. Lotsa computers to fix today. Later." Todd almost ran out the door, bumping Marc's shoulder, nearly making him drop the stack of mail.

Marc crept over to Lance Talbot's desk and tossed his mail onto the stack of envelopes still sitting in the IN box from yesterday. Holding Cory's package, he looked around for a hiding place. He crouched beside the file cabinet, opened the bottom drawer, lifted the file folders and slid the package beneath them. He slammed the cabinet door shut and let out a sigh of relief as he straightened out the mail he'd thrown in Talbot's IN box before heading out the door.

By the time he reached the cart, Marc's anxiety turned into excitement. He'd completed his project and knew Cory would be pleased. The junior copywriter position was in the bag, along with $5,000, and he was looking forward to the day he would tell his new boss Lance Talbot that he'd helped with this special birthday surprise. For the first time in months, Marc felt Fate was smiling down on him.

Two days later, as Marc wrapped a band-aid around his middle finger, he cursed the envelope that produced his third paper cut of the day. He held his hand in the air, trying to force the blood down his arm and away from the cut. Although no one else was in the room, he still felt like an idiot. He kept his arm raised even when the phone rang.

"Mailroom," he answered.

"Marc, it's Todd. You gotta get up here!" Todd sounded out of breath.

"What's going on? I'm in the middle of sorting the mail."

"Just come up to the fifth floor, NOW!"

Marc stepped out of the elevator into an eerie silence. He scanned the rows of cubicles, amazed at the sight of each employee peering over their fake walls, all of them watching two police officers and a large man in a pin-striped suit lead Lance Talbot toward the elevators. Marc searched the room for a familiar face.

"Do you believe it?" Todd whispered, running up beside him. "It's crazy." He pulled Marc toward the back of the room, away from the elevator where Talbot and his escorts were headed. Todd grabbed a grape Tootsie-Roll lollipop from the stash in his jeans pocket and practically threw the sucker in his mouth.

"What's going on?" Marc whispered. "What happened?"

"Pedophilia, that's what!" Todd threw the lollipop wrapper into the corner of the room, unable to take his eyes off Talbot. "They found kiddie porn on his computer."

Marc shook his head, trying to make sense of it. "I don't believe it. Not Talbot. He doesn't seem the type."

"Yeah, they never do." Todd moved closer, his lips almost touching Marc's ear. Marc turned away, the smell of artificial grape and cigarettes almost making him gag. "I heard they found a tape in his file cabinet too. A video of little kids having sex."

Marc felt his body go limp and he fell back against the wall behind him. Images of Cory, the Jaguar, and the envelope he placed in Talbot's file cabinet ran through his mind in one sickening instant. He let his back slide down the wall until he sat flat on the floor, hating himself for rationalizing his way through his initial fear and suspicion, queasy from the thought that he'd allowed money and success to push aside the morsel of morality he had left. He wrapped his arms around his legs, and, before burying his head in his knees, he looked up at Todd.

Todd rolled the lollipop along his lips, smiling a triumphant smile as though he'd also just made five thousand dollars.

Still damp from the shower, Marc threw off the sheet and sauntered to the bathroom. He snapped up the blow dryer, crouched down and pointed the nozzle toward the wet grout, hoping Jack wouldn't get home before it dried.

4

Speeding along the Mass Pike toward Boston, Jack opened the windows and turned the radio to full volume, hoping the cool autumn wind and blaring music would drown out his thoughts. It was almost midnight and there were only two or three other cars on the road, their taillights like distant devilish eyes watching over him. He stepped hard on the gas pedal and felt the Roadster change gears, his speedometer reading eighty miles per hour. His headlights shone on the black tar, disappearing beneath the Beamer, his tires eating up the road, spitting out the asphalt behind him. For a split second he felt in control of something and he smiled.

Then he remembered the envelope in the seat beside him, wondering where he'd hide Dana's DVD. The thought of hiding the DVD for ten years suddenly struck him with terror. Would he really be able to hold onto something for an entire decade without misplacing it? He tightened his grip on the steering wheel, remembering his last conversation with Dana and the promise he'd made. Fear was not an option; he'd have to come through – for Jenna's sake and for his sister.

The car exploded with rock and roll classics. The music so loud Jack envisioned the people living close to the Pike rising in their beds, contemplating the source of the noise and cursing the reverberating rhythm – an incessant beat rolling like thunder and leaving an eerie silence in its wake.

Elton John's "Madman Across the Water" played on the radio and

Jack felt a connection with the Madman, growing stronger with each mile of pavement that passed beneath his car. "The ground's a long way down, but I need more... Is the nightmare black or are the windows painted?"

Looking far into the distance, Jack caught sight of the flashing lights atop the Prudential Building, shimmering like a beacon, calling for him to enter their domain and choose the color of his own nightmare.

Through the din of the music his cell phone rang from inside the glove compartment. Probably Marc again. He felt bad about avoiding Marc's calls, but not guilty enough to answer the phone. He still had plenty of thinking to do. Could he give up the one person he truly loved to save his career? Would sacrificing their relationship stop the churning of J&M's most recent scandal? Jack fixed his gaze on the tiny droplets of mist hitting his headlights, looking for a sign, an answer, or just another option.

Startled by the abrupt brilliance of tollbooth lights, he braked hard to stop in time. He passed the attendant a five-dollar bill and heard her distant yell as he sped off before accepting his change. It was the last toll on the Pike and he knew he was running out of time. Nearing his exit, Jack realized he was also running out of choices.

The freight elevator jolted when it reached the top floor of his building. Jack hesitated before stepping out into the hallway, still unsure what he would say to Marc. Back and forth, back and forth, his thoughts crashed against the inside of his head. He knew he'd have to wait and see how the conversation went. This was one of the few times he couldn't make a final decision before entering the ring.

He slammed the cage door shut behind him, holding the DVD in one hand and jostling his keys in the other. Before he could find the key to the loft, the front door opened and Marc peered from behind it. Jack walked right past him, avoiding his eyes, and tossed his keys onto the glass console table. Dragging himself to the black leather sofa, he collapsed onto the supple cushions. He tossed the DVD onto the coffee table, loosened his tie and stretched his arm along the back of the couch. Marc sat opposite him in a recliner emitting classical music from the small speakers in the headrest. Still watching Jack's face, he pressed the red button on the remote control, turning the music off and adding more tension to their silence.

"I tried calling you twenty times today," Marc said. "How are you?"

Jack gazed out the window at the full moon; tracing the bluish-gray shadows that marred its surface. The moon's edges were razor sharp, the celestial body appearing flat against the night sky as it shone over the city with a pale radiance.

"I'm okay," he whispered. "Just tired."

"Can I get you anything? Some food? A drink?"

Jack shook his head without speaking.

"Do you want me to leave?" Marc's voice trembled. Jack didn't respond. "What the hell is going on?" He stood and clasped his hands behind his neck. "What is it, for Christ's sake?"

Jack's exhaustion weakened his thought process. He considered if this was the best time to bring up his conversation with David. It was already 1:00 in the morning and he'd need to start work early the next day and start mending the damage. He pulled himself up from the sofa and walked the three steps into the kitchen. Grabbing a bottle of Perrier, he unscrewed the top and finished half the bottle before realizing the liquid was running down his neck. Marc waited expectantly by the sofa.

"David came to the house today," Jack said.

"You thought he might. That was nice… wasn't it?" Marc asked, his fingers massaging the back of his neck.

"Yes, it was." As Jack sipped the water he remembered Dana in her hospital bed, struggling to wet her thin, cracked lips. He shook his head, One thing at a time. "Well, he came to pay his respects, but he had other news." Leaving the empty bottle on the granite counter, Jack crossed the living room and stood beside the windows where the moonlight cast a triangular beam on the river.

"God!" Marc yelled, his arms flailing by his sides. "What other news, Jack? Tell me what the hell's going on!"

"Mary Mulligan visited him yesterday." Jack heard a soft groan and turned around. Marc had slumped back in the chair. "Looks like you already knew that." Jack unknotted his tie, pulled it through his shirt collar, and tossed it in the general direction of a stereo speaker.

Marc stared at the oak floor, his fingers tracing invisible shapes on his baggy Lee jeans.

"I said," Jack raised his voice, "it looks like you already knew that."

"I didn't know she'd gone to see David!" Marc shrieked. "Yes, she called me into her office. But I didn't know she'd spoken with David."

Jack leaned his back against the cold window, a frigid shiver running through him. Until this moment he'd never truly suspected Marc of any wrongdoing. He pounded his fist against the windowsill.

"Are you telling me you had a conversation with Mary Mulligan and didn't tell me about it? Please tell me that's not true, Marc."

"Jack, you've been going through a lot of crap. I didn't want you worrying about this stuff. We'll take care of it. It'll work itself out, we just have to give it some time."

Jack paced the floor, mumbling to himself. When he stopped moving, he stared at Marc, trying to drill through the dazed expression and discover what he'd been thinking. "Are you out of your mind? 'Work itself out'? This stuff doesn't work out, it's worked out for you! It has a life of its own and once things get started, you're pretty much screwed. But you wouldn't know that, you're still a baby, for God's sake." He rubbed his mouth with the back of his hand. "So, be honest, Marc, who called the meeting, you or Mary?"

Marc squeezed his temples with the palms of his hands and shook his head.

"You can't be thinking I started this, Jack. You really don't believe I'd do that, do you?"

"What am I supposed to think? How did she find out about us?" Jack used every ounce of energy he had left to control his voice. "We've been so careful. Sneaking around, staying separated in public. I haven't told anyone, not even my parents." He detected a change in Marc's expression. A glimpse of remorse? An indication of shame? Guilt? "Who did you tell, Marc?" There was silence. "Marc, who did you tell?" Jack's voice echoed off the walls and fell hard between them.

"I might have mentioned it to Todd one night," Marc said under his breath. "He's one of us. He wouldn't tell anyone. I just needed to talk to someone. That's all. I'm sure he didn't say anything."

Jack leaned on the arm of the sofa for support. "You've got to be kidding me, Marc. You told Todd? That lollipop sucking freak? Todd

62

might be one of us, but there's a reason they call him The Mouth. And I don't mean because he uses it on every guy he meets. When he doesn't have something in his mouth, he's making up lies or spreading rumors."

"But you recommended him." By the expression on Jack's face, Marc knew he should've kept quiet. "At least that's what he told me."

"His parents live in the house behind Dana. He was up for the job, they knew I worked at J&M and they asked me for help. I didn't know at the time that he was such a loser!" Jack shook his head. "God, I can't believe I have to explain this to you. The point is, Marc, it's a well-known fact that Todd can't keep anything to himself. Everyone knows he's the biggest gossip at J&M. He might be the best techie around, but David's wanted him out of there for months."

Seeing Marc's eyes shimmering with tears, Jack reluctantly made his way over. He gently held Marc's head in his hands and pressed his thumbs against the falling tears, wiping them away and kissing his lover's forehead.

"It's my fault," Jack said. "I'm sorry. I should've known this wouldn't work. The sneaking around, the lying. You're only twenty-three. You're too young and so are your friends. This is big business and there's just no room for this kind of bullshit."

Jack turned to walk away and Marc grabbed his arm. "God, Jack, you act like you're fifty years old. You're only five years older than I am. And what are you saying? Are you telling me you'd give up the last six months we've spent together for your career? Am I so insignificant that you'd throw me away like a piece of trash?"

"Don't you get it, Marc? Try keeping your emotions out of this for a few seconds. Yeah, my career is on the line here – not only at J&M, but at every other agency in the city. And, if word gets out, every agency on the East Coast. I need time to sort this all out and fix things… if there's anything left to fix." Jack pulled his arm from Marc's grasp and walked toward the window. "I'm in a high-powered position. Marc. And I'm gay. In the corporate world, those two things don't go well together." Jack shook his head. "You wouldn't understand, you can't understand."

Marc squeezed his eyes. "Are you kidding me with this, Jack? I wouldn't understand?" His voice grew louder as he followed Jack's path to the window. "I'm gay, remember? I grew up in the shithole of Massachusetts with people who would've killed me if they knew who I was. I ran away from all of them, including my parents who couldn't stomach their own son. I've been clawing my way up and out ever since." He turned to see the flashing sparkle of the lighthouse in the distance. He took a deep breath and lowered his voice. "It's not just the corporate world that doesn't go well with gay. It's the whole world. You're not the only person that has their own shit to deal with. I needed to talk to someone and I chose Todd. Right or wrong, I made the decision and I'll do whatever it takes to make it right."

Jack felt a tightening in his chest, an ache in his heart. His head was full, overflowing with everything he'd been through since the day began. "It's too late, Marc. The damage is done and I have to get through this alone. And until I do…" He reconsidered his thought, thinking back to their morning together, the intense passion they shared and the commitment he'd almost made. He closed his eyes and turned away. "Until I do, we can't be together."

Marc looked to the floor, shaking his head. He started toward the door, stopped and spun around.

"What's the problem, Jack, it's not clean enough for you?"

Jack turned from the window and glared at Marc. "Clean enough? What are you talking about?"

Marc raised his arm and scanned the room with his index finger. "I mean exactly what I said: clean enough. Like this apartment, like your office, like your desk, like everything else in your life. You need to have everything in perfect order. As soon as something doesn't follow your master plan, you freak, just like you're doing now."

Marc's words hit Jack hard enough to push him against the window. He knew Marc was right, but this was different. Wasn't it? This was his career. This was the rest of his life. He couldn't allow himself to be swayed.

"What are you now, the gay Sigmund Freud? Where do you get off loading this shit on me? It has nothing to do with keeping things clean. It has to do with keeping my career. And there's no way to do that other than to maintain control."

Marc brushed the top of his hair and slid his hand into his pocket. "You said it Jack, control. It's all about control. You always need to have everything in perfect order and real life just isn't that way."

Jack felt his patience and energy flowing out the soles of his feet. He had nothing left. He massaged his temples trying to force back the pulsating emotions that resided there.

"Go, Marc. I'm done. Please pick up your stuff in the morning. I have to get some sleep."

"Jack, you don't know what you're saying!" Jack could hear the tears in Marc's throat. "Your life is in turmoil. There's just too much going on. Let's get through this together. I swear I'll make it work. I'll quit J&M. I'll give my notice tomorrow. Let me do that, Jack, please."

Jack gazed out the window again, looking to the river for strength. He wiped the tear from his eye before it fell. "I'm sorry, Marc. It's up to me from here. And I don't think you should quit either. That would only make the situation worse." His voice sounded hoarse and he rubbed his throat with his fingers. "Please, I need some sleep."

Marc grabbed his bomber jacket from the hall closet and forced himself to close the door gently until the latch clicked.

"I'm sorry Jack, I really am." He wiped his nose on the sleeve of his jacket and used his scarf to dry his cheeks. "Let's pick this up tomorrow after you've had time to sleep on it."

"No Marc," Jack said, "I'll be at J&M tomorrow. Just please get your stuff while I'm there."

"Jack," Marc moaned, "I can't believe you're doing this."

"Believe it." Jack folded his arms, hoping to keep his pounding heart from exploding through his chest. "I'm sorry."

Marc opened the front door and slowly stepped into the hallway. "I'll come by tomorrow," he said, closing the door halfway. "And I'll leave the key on the kitchen table."

In the mirror image of the window, Jack watched the door close. It took all his strength not to spin around and cry out for Marc to come back.

He was on the Boston T Redline heading toward Cambridge when the combination of tears and fluorescent lights made his eyes feel like they were on fire. Marc dashed off the T at its final Boston stop and kept running until he reached the Longfellow Bridge that would take him to Cambridge.

Halfway across, he grabbed his cell phone from the inside pocket of his jacket and flipped it open. He took a deep breath and hit the redial button, which still held Jack's number. Even before he finished exhaling, he'd already pushed cancel. Don't call him, he muttered, give him some time.

Peering over the concrete balustrade, Marc listened to waves slapping against the bridge, trying to imagine what would happen if he threw himself into the river, what he would see as the undertow pulled him into the shadows of the river. He envisioned breathing the water like air, the light above him fading with each gasping breath, leading to stillness and freedom from pain.

He lifted his head and looked to the left. Blurred lights from the MIT campus barely penetrated the mist covering the city of Cambridge. To his right stood the Boston cityscape - clear, square windowed lights dotting the sky and filling his heart with the piercing ache of loneliness.

The ringing of his cell phone shook him from his thoughts. He saw Cory's number on the display. He was about to throw the phone in the water when an awful realization struck him hard in his chest: Cory was the only person he had left. Marc flipped open his phone. "Hello?"

"Marc, it's Cory." Marc didn't reply. "I've been waiting here all night. What's going on?"

"It's not a good time, Cory. Let's talk tomorrow."

"You sound like shit. What happened? You didn't screw things up, did you?"

A warm tear crawled down Marc's face and he made a conscious decision not to wipe it away. He wanted to experience all the pain he deserved. "No! Everything happened the way we planned."

"That's cool. Glad to hear it. Now why don't you come over and we'll do a little celebrating? My girlfriend Janice is here and I have Todd in the kitchen making martinis."

The lump in Marc's throat grew larger; he thought his neck would explode. He tried to speak, but could only whimper incomprehensible sounds.

"Did you hear me, Marc?" Cory shouted. "Marc, are you there? Come by and we'll talk through the details. We're almost there! I have a lot of —"

Cory was still talking when Marc flipped the phone shut and tossed it into the Charles. He waited for the small splash before turning around and heading back to Boston.

It was 2:30 in the morning when Marc reached his apartment and saw Cory leaning against the brick wall beneath the red glow of Giuseppe's sign. He strolled past him as though Cory were a stranger, a hobo silently asking for a handout. Cory grabbed his wrist, but Marc twisted his arm and sent Cory's hand flying into the brick wall. He rushed on by, slowing when he reached the door to his apartment. Cory stood behind him as he slid the ring of keys from the pocket of his jeans.

"Look, Cory, I'm beat and I don't want to talk. I don't want to think. I just want some sleep."

Cory put his arm around Marc's shoulder and gave him a squeeze. He reeked of alcohol and cigarettes. "Hey, man, I'm here for you. I swear. I'll only stay for a few minutes. I just want to make sure everything's okay with you."

Marc unlocked the flimsy storm door and led Cory up the narrow stairwell, dimly lit by a sconce attached to the wall by a handful of electrical wires. It held two flickering, candle-shaped bulbs that barely lit the steps in front of them. Cory tripped on one of the steps and cursed as he pulled himself up, wiping the knees of his designer trousers.

When they reached the apartment, Marc opened the door and let his jacket slide down his arms and onto the floor. He plopped onto his unmade bed, laying his arms over his eyes, trying to relieve the stinging and burning.

"Nice place," Cory said, closing the door and scanning the empty walls.

Marc squinted his eyes, looking around the room. He'd bought the furniture at a garage sale: his mattress on a steel frame looked more like an army cot than a civilian's bed; the combination computer table/desk was particle board with strips of mahogany-colored laminate peeling down the sides; his television sat on a pine wood box; on top of the television stood a small framed picture of Jack and Marc. A wave of embarrassment ran through him.

"Love the décor." Cory joked, "Can't Jack keep his lover in better living conditions?"

"Shove it, Cory." Marc said, his voice thin from exhaustion.

Cory unbuttoned his brown suede jacket and leaned against the corner of the computer table. He switched the desk lamp on and off, ruffled some papers, and tried to read the notes tacked up to Marc's bulletin board.

"Calm down, buddy. You know, if I were you, I'd be looking to make as much money as possible so I could get out of this dump."

"Yeah, well the copywriting job you got me at J&M doesn't exactly pay enough for a two-bedroom condo in Cambridge like yours." Marc covered his eyes with his arm.

"That's exactly why we're doing what we're doing. This is a way for you to make the extra cash you need so you can live a real life." Cory pulled the computer chair next to the bed and sat down beside Marc.

"Why are you here, Cory? You're drunk and I'm beat. I have nothing to say."

Cory rolled his eyes. "Nothing to say? It's been six months already, my friend. This is where we make it or break it." He took a deep breath. "This is where you will or won't make your ten grand."

Marc sat up, leaned his back against the wall, and stared Cory down. "I don't want ten grand. I don't want anything from you. What I want is to go back in time and start all over again, back to when you first came at me with this screwed-up plan. I wish I'd told you to go screw yourself!" Marc forced out a long breath. "That's what I want."

"If you remember correctly, Marc, I didn't twist your arm." Cory used his hips to swivel the chair back and forth.

"Yeah, like you didn't twist my arm with Talbot."

Cory rose and slowly walked to the window where the blinking light of Giuseppe's cast a red glow on the cobblestone path below. "Let's not get into the Talbot thing again. Remember, you made five grand on that one. And don't tell me you didn't know what you were getting into."

"God damn you, Cory!" Mark shouted. "You told me that money was a promotion bonus. I had no idea it was for planting a kiddie porn video in Talbot's office! I didn't know that's how you recruited high-level executives – getting rid of the old ones so you could have your own clients take their place. I was an idiot and you conned me!"

"Okay, Okay, calm down. So I might've been a little vague. Let's say, for argument's sake that you had no idea about the Talbot deal," Cory kept his gaze on the street below. "This time you knew exactly what you were doing."

"I thought I did," Marc mumbled. Cory turned around and threw his jacket on the bed beside Marc, then held both hands against his heart and pouted in an exaggerated display of sarcasm.

"Oh, did Marc fall in love with Jacky?" Cory swayed back and forth, feigning a dance with an invisible partner. "Poor Marc. Poor Jack. Poor Marc. Poor Jack." He sang the words and laughed, dancing around the room, singing louder until the melody disappeared and he was screaming.

"Shut up, Cory! It's almost three o'clock in the morning. You're going to wake someone up!" Marc grabbed Cory's arm and swung him onto the bed, making his head slam into the wall.

"Ouch! You shit! That hurt." Cory rubbed the back of his head and checked his fingers for blood. "You're lucky I'm not bleeding. I would've sued you," He glanced around the room. "Not that there's anything here to sue you for, but I would've done it on principle."

"You? Principle? That's a joke. You're out of your mind, Cory. And you're evil, especially when you're drunk. Just get the hell out of here."

Cory sat up straight on the bed, pulling his open hands down his face, wiping away his smile. "Okay, I'm sorry, Marc. I got carried away. I'm a dick sometimes. I know that. But, look, this is big business and it's for big people."

Marc winced. He'd heard those same words from Jack only a few hours before.

"I really do feel bad that you got this thing for Fontaine, but we're too far into it. Once he's gone from J&M and my new client takes his place, we'll both be a lot wealthier. I'll get you a job at another agency, a higher paying job, I promise, and you'll forget about Jack. After that, we're done. I promise not to involve you in something like this again. Deal?" Cory reached for Marc's hand. "Let's shake on it."

Marc took a pillow and hugged it. He pressed it into his face and breathed deeply, taking the sweetness of fabric softener into his lungs. "Yea, Cory, it's a deal. Now can you get out of here please?"

Cory stood, picked up his jacket and tossed it over his shoulder, holding it with his index finger. "Okay, I'm outta here. Just tell me where things stand. How much longer do you think it'll be before Jack's out and I can bring my new guy in?"

"I don't know," Marc said, his voice muffled in the pillow. He lifted his head. "Jack said he's going to fight this, but Mulligan's a real bitch. I don't know if he's got a chance." He squeezed the pillow tighter. "I have to pick up my stuff from Jack's apartment tomorrow. He wants me out. And I still haven't decided if I'm going back to J&M. I don't think I can deal with seeing Jack. It hurts too much."

"I'll help you." Cory tousled Marc's hair and gently pushed his face further into the pillow. "I'll go with you to Jack's tomorrow and help you get your stuff. And then we'll discuss you going back to J&M. It's important for you to be there. You have to look like the victim. You can't appear guilty."

Marc looked up at Cory. The alcohol and drugs had reddened the whites of his eyes, but the cerulean blue that had captured Marc's attention that first day at the Expo still drew him in. He had no doubt about how much he hated Cory, but he also felt the familiar longing, the need for someone, anyone, to take control of his body and free his mind from the thickness of its thoughts. If it was going to be Cory, then so be it.

Cory pulled his hand from Marc's head and leaned against the wall. "This is not good," he muttered to himself. Marc looked at him quizzically, waiting for either an explanation or more physical contact. He kept his eyes on Cory's face.

"I have to go," Cory said. "I'll be here at ten tomorrow to pick you up. We'll collect your stuff from Jack's and get some lunch. Then we'll discuss your future."

As Cory opened the door to leave, Marc could barely make out Cory was whispering under his breath, but caught the words: "I definitely have to work too hard for my money," before slamming the door behind him.

Marc held onto his pillow and slid his body down the mattress. "What future?" he muttered, wondering how he could have anything without Jack; how he'd get through life knowing the pain he'd inflicted – first on a stranger and now on someone to whom he'd given his heart. Cory's words, from the first day they met, rang through his head: "I can only promise you the world, Marc Whittaker."

If this is the world, Marc thought, sobbing into his pillow, I don't want any part of it.

5

When it came to Mary Mulligan, David was certain of three things: Her stiff, pageboy haircut was ten years out of style; she seemed to enjoy owning the nickname "bitch on wheels;" and over the past twenty years she'd consistently proven herself enough to secure a niche as J&M's Vice President of Human Resources.

"We can't run a business this way, David." Mary swept aside the bangs obstructing her vision. "It hurts morale and creates a rumor-driven atmosphere. To maintain productivity, you have to nip these things in the bud."

Sitting on the antique mahogany chair facing her desk, David crossed his legs and clasped his hands in his lap. He had to restrain a grin as she leapt off her chair, reminding him of a Mexican jumping bean. Her slender, five-foot frame darting from one side of the desk to the other, impeding his view out the plexiglass windows lining the wall.

Harsh sunlight revealed the frown lines around her eyes and mouth; the cream-colored foundation she used to hide them flaked at their rigid edges. A wave of empathy overwhelmed David as he realized she looked much older than her forty-two years. Sculpted by hardship and anguish, her face wore the familiar markings of middle-aged despair – hidden by makeup and attitude.

"I hear you, Mary, and I appreciate everything you're saying," David said impatiently. "You know your business, there's no doubt about it. That's why you've been here since we opened the doors. And that's why I think you'll agree with me that Jack's an asset to J&M. The clients admire and respect him, and so do his employees. Sometimes we have to make exceptions."

Slowing her manic pace, Mary sauntered around her desk, running her middle finger along its rim. She smiled ever so slightly, tossing back her head as though her heavily sprayed hair would actually move. She leaned against the front edge of her desk and crossed her arms. After a moment of thought, she raised her head and gazed into his eyes.

"You talk about respect, David. How much respect do you think employees have for a boss who has sex with his direct reports in the bathroom?"

David didn't flinch, but had he not been sitting he would've fallen to the floor.

"Mary, please! That's crap and you know it! Jack would never do something like that. He values his job and his reputation way too much. That's just the rumor mill adding insult to injury. I don't know – and I don't want to know – who that came from, but Jack would never sink that low. It's just not who he is."

"It might not be who he is, David, but it's what they're saying." Mary leaned against the desk, facing him with arms crossed over her chest. "Okay, let's go back to the basics for a minute. There's a reason we have an employee handbook with rules and regulations. Over three hundred people count on us to keep things running smoothly. It's like a small community out there. Everyone knows everyone else's business and they rely on us to pay their wages, provide their benefits, and keep their streets clean. When there's a criminal in town, it's up to us to either jail him or throw him out."

David ran his fingers through his hair. "Cut it out, Mary. Jack isn't a criminal, for God's sake. He's having a relationship with one of his employees and…"

Mary cut him off. "Yes, something that's strictly forbidden." She grabbed the employee handbook from her top desk drawer. "On page 21, section… "

"I know, Mary, I know! Enough with the rules already! These things happen in the workplace and we just have to allow for it. All rules have exceptions. Without exceptions, we'd be living in World War Two Germany. And this sex in the bathroom thing is just preposterous. Someone's obviously out for revenge. Jack is a vital employee, and this relationship he's got going isn't enough reason to throw him out. It's not fair to him as a person or to the people who work for him. I won't allow it to happen."

Mary turned and made her way back to her chair. Tightening her fists around the end of the armrests, she looked like a queen preparing to order the beheading of one of her servants. "Then I guess you'll have to take it up with the Board of Directors." She shifted a stack of papers on her desk, pointedly ignoring him.

The muscles in David's neck tightened and pulled on his temples. Obviously Mary was finished with the conversation and wanted to get back to work. "The six of you can make the final decision," she added.

David put his palms on the edge of the desk and leaned over, his mouth less than twelve inches from her face. "The Board knows about this? You leaked it to the Board before we discussed it?"

Mary didn't speak nor did she look up from her papers.

"Jesus, this is ludicrous. What do you have against Jack? What has he ever done to you?"

She tossed the papers onto her desk and glanced at him. "It's not something he did to me, David. It's what he's doing to the company. I have nothing against him personally."

He'd known Mary long enough to recognize she was holding something back. He could press her further, but she'd only dig in her heels.

He sighed. "I'm disappointed in you, Mary. I really thought you had more compassion. I'm saddened by your total lack of understanding and empathy. J&M isn't a penitentiary. It's supposed to be a place where our employees produce great work and also enjoy their time here. This should be their home away from home, not a detention center with a warden watching their every move. And, just so you know, I'll be talking with the Board about your attitude and inflexibility – both of which don't belong at J&M."

Almost out the door, David stopped and took a few steps back into her office. He softened his voice. "Mary, I hope this crusade of yours doesn't have anything to do with Max."

Mary's head twitched as though he'd slapped her. Her mouth fell open without uttering a sound. The expression on her face told David he'd struck a nerve, so he closed the door and walked back to his office.

Other than the pile of condolence cards neatly stacked on his desk, Jack was surprised to find his office exactly as he'd left it three days earlier.

"I had the maintenance people put all the plants and flowers in the cafeteria." His assistant Monica stood behind him, carrying storyboards in one hand and a cup of coffee in the other. "I knew you wouldn't want them messing up your office." She handed him the coffee and smiled. "How are you?"

Jack sipped the coffee, cupping his hands around the mug to warm his fingers.

"Just fine, thanks." He tapped the pile of cards with his finger. "I guess I'll have to send thank-you notes to all these people."

"Already done," Monica said.

Jack took another mouthful of coffee, walked to his chair, and slid the heavy, leather bag off his shoulder, letting it drop to the floor. "You really are the best. Thanks, Monica."

He thumbed through a mound of telephone messages tucked inside the corner of his desk blotter, mostly from clients expressing sympathy. As he began reading the others, Monica plopped down in the chair beside his desk.

"No one expected you until Monday, Jack. Being that it's only Friday, your schedule's clear and you really don't need to return those messages yet. Why don't you take it easy today and catch up on things?"

Jack knew he'd be doing more than just catching up, and Mary was first on his list. He'd spent most of the night composing the perfect speech, word for word what he'd say to her, and practicing an even tone so she wouldn't sense his vulnerability. Jack knew Mary wasn't the type of person to change her perspective based on emotion. The worst thing he could do was have her try to find her own sensitivity – something buried so deep, he figured, she'd lose her patience before he even got the words out. By memorizing and practicing his delivery, he was also able to keep his focus off Marc.

"Definitely a day to catch up," he said, reaching for the storyboards on Monica's lap.

She eagerly gave him the boards, exposing the long, smooth legs Jack heard discussed repeatedly in the men's room. As he took the sketches from her, he noticed a quiet sadness in her expression. Her brown eyes, usually wide and filled with anticipation, appeared small and slightly drooped. She bit her bottom lip and busied her fingers by pushing loose strands of blonde hair behind her ears.

"What's up, Monica? What's wrong?"

She shrugged. "Nothing. I'm just not sure what I can do for you."

Jack smiled and leaned back in his oversized leather chair. "Just keep doing what you're doing, Mon. If I need anything, you'll be the first to know."

She turned toward the door, inspecting the office traffic. When she saw the doorway was clear, she moved the chair closer to Jack's desk. "Jack, there's something else. It's about Marc."

Acting nonchalant, he put the storyboards down and leaned his head on his hands. "What about Marc?"

"He called and said he wouldn't be in today. Something about moving. I can't remember exactly. He was mumbling and he sounded kind of nervous, maybe even scared."

Jack rubbed his chin, pretending to wonder. After a few seconds, he shrugged. "I guess we'll have to get by without him today."

Monica pulled the hair from behind her ears, twisting it with her fingers.

"What, Monica? What is it?"

"Okay... well... you know how it is when you're out for a few days.

Like me… I know when I'm out sick or on vacation, people say things about me because I'm not here. You know, they'll say something about my short skirts, my blouses, my makeup, whatever. When I'm not here, people think they can say things about me and I won't know. But that's not the way it works. I always find out what people say, because someone ends up telling me."

Jack faded out for a moment, but came to attention when he heard Marc's name.

"…and he said you and Marc, well, you were having a relationship. And you know, your personal life is your personal life. I'm not one to judge. But he also said some other things that…" Monica stopped mid-sentence and covered her mouth with her hand. "I'm sorry, Jack. This is your first day back. I really shouldn't…"

"No, Monica. I want to hear what's being said. I need to hear it."

She stroked her hair back. With every second she hesitated, the drumbeat in Jack's chest grew.

"He said something about you and Marc having sex in the bathroom." Monica hunched her shoulders and covered her eyes with her hand.

"What!" Jack jumped from his chair. "Are you kidding me? Who told you this?"

Monica jumped back in the chair and sat straight up. "It was Walt. But he said he heard it from Susan. When I confronted her, she said she'd heard it from Brenda who was talking to Todd and —"

"I should've known. That little…" he pounded his desk and looked at Monica. Her sad expression had turned to one of fear.

"I know, Jack, I know. It's crazy! But I thought you should know

81

what they're saying. I tried to deny it as much as I could, but who am I? I didn't know what to say."

"I can't believe this. I'm a VP, for Christ's sake! You'd think they'd have some respect. If I get my hands on Todd, I'll fire him myself. I should've never gotten him that job." Jack felt himself losing control. He paced the floor, looking out the windows, at the ceiling, back to the floor. As if things weren't bad enough, the rumor mill was mincing up the truth and spitting out untruths – evil lies that he feared would cost him more than his job. "I have to find Mulligan," Jack started toward the door, "now!"

"Wait, Jack." Monica stood and blocked the doorway. "You'd better calm down first. You need to sit and organize your thoughts before you take on Mary. Maybe check out the storyboards first, read some copy, make sure the team's on the right track. If you meet with her in this state of mind, you're going to screw yourself."

Jack knew she was right. Feeling like a disciplined five-year old, he turned, walked back behind his desk and sat down.

"I'll shut the door and leave you alone for a little while." Monica stuck her head through the half-closed door. "We'll talk more about it later… if you want. But right now I think you'd better focus on something else for a while. I'm sorry I said anything. I should've waited."

"No, Monica, I'm glad you told me. I need to know these things. Thank you… again."

Monica waved and closed the door.

I'm behind the eight ball already, Jack thought. He picked up the storyboard sitting on top of the file and scanned it. He grabbed his leather bag from the floor, pulled out a yellow legal pad and started to scribble his thoughts. But it wasn't any use. He couldn't get what Monica told him out of his head. Her words echoed through the room, stirring up the same long ago feelings he experienced when the rumors in high school echoed throughout those hallways – people he didn't even know spreading stories about his sexuality, unfounded tales that made their way back to him through others who called themselves his friends.

He never understood how the rumors got started, especially because he'd hidden his feelings so well, acting like everyone else and promising himself not to act on his desires until he escaped the binds of Small Town USA.

"Dana told me what's going on at school," his mother said, following him up the stairs to his room. He'd just walked home from school and going through a Lisa Fontaine life inquiry was not on his top-ten list of pleasurable activities.

"I don't want to talk about it," he snapped. "And tell Dana to keep her big trap shut." The day had been embarrassing enough. His parents' discovery of what had been going on at school was the icing on the cake. Jack wanted to crawl in a hole and die. Of course that would be after he threw Dana down the stairs.

His mother sat down on the corner of his bed and patted the space beside her.

"Please sit for just a minute, Jack," she said, crossing her legs and resting her clasped hands on top of her knees.

Jack sat next to her and she rubbed his leg. "I'm not going to make this long, Jack, I just have one thing to say." She straightened her rose silk blouse and looked right at him. "Actually, I have two things to say. The first is that your father and I want you to know that we love you, no matter who you are or what you do." Jack opened his mouth, but his mother cut him off before he had the chance to speak. "I'm not saying that we believe the rumors, Jack. I'm just saying that to us, you're our Jack and that's all that matters. And when and if you're ready to talk about anything, we're here."

Jack pictured himself falling backward onto the bed, crying, screaming, letting out all the emotions he'd pent up for so long. The anger and humiliation, the pain and loneliness. He wanted to spew it out like an erupting volcano, letting it go until he was empty, free from the self-loathing muck that clogged his veins every day of his life.

But Jack nodded, using his hand to say, "Continue."

"And, secondly, it's apparent why these kids say things about you." Jack saw himself pushing Dana down the stairs, laughing as he informed her that this was her punishment for sharing his life. "You're sensitive, you're sweet, you're smart and you keep up your appearance. They're jealous and envious because they have no idea how to be you."

Jack lay back on the bed and waited for her to continue, but she didn't. He bent his neck and looked up at her.

"That's all." She smiled. "Believe it or not, I'm done." Lisa stood and walked toward the hall. "We love you," she said and closed the door.

Jack sat up, feeling the perspiration under his arms from anxiety and humiliation. He looked around his room wondering why, with all the cool posters and sports paraphernalia scattered around, people still considered him different. It seemed no matter how hard he tried, he could never fit it. He took off his sweat-stained shirt and threw it on the bed, seconds later falling on top of it and soaking it with tears.

Sitting in his office, he was sweating now, too, except this time it was from anger and fear. Ten years later and I'm still fighting the same battles.

He glanced at the framed awards on his wall, precisely arranged according to date his perception of their distinction: Clios lining the top row, Addys filling the second, Edisons below those, along with other miscellaneous marketing and advertising honors. Glints of sunlight reflected off the glass frames and onto the ceiling, creating vertical bars of prismatic radiance.

"Rainbow swizzle sticks," Jack thought aloud, wondering how Samson Bottling, one of J&M's largest accounts, could utilize rainbow swizzle sticks to market their new line of hard liquor. He grabbed his leather bag from the floor, pulled out a yellow legal pad, and scribbled his thoughts. "Neon… square… loops intermingling…" he muttered to himself as he wrote. "Use as incentive for bars, restaurants, clubs, promotions, etc." He glanced again at the colored reflections on the ceiling and followed them back to their source – the awards he'd won over the past four years. He leaned back in his chair, tapped the pen on his chin in a syncopated rhythm and wondered if he'd ever win another award. Forget the awards, he whispered, will I even have a job?

Knowing how quickly J&M's rumor mill processed information, he'd have to take immediate action before other executives got wind of the bogus bathroom story. Taking Monica's advice to calm down might work if he wasn't dealing with Mary, the bitch on wheels, but he couldn't leave anything up to chance… or time. He grabbed the phone and pushed the speed dial that connected him with David's personal extension.

"Hey, Jack, I didn't expect you here this early. Come on by and let's talk."

"David, I was hoping we could meet and then speak with Mary, preferably this morning. I just heard about a rumor that's spreading and I want to reach her before she hears it."

"You mean the bathroom story?"

"Shit." Jack sighed.

"Shit is right. Get in here. We need to talk."

Jack hung up the phone and scrambled to his feet. Briskly walking down the corridor to David's office, he smiled and waved at people in the hallway, trying to appear confident. Any sign of weakness would be like blood in the water for a school of sharks.

"We're too late," David said. "She's already leaked it to the Board." Jack slumped in his chair. Can this be real? Is this really happening? He scanned David's office: The Renoir still hung behind David's desk; the dozens of awards still adorned the wall beside one of the tall windows; and the pendulum of the miniature grandfather clock sitting on the corner of his desk still swayed from side to side. Shit, he thought, this is VERY real.

"How could she do it?" Jack asked. "Does she hate me that much that she'd go to the Board without talking to me first?"

"Or to me, Jack." David crossed his arms and tilted back his chair. "And that's a whole other issue that I'm going to deal with. But right now – first things first. I'm meeting with the Board at ten o'clock. Your situation is just one of the items we'll be discussing. I just need you to remember one thing." David placed his elbows on the desk and leaned forward as if he were going to share the secret of life.

"What is it, David?" Jack scooted forward in his chair.

"I'm the president of J&M, not the sole owner. I have a say in what goes on and I'm in on the important decisions, but my vote is one of six. Five other people have a say in what happens — four narrow-minded men, and, of course, Meredith."

Jack wiped his forehead with the back of his hand and wondered if the heat was set too high. Or did he have a fever? Another anxiety attack? The wife of David's deceased partner, Meredith Johnson, had been the force behind establishing a Board of Directors the day after they found her husband face down on his desk, dead of a heart attack. David's compassion for Meredith, along with his inability to locate financiers who truly understood the business, forced him to capitulate to her selections. Since the Board's formation, every meeting had been argumentative, resulting in weak compromises and half-assed solutions.

"They don't get it." David sighed. "They never have. They're into making money for sure. But because this is such a high-profile business, status and reputation often overpower their greed, if you can believe that. Maybe it's because they're all so freaking wealthy. If J&M went down, they'd still be sitting on a stack of cash."

Jack pulled himself up from the chair and walked to the window. Leaning his shoulder against the glass, he looked down at the Charles. The water was choppy, foam spraying high in the air from the crashing waves, like the waves in his head, splashing and splattering warm liquid against the walls of his skull. "I'm screwed, aren't I?"

"Not yet, Jack. I'm just telling you how it is. I want you to be prepared in case I can't talk some sense into them. This won't be the first time I've taken on the entire Board – it's something I'm used to. I'd say I'm batting four-fifty with them for the month. The trick is to raise the average and make them see how much we'd suffer without you, which in turn would hurt their wallets."

David walked over to Jack and gently rubbed his shoulder. Jack wanted to turn around and hug David, but he knew he had to restrain himself. There were enough rumors floating around. He ducked away, leaving David's hand in mid-air as he rushed to the door. Stepping into the hallway, he offered David a nod of thanks and headed back to his office, wondering how he'd survive the day.

Peering through the narrow panel of glass beside the conference room door, David shook his head, amazed at the sight before him: Meredith Johnson sat regally at the far end of the conference table in a dark blue pinstriped suit that, for a fleeting moment, David thought he recognized as one of her deceased husband's client presentation outfits. To her left, Arthur Kennedy perched himself on the edge of the table, his back to the others as he held his cell phone to one ear and stuck his finger in the other in order to mute the surrounding noise. David figured he was probably talking to his stockbroker, selling his J&M shares before the sordid news hit the street. Across from Arthur, James Stratford hunched over a stack of papers, pushing the buttons of the oversized calculator that was by his side wherever he traveled. As chief financial officer, James was responsible for J&M's bottom line, and, knowing his relentless drive to prove himself, David wondered if the mound of papers he'd brought with him contained calculated proof that Jack's asset status had moved to the liability column. By the glistening beads of sweat on James's balding head, David began to fear the worst.

Behind Meredith, gazing out the floor-to-ceiling windows, the Kennedy brothers, Jon and Ross, stood with their hands clasped behind their backs, apparently nodding in agreement to something one or the other had said. From the day their inherited fortune landed them on J&M's Board of Directors, they hadn't once disagreed with one another on a single issue. It took only a quick glance and nod for each to know what the other was thinking, and David spent the majority of these meetings trying to sway Ross, the older of the two, toward his own way of thinking. The Kennedys based their decades of lucrative business endeavors on "respecting their elders," listening and learning from family members who possessed the experience and wisdom of their age. Although Ross was only a year older than Jon, they held to this tenet like dogs with bones and David knew that once he convinced Ross on any issue, he'd have two votes in his favor.

About to turn the doorknob, David stood motionless as Mary Mulligan walked across his line of sight. What the hell is she doing here? It immediately became clear that the Board must've called her to act as the star witness, the leading expert in the field of Corporate Ethics, who would attempt to hang Jack out to dry with her HR handbook and college dissertation on Organizational Behavior. As if she'd heard his thoughts, Mary turned to the door and nodded. Her face was drawn, a hint of sadness surrounding her eyes. Her expression reminded David of a night, ten years earlier, when she appeared on his doorstep, drenched from a downpour, her body trembling uncontrollably from the late autumn chill and the horrific scene from which she'd been running.

He motioned for her to exit the conference room and meet him in the hall. With a huff she obeyed, and, before fully closing the door behind her, she'd already started to whisper her tirade.

"What do you want, David? They're waiting for you. There's a lot to discuss today and I – "

"In a second, Mary!" David interrupted. "First I have one question and I'd like an honest answer."

"What is it, David?" She sighed, glaring at the curious faces passing them by.

"I want to make sure this isn't about Max," he said, trying to conceal his anger by infusing a soft tone to his voice.

Mary threw back her head and forced a chuckle. "Don't be ridiculous, David. That was ten years ago and I've gotten past it. This whole thing is about decency in the workplace. That's all."

"Mary, to be honest, I don't think you've gotten over it. And I have a strong feeling you're using this opportunity to seek revenge for Max's adultery." Mary twisted her head toward the conference room door. "I understand it was devastating, especially catching him with another man, and in your own home, on top of it. That sort of thing leaves wounds that take years to heal, if they heal at all. But you need to understand that this is Jack we're talking about, not Max."

"You're wrong, David," Mary said adamantly, crossing her arms.

"I don't think I am, Mary. You keep bringing up decency and I believe you think that being gay is indecent. I'm not sure if you thought that way before the Max ordeal, but, by the way you've been acting, I have no doubt homosexuality sickens you. And that's perfectly understandable considering what you've been through. But it's showing prejudice, and, as the person in charge of Human Resources, it's something that should never be part of your decision-making process."

"You're wrong, David," she insisted. "We're talking about decency in the workplace, that's all. You're stepping over the line here and I refuse to listen anymore."

Mary turned and opened the door.

"Decency is one thing, Mary, vengeance is another," David whispered, following her into the room. "Please try to differentiate between the two."

As they entered the room, the Board members looked at them in silence without any sort of welcoming glance or gesture. David met their stoicism with a smile, so forced and out of place, he panicked, worried that he wasn't going to be able to keep his breakfast down.

6

Cory's dream was to hit it big, find the opportunity that would bring him the cash he needed to retire at thirty and live the life of luxury he deserved. He knew he couldn't continue his current schemes. Sooner or later someone would catch on, and he'd either lose his job or end up in Devens Federal Prison – the institution his father called home for two years before the guards found him hanging from the sweaty pipes of the mess hall ceiling. Cory promised himself he'd never end up like that. He'd never get caught.

"That asshole!" he yelled over the rumbling of the car's engine. Although he'd been a little smashed the night before, he clearly remembered telling Marc he'd pick him up at ten o'clock, but Marc hadn't answered his phone or responded to Cory's fist pounding on the door. As he continued knocking, Cory heard the shuffling of slippered feet along the broken tiled floor below. He looked down the staircase and almost laughed at the troll-like woman contorting her neck, trying to see who was causing the racket.

"Whatta you bangin' about?" the woman shouted, her accent so thick with vowels Cory had trouble understanding her. "Whatta you wanta with Marco? He'sa not here."

Cory peeked down the rickety steps at the chubby, middle-aged woman, a red kerchief wrapped so tightly around her head that her eyes protruded from their sockets.

"I'm sorry, ma'am," Cory said, turning on his charm. "I'm supposed to pick Marc up this morning and he's not answering the door. I'm a little worried about him."

She slapped the air with her hand. "He'sa not here, I said. He lefta, dis mornin, bout an hour ago. I gava him a muffin to take with him. So skinny, you know. So skinny." She shook her head and slapped the air again, this time with both hands.

Slowly, Cory descended the stairs. When he reached the woman, he examined her paisley housecoat: frayed at the edges with long threads hanging loosely to her knees. She had to be less than five feet tall, forcing him to bend over to grab her hand, which he tenderly kissed. He peered into her eyes and revealed his straight, white teeth. Immediately her expression softened and she stared at the floor in modest embarrassment.

"I know, Signora," Cory said, "he's very skinny. I wanted to take him to breakfast, you know, fatten him up a little. Do you know where he went?"

She shook her head, searching for something in his eyes. "No, I donta know where. He had a bagga with him, a suitacase, you know, something to carry clothes in. He hada very sad looka on his face. I felta bad for him. He's soa sad all the timea, anda so skinny, so skinny."

Cory felt his face grow hot. Not only had Marc blown him off, but he'd lost his chance to snoop around Jack's apartment. In the past he'd searched through the belongings of strangers and found valuable information. He'd known this was his opportunity to snoop through Jack's apartment and he wasn't going to let it pass him by.

Cory hid his frustration by widening his smile and kissing her hand again. "Thank you, Signora," he said in a sultry tone. "I'll find Marc and I'll be sure to get him some breakfast."

She smiled back, her hand hanging in mid-air after Cory slipped past her and ran to his car.

Cory pressed his foot on the gas pedal, revving the engine to relieve his growing tension. As he mapped out the fastest route to Jack's apartment, his cell phone rang. The display showed his home telephone number.

"Hey, Janice," he said. "What's up? I'm kinda in the middle of something."

"I just wanted you to know I didn't go to work today," she said, her voice raspy and filled with phlegm, a sound with which Cory had become despairingly accustomed. "I'm still in bed."

"What's wrong?" he asked.

"Too much alcohol, I think. Or maybe it was the coke. I don't know." She cleared her throat and swallowed so hard Cory almost gagged. "I didn't even hear you leave this morning."

"I have a lot to do, Janice." He glanced at the dashboard clock. It was ten-fifteen and his agitation was building. "I'll stop by later and bring you some soup or something. Get some sleep. Gotta go, love ya." Without waiting for a response, he flipped the phone closed and flung it onto the passenger seat. He stepped on the clutch, slid the car into first gear and sped down the narrow street, leaving in his wake a cloud of smoke and a middle-aged woman from Sardinia longing to be twenty again.

On his way to Jack's apartment, he decided to call Mary Mulligan. Three weeks had passed since he stopped by J&M to introduce himself, and this was the perfect time to check in with her. He remembered scrawling Mary's phone number on the back of one of his business cards and he searched for it - fingering his way through gum wrappers and receipts stuffed tightly into the narrow compartment above the ashtray on the dash. "Bingo!" he exclaimed, holding the card up to the light. He dialed the number and stuffed the card into the pocket of his shirt. After assuring her assistant Nancy he'd only take a few minutes of Mary's time, she transferred his call.

"Funny you should call, Cory," Mary said. "There might be an opportunity for you here. I can't give you the specifics, but I have your number and I'll call if things go the way I think they will."

Cory felt the adrenaline shoot through his veins. Slam dunk!

"I thought so." He banged his forehead with his fist, "I mean, there's always an opportunity at a company the size of J&M. By the way, I'd like to take you out to lunch sometime soon – tell you a little about the firm and myself. If I don't hear from you within a week or so, I'll give you a call, okay?"

He slipped the Jaguar into a parking space across the street from Jack's building and peered up at the apartment. No sign of movement, no indication Marc was inside.

"Mary? Are you still there?" he asked, impatience eating a hole in his stomach. He had to get upstairs.

"Uh, yes, Cory. I'm sorry. Just got caught up in something. I'll wait for your call. Goodbye."

He flipped the phone closed and slid it into his jacket pocket. The small shops and mini-marts lining the sidewalks on both sides of the street were bustling with activity and Cory's envy surfaced with a vengeance. This was Boston's Back Bay section, an area designed for the wealthy – the social elite who had everything they could ever desire at their fingertips, never having to walk more than a few feet to fulfill their needs. At that moment he made a promise to himself to investigate the community and find out what he needed to do to become a part of it. This, he decided, was where he belonged.

He leapt out of the car, dodging an onslaught of traffic as he ran toward the giant apartment building across the street. He peered through the oversized glass doors into a vestibule leading to another set of bevel-edged glass doors with gold-plated handles. The right hand wall of the vestibule contained mail slots, small buttons, and apartment numbers. Looking further into the lobby, he cupped his hands over his eyes to deflect the glare and caught site of a doorman's cap, the rest of his body hidden behind a wooden podium. Cory bit his bottom lip – someone would have to buzz him inside before he could even get near the elevator. Pretending to search for keys, he smiled at a tall, slender woman walking down the street toward him. Her flowing blonde hair, tied back with a bright purple scrunchy, thrashed behind her like the back end of a mare. He gave her a nod and pulled open the first door, allowing her to pass beneath his arm.

"Forgot my key," he said, feigning embarrassment.

"Been there!" she offered a flirtatious smirk before the doorman waved and buzzed them in. Together they walked past the doorman and onto the waiting elevator where Cory exhaled a silent breath of relief.

"Thanks," he said. "I thought I'd be stuck out there forever. That doorman of ours isn't the most alert guy around."

"Isn't that the truth?" The woman laughed. She pressed the button that would take her to the fourth floor and searched her leopard-skin pocketbook for her keys. "I can't seem to find my keys either," she said, half-panicked.

He smiled. "Looks like it's catching. My name's Tom," he said, sticking out his hand.

She pulled her fingers out of her handbag and shook his hand. "Teresa," she said, "Apartment four-twelve."

Cory rubbed the top of her hand with his thumb, glancing at the panel of buttons behind her. "Apartment seven-fifteen," he replied, almost inaudibly, hoping she didn't know who lived in that apartment.

He didn't let go of her hand until the elevator came to a gentle stop. Just before the doors opened, Teresa dangled keys from her bony fingers. "Tada!" she sang, as though she'd just pulled a rabbit from a leopard-skinned hat.

"Let's hope I get as lucky," Cory replied, pretending to search through his jacket pockets.

"Maybe I'll see you around," she said, stepping out of the elevator.

"Definitely!" Cory said, digging his fingers deep into his pants pockets. "Maybe sooner than you think if I don't find my keys."

Teresa smiled and walked away, disappearing as she turned left down the fluorescent-lighted hallway. As soon as she turned the corner, Cory concluded his bogus key search and rubbed his hands together. "Maybe sooner than you think." He pressed the penthouse button and fixed his hair in the reflection of the metal doors that took forever to close.

The door to Jack's apartment was slightly ajar and Cory hesitated, wiping the perspiration off the back of his neck with his clammy palm.

What if Jack's in there? What if he's got cleaning people working? What if Marc didn't even come here in the first place? Each question was like a hot poker stinging his skull. He placed his ear to the door, standing rigid, alert for any sound. After a few moments, Cory gently nudged the door and let it swing open.

He immediately recognized Marc's jacket draped over one of the dining room chairs. Sandwiched between the sofa and recliner, a plaid suitcase rested on the floor. Cory lifted each foot slowly, creeping into the apartment and silently praying the wooden floor wouldn't creak. Before he reached the sofa, he came to a halt, and craned his neck, straining to hear. "Marc?" he called with such restraint he could barely hear himself. "Marc?" he repeated, this time with more force, "are you here?" There was no response. "Is anyone here?"

Things felt wrong. There was coldness in the air, an inimical sensation he hadn't expected. Initially he thought the feeling was his own anxiety, but he never gambled with his intuition. If he was going to nose around, he knew he'd have to do it quickly before whoever left the door open returned.

On the granite sofa table, between a DVD and an oversized, half-filled coffee mug, Marc's keys spread out like the fingers of an open hand. Cory tiptoed through the living-room, glancing back at the door every few seconds to make certain he was alone. When he reached the panel of windows overlooking the city, he inhaled deeply and took in the view. "Must be nice," he muttered. He squinted into bright sunlight that polished the Charles with a blanket of orange chrome. This is where I belong, he thought again. I deserve a view like this.

Through a doorway on the right he spotted a nightstand and the edge of a bed. After another quick side glance at the front door, he scuffled into the room.

At first he thought the covered mound was simply a crumpled blanket on the unmade bed. But, stepping over the pile of clothes, he glimpsed an arm dangling down the side. Cory felt every muscle in his body constrict; visions of Sunday visits to Devens to meet his father flew like photo-filled flashbulbs past his mind's eye. He tried to ignore his rising goose bumps and moved closer to the heap of tangled blankets and sheets. A bottle of pills lay on the Oriental rug beneath the king-sized platform bed. With the precision of a surgeon, he used his thumb and index finger to pull the comforter toward him, exposing the body.

"You have GOT to be kidding me," he said out loud. "This is like a bad freakin' movie of the week."

Except for his trembling eyelids, Marc lay naked and motionless, one arm and one leg wrapped around a king-sized pillow. Cory knelt and put his ear to Marc's nose. A slight sense of relief passed over him when he heard the breath, shallow as it was. With his knuckles, he rolled the pill bottle across the floor so he could see the label. Although the words were smeared, Cory made out Jack's name and the word Diazepam. "Valium," he whispered. "God, what an idiot."

Cory glanced at the phone sitting on the nightstand and, for a fleeting moment, considered calling 911. He trashed the thought, knowing if he made the call there'd be no way to distance himself from the situation. "What were you doing here?" "What's your involvement with Marc Whittaker?" "How do you know Jack Fontaine?" "Who?" "When?" "Why?" The spit from the imaginary police detective hit his face, forcing him up against the wall.

Cory shook his head and lifted himself up. "This could actually help the cause," he whispered. "Now it's a real scandal."

He studied Marc's skin, a color so bloodless his body was almost absorbed by the whiteness of the sheets. With his hand still trembling, Cory reached over and placed his hand in the curve of Marc's neck. Still warm.

He pulled his hand back and wiped it on his jacket as though he'd just extracted it from a vat of toxic liquid. "You'll be okay," Cory whispered, pulling the cover up to Marc's neck. "Jack will take care of you." He was astonished at himself for actually hoping his prognosis was correct.

Stepping back into the living-room, Cory saw a flicker of sunlight bounce off the shiny edge of a DVD. Using old tissues from his jacket pocket, he lifted the DVD from the table and looked for a label, anything to reveal its contents. Nothing! Damn it! Probably gay porn anyway.

Still holding the DVD, he gently tapped it against his forehead and considered the options. He walked to the front door, nudged it closed with his shoulder, skulked back to the sofa, and sat down across from the DVD player.

"A quick preview couldn't hurt." He pushed the DVD into the slot and leaned back into the plush leather cushions.

An oblong, mahogany conference table filled most of the windowless room. The occupants could barely move their chairs without banging into a wall or colliding with someone. Eight-by-ten framed prints of past ad campaigns blanketed the walls, adding to the closeness of the room and making it seem even smaller. Ten of Jack's group leaders sat around the table, waiting in silence, until the petite brunette stretched both arms above her head.

"This room gives me claustrophobia," she said to no one in particular.

Low sighs and grunts echoed her thought.

"Marisa, a baseball stadium would give you claustrophobia," Eric said, smearing the table's glossy veneer with the moist tip of his index finger.

Marisa glared at him. "It's too early for you, Eric," she retorted.

"Marisa, I hate to tell you this, but it's after eleven. Hello… time to wake up!" The others sitting around the table smiled, no one daring to laugh aloud, knowing the couple's past and unwilling to take sides.

"I just said this room gives me claustrophobia, Eric!" she started. "Why do you have to –"

She halted the exchange the moment Jack entered the room. He marched to the front, placing a pile of storyboards and comps on the table. Slipping his hands into the pockets of his black khakis, he scanned the room and offered everyone a slight smile.

"I'm sorry we had to meet in this room," he said, giving Marisa an inconspicuous glance, "but the Board commandeered the large conference room and this was the only other place available. We'll keep the door open for this meeting. We wouldn't want anyone passing out."

"It's okay," Marisa said. "We can deal."

Jack nodded and forced a laugh. "Thank you, Marisa. And now that you're happy, we can start." She rolled her eyes in response. "First I want to thank everyone for the condolence cards and notes. I appreciate all of them very much." Except for Marisa, everyone looked down at the table. Jack sensed their discomfort and banged his fist on the table. "Now, back to work!"

He held up the board from the top of the stack, viewable from all sides of the room. They examined the sketch – a bottle of brandy surrounded by snifters – with the headline: The Definition of Smooth. Jack scanned the faces before him and rested his eyes on Walter, leader of the Samson Bottling creative team.

"What do you see here?" he asked the room.

Walter leaned back in his chair and jerked forward when he hit the wall. Regaining his composure, he folded his arms on his chest and took a deep breath. Jack recognized Walter's typical defensive posture, but held his stare anyway.

"Brandy is smooth. People want smooth. They want to know each sip of brandy will feel like velvet on their tongues," Walter said, speaking to Jack and to everyone else in the room. "Hence, the 'smooth' positioning."

All heads turned to Jack. Be gentle, Jack reminded himself, be kind.

"Got it, Walt. I definitely understand where you're heading with this. However, let's think back to our presentation with Samson's marketing people. We decided the focus of the campaign would be pleasure and enjoyment. Drinking alcohol isn't about glistening snifters or pretty bottles – it's about people enjoying themselves and feeling good. I don't see one person in this ad… no couples sitting by a fire, no small get-together or cocktail party with smiling people delighting in one another's company. There's no warmth in this ad, and definitely no sign of enjoyment. Sure, the concept shows smooth, but that's only one aspect of the product. The ad needs to show the end result of smoothness… how the experience of drinking the brandy will enhance the drinker's life. It has to…" Jack stopped in the middle of his sentence and looked down at the table. He realized he was breaking one of his strictest rules: Let them figure it out on their own – a rule David had consistently adhered to while mentoring him. Still standing, Jack tapped the stack of storyboards and comps with his middle finger. "Unfortunately, I have the same problem with every concept in this pile."

Marisa's eyes widened. She pulled her hair back into a ponytail and brought it around her neck, letting it cascade down her left shoulder. "Even the candy ads from my group?" she asked.

"Even the candy ads from your group," Jack echoed.

"But we show kids having fun! Loving the candy, enjoying themselves."

Jack thumbed through the heap of boards, pulled out the Chaco chocolate ad and showed it to the room.

"What do you see?" he asked Marisa.

"Like I said, I see kids having fun and loving the candy."

"Yes, the kids are having fun… lots of fun. But what I'm focusing on is the mess they're making," he added. "Look at the candy stains all over their faces." He pointed to a toddler standing in the center of a circle of children. "And look at this kid – he's got chocolate on his shirt. You've got to remember, this isn't an ad for kids, it's for their parents. One look at this picture and they'll turn the page – either because they think it's an advertisement for Tide laundry detergent or because they don't want to have to clean up the mess their kids will make with Chaco candy."

"I totally disagree, Jack," Marisa said, braiding her hair.

Jack glanced toward the ceiling and took a deep breath. "I'm sorry to hear that, Marisa, but, unfortunately for you, I don't care," he snapped. "You know better than this," he said, banging the sketch with his hand. "This is sloppy work. Period. And I'm sure our contacts at Chaco would think the same thing. But, thankfully, they won't see this. They'll be seeing something a lot more creative… by the end of the day."

The room was silent except for muffled voices coming from the hallway and the sound of copy machines squeaking paper through their grips. Jack slowly paced the front of the room and wiped his forehead with the back of his hand; the fear that he'd returned to work too soon numbed his legs. The walls were moving inward, squeezing the oxygen from the room and the air out of his lungs. His head started to spin and he leaned his shoulder against the wall.

"Jack." Eric got up. "Are you okay?"

Dana… Jenna… Marc… Mary…the people and circumstances of his life crashed against one another in his mind, all catching up with him at once. Anxiety began to overwhelm his logic and he felt the sudden need to be alone, to sit in darkness and focus his mind. But this wasn't the time or place; the room was filled with people he had just offended and chanting meditations would only add fodder to the rumor mill. He rolled against the wall, from his shoulder to his back, facing the wide-eyed employees.

"I'm fine, Walt," Jack said. He pinched his nose and pressed his hand against his mouth. "I'm sorry, everyone. I have to go." He squeezed past the back of a few chairs, leaving some of the hanging prints swinging on their hooks. When he reached the exit he turned around and forced a smile. "New concepts by tomorrow morning, please."

He raced down the hallway towards his office and held up his open palm as Monica tried to give him his messages. "Not now," he muttered.

Jack slammed his office door and switched off the lights. He pushed the lock button on the doorknob and closed the vertical blinds to block the view of the outside corridor. Walking to his desk, he considered calling his parents, but quickly dismissed the idea, not only because he needed more than emotional support or fitting platitudes, but because they were in the midst of their own private hell. They'd just buried a daughter and he thought it unfair to add another burden to their shoulders. He plopped into his chair and hadn't even closed his eyes when he heard someone trying to turn the doorknob. He ignored the knocking until the muffled voice on the other side of the door compelled him to stand. "Jack, it's me, David. We need to talk."

Smoothing his hands against the coarse fuzz covering his head, Todd cursed his father. "Damn genetics," he whispered to himself. The decision to shave his head was difficult – months of uncertainty, wondering if he should let creeping baldness gradually steal his hair, or take action and disguise his thinning locks with a buzz cut. Yesterday he'd watched the wispy tufts of hair fall to the salon floor and he could still feel the razor's vibration. He gazed into the small mirror tacked to the wall in front of his desk and sighed, still questioning his decision.

"I like it," Mary said.

Startled, Todd jumped and looked in the mirror behind his own image. Mary Mulligan stood within the narrow pathway of J&M's giant computer servers, hands hidden behind her back. She looked like a four-star general standing at attention, on the verge of executing her next command. In the eight months since he'd started at J&M, this was only the second time he'd seen Mary inside the computer room. The first was a few months earlier when he'd spent the entire night repairing the e-mail server. Mary had burst into the room at seven-thirty am, demanding to know when she'd be able to spread her impersonal communications to the rest of the world. As luck would have it, he had the server up and running only two minutes before her dramatic entrance.

"Thanks," he said, swiveling his chair to face her. "I blame my father for this."

"What do you mean?" Mary walked toward him, hands still clasped behind her back.

"I'm only twenty-five and I'm losing my hair. It's genetics. My father's bald and so was his father. I've been cursed. So who else do I blame?"

"Actually," Mary smiled, "I've heard baldness comes from the mother's side. But it doesn't really matter, Todd. You'll find a lot worse things to blame your parents for. Don't waste it on your hair." She looked down at him as she leaned on the desk. "I think it looks good."

Her words surprised him, an apparent attempt to offer sincere advice. She still made him feel cold inside, but he decided to accept any hint of warmth she was willing to offer. "Thanks again. Now, how can I help you today, Ms. Mulligan?"

Mary glanced around the room, then back to Todd. "Are we alone?"

"Yup. Keith is out among the ranks doing house calls and Marty is —"

"Good," she interrupted. "I have a question for you."

"And I hope I have some answers. Shoot."

"What you saw in the bathroom that day," she said, looking around the room again. "Did you actually see what you reported? I mean, did you see it with your own eyes or did you only hear something?"

Todd ran his palm along his stubble, worked his hand down the back of his head, and grabbed his neck.

"I saw it, Mary. I saw it with my own eyes." he dug his fingers into the tense muscle holding up his head. "And like I said, others saw it too. Not that day, but other times, usually after hours. But I can't give you names. If they want to tell you, they can, but I don't want to get anyone in trouble."

Mary shifted her position on the edge of his desk, folded her arms across her chest, and peered down at him. "How well do you know Cory Daniels?" she asked.

Todd was floored. Why was she asking these questions? What did she know? "Not that well," he replied, trying to hide the tremble beneath his voice. "I mean, we're not friends or anything. He helped get me this job. Actually, I haven't spoken to him since. Why?"

"Just wondering," she said vaguely. "I was looking through some files yesterday and noticed you and Marc both came from Stetson and Cory placed you."

Todd leaned back in his chair. "But Jack recommended me too. That's in the file, right?"

"Yes, it is. That's why it's so surprising that you'd snitch on him like this." Mary lifted her eyebrows awaiting his response.

"I know," Todd said, looking to the floor, "I feel bad about it, but it's just not good for J&M to have those things going on in the workplace. I did it for the good of the company."

Mary felt the insincerity of his words permeate her skin and she quickly changed the subject.

"Did you know Marc while you were at Stetson?"

"Barely. I was computers, he was mailroom. We never had much contact. They didn't have computers down there, at least not the kind I could repair. I'd see him once in a while, delivering mail or eating lunch, but that's about it. Why?"

Todd's thoughts were spinning. He grabbed a lollipop from his desk drawer, almost forgetting to unwrap it before placing it on his tongue. He knew Mary was a shrewd woman, but he and Cory had been so deliberate, so detailed in their strategy, he couldn't imagine she'd figure it out. Unless . . . his heart skipped a beat. Unless Marc had said something to her, surrendered his guilt by vomiting up the entire scheme during an inquisition similar to this one.

"I'm just curious," she said as she rose and pressed out the wrinkles of her skirt with her hands. "Thank you and…" she pointed to his mouth, "I've been meaning to ask, what's with the lollipops? I never see you without one."

Todd smiled, took the sucker from his mouth and twisted it within his fingers.

"I like 'em. They help me concentrate."

"Better watch your teeth. Too much sugar and they'll rot away." Todd knew Mary didn't give one iota about his teeth; she was obviously heading somewhere with this. He nodded, waiting for her to continue. "Sometimes people develop bad habits to relieve stress. For instance, when some people get nervous they eat a lot or smoke cigarettes."

Act cool. Just stay cool.

"Well, I must be an extremely nervous person, because I do both," he replied, tossing the lollipop back in his mouth, catching it with his tongue. "Add my suckers to the mix, and I'm one total neurotic."

Mary gave him a smile that told Todd she'd rather stick the lollipop down his esophagus than continue their conversation. "Thanks for the info, Todd. Have a good day," she said, turning around toward the door.

Todd smiled without saying a word and watched her march out of the room without even a glance behind her. He looked in the mirror and lifted his top lip to examine his teeth. A little yellow, maybe, but not rotting. Bitch. He chewed down hard on the Tootsie pop and dialed Cory's number.

"What else did she say?" Cory asked, turning on his flashers and pulling to the side of the road.

"That's it. She was vague. I'm not sure if it was just curiosity or she's actually on to something. All I know is, she threw me for a loop and I almost crapped in my pants. Have you talked to Marc? Do you know if he confessed anything to her?"

"Marc didn't say a word." Cory ran his fingers through his hair, fighting the thought of Marc's naked body and pushing past the pang of guilt about leaving him to fend for himself. He's a big boy, Cory rationalized, letting loose strands of wavy hair fall in front of his eyes. "Trust me, he didn't say anything."

"I hope not. What are you going to do now? Is there any way to fix this, just in case?"

Cory observed the passing cars, envious of the people who were accomplishing tasks and would soon arrive at their destinations. For the first time in his life he felt dazed and a little baffled. There was no doubt he needed to handle the Mary situation, that he knew. But what would he do about the DVD he just viewed? He couldn't just sit on the sidelines – this was too big.

"Are you there, Cory? Come on, I have to get back to work. Tell me what to do."

Cory shook his head and squeezed the phone. "Just go back to what you were doing. Pretend nothing happened, Todd, stay cool. The more uptight you get, the quicker she'll see you're up to something. Take some deep breaths or something. I'll call you later."

Cory hung up the phone and turned off the car's engine. A light rain began to fall, spattering against the roof of his car. Through the tinted sunroof he watched the grayish-white, low hanging clouds swiftly moving eastward. They were traveling somewhere – across the city, over the river, perhaps holding together long enough to reach another state. And Cory was determined to do the same.

7

"Three months. That's all, Jack, just three months," David said, closing the door behind him. "Can I turn on the lights? It's like a cave in here."

Jack nodded indifferently.

With the sudden onslaught of light David quickly lifted his hand to shade his eyes. "They wanted permanent dismissal," he said, "but, after a lengthy speech by yours truly, they opened up to a three-month leave of absence – just until things quiet down a bit. I think we did pretty well, don't you?"

Jack staggered back to his desk and fell into his chair. "Three months, three years, either way, it's a done deal," he whispered.

David furrowed his brow and sat down in the chair across from Jack. "What are you talking about? I know this whole thing was blown out of proportion, but considering the uptight people we're dealing with, I think a three-month leave is a good thing. It's just a blip on the radar, a little time for you to relax and do something you enjoy. Six months from now, no one will even remember this."

Jack leaned back in his chair, resting his head against the soft leather cushion supporting his neck. His body was so numb he couldn't tell if his face held a smile or a grimace; he had to judge David's expression as an indication of his own.

"Jack, are you okay? Say something, talk to me."

"Like I said, David, three months or three years, it doesn't matter. It's a stain on my character – something people will always remember.

By throwing me out for three months, the Board is saying I'm guilty."
Jack leaned his elbows on the arms of his chair and pressed the tips of
his fingers together. "And when I return, it'll be impossible to regain
the respect of my department… or anyone else for that matter. They'll
always have something to hold against me when I criticize their work
or their attitudes. 'How can this sexual deviant tell me what's right and
what's wrong?' That's what they'll be asking themselves every day until
I'm gone for good." Jack let his hands fall to the sides of the chair and
sighed. "Let's face it David, it's over."

David shook his head feverishly. "That's bullshit, Jack. And from
what you're saying, I think three months off will be good for you. It
sounds like everything's catching up with you and you need a good
rest. Take the time to get over Dana's death and everything else that's
going on in your life. Once your head's clear you'll see things
differently. I guarantee it."

Jack pushed his breath through his tightened lips. "David, I
appreciate everything you've done for me, from the day I started until
this moment. But you're right, I'm beat. And I don't think three
months will make things any better. You know, I'm starting to wonder
what the hell everything's all about anyway – why we work so hard,
why we go through all we do, the suffering, the heartbreak, the anxiety.
It doesn't make sense to me. In the end, it all winds up the same – we
die, with nothing to show we were here but insignificant possessions
we pass on to other people. The whole thing is ludicrous."

David walked around the desk to Jack's chair. He crouched to meet
Jack's eyes.

"This is not you talking, Jack. This is fear talking. It's

her lips and emptied it.

She'd purchased the apartment the same day her divorce from Max had become final. After the papers were signed and the lawyers left the room, Mary slid her pocketbook strap over her shoulder and headed for the door, unable to look at her newly estranged ex-husband.

"Wait, Mary," he called, rising from his chair. "I just want to say – "

"Don't!" she said, looking past him, out the window, at the attorneys shaking hands, probably heading out for a mid-morning liquid lunch, she thought. "There's nothing to say."

"But there is," he paused and cleared his throat. "I'm sorry."

Mary fingered the clasp of her pocketbook, looking for anything that would divert her attention from the situation and move her closer to the door. She wanted to respond, but her emotions squelched any sensible words.

"I'm sorry," Max repeated. "I just hope that one day you'll forgive me."

Her words surprised even herself. "I do forgive you," she uttered, unsure if what she'd just said was true. "It's my fault. I should've known what was going on. I had a feeling… something inside… I denied it… hoping…" She felt the weight of tears forming along her eyelids and cupped her hand over her mouth. Running to the door, she turned to look at Max who, she was relieved to see, had a tear running down his cheek.

"I have to go," she said, darting into the hall and slamming the door behind her.

She hadn't seen Max since that day almost ten years ago, but the burning sensation that had invaded her chest during their last meeting had never subsided even slightly. And the anger she'd felt sifting into her bloodstream the moment she'd caught him with another man flowed through her body today with the same intensity as a decade ago. She poured another glass of wine and sunk deeper into the chair.

The chatter in Mary's head grew louder. The senseless din was now composed of a single voice: David Macrae, accusing her of persecuting Jack in order to get back at Max. As his voice roared so did her pain, forcing her to jump from the chair and flee into her bedroom, leaving the blanket that warmed her shoulders lying on the cold, uncarpeted wooden floor.

She sat down at her makeup table, promising herself not to look in the mirror. Reaching for the mahogany jewelry box, her fingers scraped along the top of the table, scattering eyebrow pencils, mascara, face powder and every other war paint instrument she'd been using to disguise her pain. Delicately, she pinched the miniature ballerina standing atop the jewelry box and pulled upward, releasing an off-key version of Elton John's "Tiny Dancer" while at the same time exposing unmatched pieces of jewelry. She slipped the gold wedding band onto her left ring finger and studied her hand, pretending, for one brief moment, that any second Max would walk through the front door and tell her about his day. She took a sip of wine and wiped the teardrop falling down her cheek with the back of her hand.

Grabbing the jewelry box's false bottom, she lifted it slowly and pulled out the photo she'd so often held to her chest as she fell off to sleep: She and Max, standing proudly atop a butte somewhere in New Mexico, smiling at a stranger kind enough to take a few minutes out of his tranquil meditation to snap the photograph. A stranger she yearned to meet with one more time so she could ask him to recall the moment and give her a detailed account of what it was like to see her smile.

Slipping the photograph into her shirt pocket, she stumbled into the living room and refilled her glass. A strong gust of wind pushed rain hard against the windows, startling her and causing her to spill wine onto one of the manila folders lying on the coffee table. She smeared it with her fingers, hoping she'd be able to find an extra folder into which she could transfer its contents. She glanced at the folder's tab which read Todd Lindsay and opened it up, fingering through the papers inside. On the table below sat two other folders, one tab read Marc Whittaker, the other Jack Fontaine. Setting the glass on the table, she snatched the blanket from the floor and rewrapped it around her shoulders.

She pushed the back of her head into the chair's pillowed headrest, remembering why these folders were in her home: During her conversation with Cory, she'd felt a wave of suspicion. There was something in his tone, an indication that he was aware of something he shouldn't be privy to. At first she denied her hunch, but, after speaking with Todd earlier that morning, she was convinced there was some sort of collusion taking place. Further, her intuition had forced her to doubt Jack's guilt, and, as Vice President of Human Resources, she knew it was her job to get to the bottom of things.

The sound of David's voice had disappeared from her head. She wondered if it was because she realized he might be right about her using Jack's situation to get revenge on Max. Through her shirt, she rubbed the photograph in her pocket. She gathered the three folders into a pile and placed them on her lap, still unwilling to completely concede to David's accusations, but knowing, deep inside, that her responsibility to J&M must take precedence over her personal vendettas. If there was one thing she was convinced her employees deserved, it was the truth. After all, she thought as she started to sift through Todd's file, they were the only people she had left in her life.

Pelting rain struck the windows like liquid bullets, blurring the view and creating a dismal emptiness throughout the loft. The first thing Jack noticed as he closed the door behind him was Marc's jacket and suitcase.

"Shit!" he whispered. It was almost four in the afternoon and he figured Marc would've collected his things hours ago. He dropped the box of office trinkets he'd brought home onto the dining room table, slipped off his coat, and threw it onto the sofa. Shit! I really don't need this right now!

He crept over to the windows, straining to look into the bedroom without actually going in. A gust of wind drove the rain hard against the glass. Jack jumped backward and grabbed his chest. He knew he was too highly strung and needed to compose himself before facing the last event of his already nightmarish day. Taking two deep breaths, he raked his hand through his hair and marched into the bedroom.

"Marc," he called. Silence. "Marc?" Jack glanced around the room. The only evidence of Marc was the pile of clothing on the floor and the unmade bed. "Marc?" Jack called again, slowly making his way to the bathroom.

He could feel the heat of the blood rushing into his head as he opened the door and saw Marc naked, hunched over the toilet, both

118

arms hugging the rim as though he held the commode to the floor. Jack stooped beside him and gently rubbed his back. It was moist with sweat and Jack felt a slight tremor beneath his skin.

"Marc... what happened? What's wrong?"

Marc tried lifting his head, but immediately turned away, surrendering to a convulsive dry heave. Jack grabbed the towel from behind the door and draped it over Marc's back. Marc attempted to speak again, but his words were buried in the commode's basin.

"I can't hear you," Jack said, fingering the damp hair that covered Marc's brow. "I don't understand what you're saying."

Marc raised his hand from the toilet's rim and pointed out the bathroom door to the floor beside the bed.

"Shit!" Jack ran to the empty bottle and picked it up. "My Valium." he said. He closed his eyes and desperately tried remembering how many pills had been left in the bottle. Five? Seven? Twelve? On all fours, he crawled back to the bathroom and pulled on Marc's shoulder so he could see his face. "How many did you take?"

Marc's eyes were bloodshot. His face was colorless and his lips a deep scarlet. Jack swept the hair away from Marc's eyes and used the towel to blot the perspiration from his forehead.

"How many?" Jack asked quietly.

Marc closed his eyes. "I don't know," he sputtered, reopening his eyes and trying to focus on Jack's face, "Five... seven... whatever was left." Marc let his head fall against Jack's chest. "I'm sorry... I'm sorry... I'm sorry," he cried until sound could no longer escape his parched throat.

Jack picked up the towel and draped it around Marc's shoulders, instinctively wrapping his arms around Marc and rubbing his back. Jack could feel the vibration, the final tremors of a body trying to rid itself of poison.

"I'm calling 911," Jack said, lifting Marc to his feet.

"No," Marc yelled. "Everything's out. I'm just dizzy and sick to my stomach. Please, Jack, don't call anyone."

"Okay, okay," Jack consented reluctantly. "Let's get you into bed."

With one hand on Marc's elbow and the other coiled around his waist, Jack brought Marc to the bed and laid him down. He covered him with the blanket and sat beside him, wiping the damp strands of hair from his eyes.

"Why would you do this, Marc?" He gently stroked the side of Marc's face, which was slowly regaining a hint of color. "No one is worth it. No one… especially me."

Marc wiped a tear from his eye. "I'm sorry, Jack. I'm sorry for what I said. I'm sorry for being such a bad person. I'm sorry for what I've done… to the one person I love… to the only person who…"

Marc buried his head in the pillow and sobbed.

"Shhhh, we'll talk about it later." Jack tucked the blanket under Marc's chin. "Right now, you need some rest."

He stood and walked to the window, twisting the Levolor rod and closing the wooden slats to darken the room. As he shut the bedroom door behind him, he could still hear Marc sobbing, "I'm sorry for what I've done."

Walking into the living-room, Jack gazed out the front windows. Wisps of white rain clouds floated through the charcoal-gray sky like tug boats adrift in a stormy sea. Through the droplets of rain that clung

120

to the glass, Jack watched the clouds blow through the sky – some torn apart by hateful currents of wind, others fighting to hold their form and survive as long as they could.

He grasped the wooden beams separating the windows and leaned his face against the chilly glass, wondering if he had the strength to survive. Or would his spirit be annihilated like the clouds in the sky, leaving behind an unrecognizable cluster of dust and debris? He didn't have an answer, but, for a quick instant, he sensed the outcome was completely out of his hands.

After he opened his eyes, it took Glen a few seconds to realize where he was. Having fallen asleep in Dana's favorite living room chair, he'd dreamed of her – the two of them walking hand-in-hand along the white sands of a Bermudan beach during their honeymoon ten years before. Holding their clasped hands in front of him, Glen cocked his head at the water. It wasn't the transparent, exotic turquoise color he remembered, but a sapphire blue, an opaque cerulean hue with misty undertones of mint green. The sky was the same color as the water, making it almost impossible to tell where the sea ended and the sky began.

He tightened his grip on Dana's hand as he brought it to his chest and studied her face. She looked exactly as she did the first day they'd met – high cheekbones and chocolate brown eyes as wide as the future that lay before them. Caramel-colored from the sun, her long hair blew behind her in the warm tropical breeze. She smiled, but Glen did not – he wouldn't allow himself to. Nor would he allow himself to speak – he knew, deep down, Dana was dead, and, in speaking to her, he'd be admitting to madness. Yet the elation welled inside of him, begging for release, urging him to ignore logic and give in to the wondrous moment. As he opened his mouth to speak, Glen caught a glimpse of Jenna passing across Dana's excessively large pupils – a vision of the life they conceived together – floating through her mind's eye. In the next instant, his mind fell into a whirlpool. Swirling... twisting... turning, as though his soul dropped from the weightlessness of the surreal into the netted fabric of life, heading down... down... down, back into his waiting flesh.

When he opened his eyes, the room was dark and the glowing digital clock read four-thirty pm. He lay in a fetal position – his left foot dangling off the ottoman, his right leg the only part of his body covered by the red plaid mackinaw blanket. He realized he'd slept for over two hours and leapt to his feet.

"Shit," he whispered, and flipped up the light switch by the stairs. Windswept rain struck the panes of the bay window behind him. "Shit," he said again, concerned the cement he'd used to fill the basement wall cracks last week wouldn't hold. It'd been raining since early morning and he feared a flood was inevitable. He knew he had to examine his handy work, but decided to check on Jenna first. He'd put her down for a nap right before he passed out. If she slept too long, he'd never get her to bed again by her usual eight-thirty bedtime.

On the table beside the staircase, the telephone receiver was off the hook. He'd meant to give himself a break from the constant ringing, calls from friends and neighbors offering condolences and checking up on him and Jenna. He placed the receiver back into its cradle and slowly climbed the steps, praying it wouldn't ring before he reached Jenna's room.

He crept toward her bed. Fumbling to find the switch on her bedside lamp, he hit the lampshade, causing it to bang against the wall.

"Shhhh," he said, turning on the light, "it's okay, sweetie."

Looking down at the bed, he covered his mouth to hold back a scream – it was empty except for a few stuffed animals and the ruffled sheet that held the outline of her tiny shape. Glen removed his hand from his mouth and grabbed the back of his neck.

"Jenna?" He threw the blanket from the bed. "Jenna?" he shouted, looking under the bed. Panic set in, his heart pounded and blood pulsed into the cul-de-sac of his eardrums. Throwing open the closet doors, he called her name again, struggling to keep the fear from his voice. "Jenna!" he was screaming now, flying down the stairs, turning on every light switch he passed. "Jenna! Sweetie! Where are you?"

Glen's arms flailed insanely, his voice quivered as he tore through every room of the house. He ended up in back in the living-room, knowing his last hope was the basement. When he skidded into the kitchen and opened the basement door, he knew, even before he turned on the light, that he was the only one in the house.

"Jenna!" he screamed so loud he started to choke. He grabbed the half glass of water beside the sink and gulped it down. Trying to figure out his next move, he looked out the window above the sink and saw movement in the backyard – a dusky figure sitting motionless on top of the stone retaining wall running along the backyard. Throwing the glass in the sink, he ran to the french doors, slid them open and scurried onto the deck.

"Jenna!" he screamed.

The figure moved slightly, and, although it was nearly dark and the wall was more than twenty-five yards away, he made out the yellow of Jenna's raincoat.

His feet sloshed in the soaked grass as he ran to her, screaming her name, unable to differentiate his tears from the cold raindrops streaming down his face. When he finally reached her, he hugged her tightly, almost squeezing the breath from both of them.

"Hi, Daddy," she said innocently, hugging him back.

He held her in front of him, trying to see her face through the thick shadow of rain and dusk. Strands of wet blonde hair fell from inside her hood onto her face. She tried to push them back.

"Jenna, you scared me to death! What are you doing out here? It's pouring."

"Mommy told me to protect the birds," she said, pointing to the birdbath a few feet behind Glen.

"What?" Glen asked, the rain soaking through his shirt.

"I think I had a dream, Daddy, but I'm not sure it was a dream." Jenna tried desperately to keep her hair from escaping her hood. "Mommy said I should protect the birds."

Glen didn't like where the conversation was going. He grabbed her hand, and pulled her toward the house. "Jenna, there are no birds out here! It's raining, for God's sake. They're in their nests… staying warm and dry the way you should be."

Jenna didn't reply. She kept her eyes on the ground passing beneath her as Glen pulled her to the deck and into the kitchen. He slammed the door shut, led her to one of the chairs surrounding the small glass table, and unzipped her jacket.

"Jenna, please, don't ever do that again!" He tried to hide his fear by speaking sternly. "Never leave this house without telling me."

"But you were sleeping," she whined. "I didn't want to –"

"It doesn't matter what I'm doing. You never leave this house without asking my permission. Do you understand?" He slipped off her coat and let it drop to the floor. Mickey Mouse's face smiled up at him. DisneyWorld – the family's last trip before Dana got sick, before this whole nightmare started, before...

"I'm sorry Daddy." Jenna was on the verge of crying. He drew her to him, closing his eyes as she nuzzled her face deep into his neck. "But Mommy said the birds were in trouble and I should watch out for them."

Glen shivered and gently pushed her back. "Jenna, we discussed this, remember? Mommy's in Heaven where it's beautiful and peaceful, keeping an eye on us and making sure we're okay. I don't think she'd want you sitting out in the rain on such a cold, stormy night. You could get sick and she wouldn't like that, would she?"

Dazed, Jenna shook her head.

"You must have had a dream. It was a beautiful dream because Mommy was a part of it. But –"

"Daddy, it was real," Jenna argued. "I... I think it was real. It was so dark. But she sat on my bed... she talked to me... she told me to go to the wall and protect the birds."

Glen grabbed her arms and lifted her off the chair, placing her feet on the floor. Although his heart ached and his head was spinning, he could feel his tolerance giving way. He unbuttoned Jenna's soaked shirt and tossed it on top of her jacket, hiding Mickey's face.

"Let's get you into a hot bath," he said, snatching a towel from the hallway closet. "I want you to finish taking off your clothes." He wrapped the towel around her bare, damp shoulders. "While you do that, I'm going to get into some dry clothes myself. When I finish changing, I want to see you in the bathroom with the hot water running in the tub. I know you know how to do that, right?"

Jenna nodded, droplets of rainwater falling from her hair into the small puddles already forming on the kitchen floor.

"I'm trusting you, Jenna," Glen said, kissing the top of her head.

He turned around and made his way to the stairs. Holding onto the banister, he took a deep breath, allowing his heart to beat again. He fell onto the third stair up from the bottom of the staircase and cupped his head in his hands.

"Help me, Dana," he muttered.

He jerked his head to the left. If the rain wasn't slapping so hard against the windows, he would've sworn he'd heard a soft whisper, a gentle, "It's okay" coming from the wall beside him

The next day was warm for the last day of September. On the radio alarm that awakened Glen, a weatherman announced the temperature might reach eighty degrees; the front that passed through the night before opened the way for a northerly flow of deep southern air and temperatures would hover above normal for the rest of the week.

Glen sipped his coffee and silently cursed the meteorologist. He'd been looking forward to a pre-autumn chill – the perfect excuse to watch the world pass by from the isolation of his living-room. With the weather warming up, he'd have to face the neighbors; hear children playing up and down the street; breathe the warm, humid air that would remind him of his last days with Dana.

He slid open the patio doors, stepped onto the deck, and gently closed the doors behind him, trying to subdue any noise that might awaken Jenna. He scanned the backyard and stopped drinking his coffee, mid-sip, when he saw a hollowed out section of the retaining wall directly beneath the spot where Jenna had been sitting the night before.

"What the hell?" he whispered, placing the coffee mug on the plexiglass table.

Nearing the wall, the first thing he noticed was the rocks. Once a part of an eight by three foot section of wall, they were now strewn across the grass. He stepped over the large stones and bent down to examine the opening, peering straight through the hole into his neighbor's yard. He ran his finger along its edge, damp fragments of mortar clinging to his skin. Wondering if this had always been a weak spot in the wall, he dropped to his knees and slid his head and torso through the opening. Scattered rocks also lay on his neighbor's lawn and Glen's suspicions grew. The hole was too clean, its edges too smooth. He'd built this wall himself and couldn't imagine anything but a tidal wave could break through the stone and mortar.

He backed out of the hole and wiped his hands on his pants as he stood. His thoughts swirled. What could have caused this? Why this one spot? Was it an animal? A person? He looked back at the house and caught sight of Jenna waving from her bedroom window. Glen returned the wave and walked back to the deck.

As he entered the house, he heard the pitter-patter of Jenna's feet running down the stairs. He met her in the living room with outstretched arms. Lifting her above his head, he kissed her stomach peeking through her pink pajama top covered with tiny white bunny rabbits.

"How'd you sleep?" he asked, gently lowering her bare feet onto the carpet.

"Good," she said.

"I'm not convinced," Glen responded, noticing the sadness in her expression, the wet around her eyes. He could tell she'd been crying. "How 'bout I make you some pancakes?"

"I'm not hungry," Jenna said, jumping onto the ottoman.

"I figured that." He rubbed his chin, feigning deep thought. "I'm not hungry either," he said, "but we have to eat or we'll become invisible."

"That would be fun." Jenna wiped her eyes with the back of her hands.

"It might be fun, but it's not okay. We have to stay strong and healthy," Glen said, though he knew exactly how she felt.

"What happened to the wall?" Jenna asked. "Did I break it?"

Glen smiled and smoothed her hair.

"No, sweetie, you didn't break it. To be honest, I don't know what happened. Maybe the storm was so strong it loosened the cement around the rocks and they fell out. That's probably what it was," Glen said, trying to convince both of them.

"Maybe," Jenna yawned.

"Okay, do you want BIG pancakes or small pancakes?"

"Medium," she said. "Will you make them like Mommy?"

Since the day Dana first entered the hospital, Jenna had asked questions like that; questions that pierced Glen's heart like a hot dagger. He turned around and walked toward the kitchen, not wanting Jenna to see his pain. He wondered if she knew how much he was hurting; if she understood that every mention of her Mommy loosened an already eroding log in his dam of tears. She was a smart little girl, but maybe she wasn't as intuitive as he thought, or hoped, she would be.

"I'll try," he said. "I'll try."

When he was out of earshot, Jenna stood and pulled her pajama top, stretching it down to her knees and squatting down.

"I know you will, Daddy," she said.

8

The sky was filled with haze, a light fog sweeping across the surface of the Charles. Marc watched the tumbling waves, knowing this was probably the last time he'd see the river from Jack's apartment. Dizziness ran through his head, a mild buzzing he feared would end up in his stomach. He wiped the perspiration from his forehead and clenched his teeth, determined to fight the nausea until he reached his own apartment. Turning to retrieve his jacket and suitcase, he caught his reflection in the glass of the framed Van Gogh.

"Shit," he muttered. He looked like a homeless person – disheveled hair, an extra-large, dirty sweatshirt reaching mid-thigh, and hollow eyes devoid of emotion. All his fears about hitting bottom were gone; he was already there, so far into the shadows the only sensation left was a tingling numbness.

He looked away from his reflection and crept toward the front door. Just get home, he thought, just get out before Jack wakes up. Grabbing his keys from the sofa table, he tossed his jacket over one shoulder and picked up his bag.

"Hey!"

He turned around. Jack stood beside the dining room table, wiping the sleep from his face. From his crumpled clothing and the shirttail hanging over the waist of his pants, it was obvious he'd fallen asleep in his clothes. "Where are you going?"

"Home," Marc said, tightening his grip around the suitcase handle.

"You look like shit." Jack peered down at his own wrinkled clothes.

"I'm one to talk." he laughed. "Let's have breakfast first, okay?"

"Look, Jack, I shouldn't be here. I'm just going to go and –"

"Come on, Marc, just some coffee. And I'll make you eggs with all the extra butter you like so much. Then you can go. You've got to get something in your stomach or you'll be heaving all over the T."

Marc threw his jacket over the arm of the sofa and tossed his keys back onto the table. "Okay," he said, "but not eggs or I'll be heaving before I even reach the T."

The toast rested on a large saucer in the center of the glass table, the tension as thick as the stick of butter sitting between them. Marc waited for Jack to speak, sipping black coffee and avoiding Jack's eyes.

"I guess I left it in the toaster too long," Jack said, pushing the plate of slightly burnt toast toward Marc. "Try it... a little butter should cover the taste."

Marc smiled and brought the toast to his lips. The smell screamed out to him: If you want to puke all over the table, take a bite, go ahead, take a bite. Marc let the bread fall onto his plate.

"Not yet," he whispered, swirling the bitter coffee around his mouth.

Jack took a large bite of toast and washed it down with a slug of orange juice. "What's all over your shirt? You look like you've been mud wrestling."

Marc looked down at his sweatshirt. He wiped his hands over the stains, embarrassed by his apparent grunginess. Just another reason I'm not good enough for him, Marc thought.

"Yeah, that's what I've been doing," he replied. "From an overdose to the wrestling ring in one night."

Jack threw his toast onto the plate and looked out the window. "Do we talk about what happened yesterday?" he asked.

Marc shook his head.

"Do we talk about why you think you're such a bad person?" Jack probed further.

"I'm a loser?" Marc asked, the question sounding more like a pronouncement.

"No self-loathing crap today, Marc," Jack said, gently touching Marc's arm. "I want you to talk to me. And look at me, for God's sake! You're making me nervous."

Marc gave his usual prolonged blink. He locked on to Jack's eyes and felt a sharp pain in the center of his stomach, unsure if it was guilt, fear, or the knowledge that he'd lost the one true love of his life. Whatever it was, the longer he looked at Jack, the more the pain increased. He looked back down to the table. "Why aren't you at work?"

"I'm on a leave of absence."

Marc's eyes widened.

"The Board wants me out for three months until things calm down. They say three months, but I doubt I'll be going back. I'm not even sure if I want to go back," He added in a whisper.

Marc shot up, holding onto the table to keep his balance. "I have to go!" He staggered toward the door.

Jack stood and grabbed Marc's arm. "Where are you off to?"

"To set things straight," Marc replied. "It's not fair."

Jack spun Marc around so they faced each other. He raised his hand to move the hair dangling over Marc's eyes, but Marc stopped him.

"What do you mean 'set things straight'? There's nothing you can do, Marc. David did all he could. What can you do that he couldn't?" Marc twisted his arm to loosen it from Jack's grip and turned his back.

"I'll tell the truth, that's what I'll do. I'll tell everyone what's really going on, what really happened, and they'll take you back. They'll beg you to come back."

Marc felt Jack's hands on his shoulders, pulling him back with a force that wouldn't allow him to move. He turned around and swallowed his tears at the sight of Jack's bewildered expression.

"What are you talking about?" Jack asked, pressing his fingers into Marc's shoulders. Marc didn't respond. "Whatever it is, why don't you tell me first?"

Marc's eyes swelled with tears.

"Because I don't want to see your face when you find out."

Jack gently pushed Marc down onto the sofa and took a few steps back. "I'm waiting," he said, looking up at Marc. "I think it's time you talk to me." He felt a slight tremble in his stomach, a growing fear of something he'd sensed for months but had smothered with his consuming affection. From the expression on Marc's face, he knew he shouldn't have denied his instincts.

"There's this guy, Cory Daniels." Marc cleared his throat, "He's an executive recruiter... at least that's what he calls himself."

With his eyes fixed on the table, Marc described his own desperation for money and the need to find a hole in the corporate maze – a way to prove himself as a top-notch copywriter. He spoke of Cory's web of lies and promises, his blueprint to oust Jack from J&M and replace him with one of his own, high-paying clients.

Jack held his head, the shock and surprise of Marc's words drowning him in his own thoughts. At first he couldn't absorb what Marc was saying. The lies, the deceit, his own stupidity – how he'd actually considered taking Marc back and giving their relationship another try. Marc's voice slammed against the inside of his head, each word another slap in the face, another jab in the heart.

"And then," Marc stammered, taking a deep breath, "and then I realized I couldn't go through with it because... because... I fell in love with you."

Jack stared into Marc's eyes, almost unable to breathe. He inhaled only as much air as he required to speak.

"When did you meet him?"

"About ten months ago, at the Career Expo."

Jack knew the answer to the question he was about to ask and shook his head as the words flew off his tongue. "Does the name Lance Talbot mean anything to you?"

Marc shifted uncomfortably on the sofa, continuing to stare at the table in order to avoid Jack's eyes. He bit his bottom lip without responding.

"Your resumé said you worked at Stetson," Jack said. "Around the time Lance was thrown out on bullshit kiddie porn charges." Jack moved to the edge of the recliner. "Did you know him?" Silence. "Did you know him, Marc?"

"Yes! I knew him!" Marc snapped. "But I had no idea what was going on! Cory tricked me! He got me the mailroom job and showed up one day with a videotape. He said his boss and Talbot were friends and it was a videotape of them as kids or something. He wanted to give it to Talbot as a surprise and asked me to hide it in his file cabinet. I was an idiot – I believed him."

Jack turned toward the windows, trying to see through the haze. Things were starting to come together, piece by piece, and it sent a wave of rage through his body.

"Stetson was a big client of ours. I worked closely with Lance. I knew the charges were crap." Jack turned to look at Marc. "Do you have any idea what you've done? The lives you've ruined? The people you've hurt?"

"I told you, Jack, he tricked me! I had no idea what he was making me do. As soon as I found out what happened, I quit Stetson. The whole thing made me sick. Especially knowing I was the one who hid the videotape in his office."

Videotape! The words hit Jack like a sledgehammer across his chest. He ran to the sofa table and felt sweat form on the back of his neck when he realized Dana's DVD was missing.

"Where's the DVD?" Jack screamed.

Marc inched back into the sofa, moving away from Jack's sudden outburst.

"What DVD?" he asked, holding tightly onto the arm of the sofa.

"Dana's DVD, God damn it! She left me a DVD. Where is it, Marc? I haven't touched it since I brought it home and you were the only one here!" He hovered above Marc, leaning against the back of the couch. "This is your chance to make up for what you've done to me! Now where is it?"

"Jack, I swear, I have no idea what you're talking about. Yeah, I was here, but I just packed my stuff and –" As he spoke, Marc glanced at the DVD player sitting on the shelf below the flat-screen television. He looked at Jack and pointed to it. "It's blinking. And look, it shows there's a DVD in it. Maybe you watched it and just don't remember."

Jack turned and knelt by the player. "I'd remember watching it, Marc, trust me." He pressed the play button and saw the numbers on the digital display read 1.02.30. "Someone watched this DVD," Jack yelled. "Somebody watched this DVD, Marc!"

"It wasn't me!" Marc cried, "I swear! I was unconscious, remember? How could I have –" He turned to look at the front door. "Cory!" he yelled, "It had to be Cory!"

Jack hit the EJECT button. "Cory, huh? How'd he get in here? Why would he watch this DVD? Marc, you're grasping now. I don't know what you're up to, but you'd better go. I'm done with you and this whole thing."

"Jack, please believe me. Cory was supposed to help me get my things yesterday morning. I probably left the door open and he snuck in while I was passed out. It's the only thing I can think of, Jack. I swear, I didn't watch the DVD. I didn't even know there was a DVD."

Still watching the digital display on the DVD player, Jack shook his head waiting for the DVD to pop out.

"And why should I believe YOU?" he asked. Jack jumped to his feet and grabbed the DVD.

Marc stood and grabbed his jacket and suitcase. When he reached the door, he turned to face Jack. Jack could see he was desperately searching for the right words, anything that would exonerate him from the accusations. In the back of his mind, he hoped Marc would find those words.

"You shouldn't," Marc said, "and that's why I'm a loser."

This time he made sure he heard the lock click when he closed the door behind him.

Crouching before the gaping hole, John Fontaine rubbed gray pieces of mortar between his fingers, watching them disintegrate and fall into the grass below him.

"It's a big hole, isn't it, Grandpa?" Jenna asked, leaning on her grandfather's shoulder.

John turned to Jenna and smiled, planting a kiss on her soft cheek. "It sure is, sweetheart. One of the biggest I've ever seen." He ran his fingers along the inside of the hollowed out stones one last time and raised himself up. His knees cracked, sending a sharp pain up the front of his leg. Holding onto Jenna for support, he led her through the tangled brush and leaves, the dried out remains of countless autumns. They headed back toward the house where Glen and Grandma Lisa waited in silence, sipping coffee, gazing in different directions.

"Okay," Glen said, grabbing Jenna's hand as she bounded up the four steps leading to the deck. "What does the master contractor conclude?"

"Well," John replied, lowering himself onto one of the pine chairs surrounding a circular pine table, "it's very strange. I've been in construction long enough to know that even a sweeping rain couldn't cause something like that. It's the kind of hole a wrecking ball would make after smashing the side of a building. But the difference here is the top of the wall didn't collapse. The hole is too deliberate."

"Plus," Glen joked, smiling at Jenna, "I think we would've heard a wrecking ball come through the backyard."

"Exactly," John said. "That's why the only other conclusion I can come to is that this hole was manmade. It's like someone used a chisel, a drill, or even a hammer. I'm not sure, but the stones aren't damaged enough for me to think this was caused by any type of mechanical equipment. Even more confusing, the mortar around the hole looks fresher than the mortar in the rest of the wall. It's as though that entire section of wall was recently patched or rebuilt with fresh cement before this hole was made. I can't say for sure –"

"But, John," Glen interrupted, "I haven't touched that wall since you and I built it eight years ago. And look at it, it's hidden by bushes and leaves. Sometimes I even forget it's there."

"Me and Mommy used to play there all the time," Jenna said, walking to John and trying to climb onto his lap. He pulled her up and let her snuggle the top of her head under his chin. "We played all kinds of games there."

John looked at Lisa who sat beside them, forcing a smile as she placed loose wisps of Jenna's hair back behind her ears.

"What kind of games, Jenna?" she asked, her voice quivering with emotion.

"All kinds. Hide and seek. Tag. Mommy sometimes made a small hole and put a nickel or a dime in it. Then she'd cover it up again and give me clues so I'd know where to find it. That was my favorite game."

John smoothed his hand over the top of Jenna's head. So unfair, he thought, for everyone.

"Maybe that's why she told me to protect the birds," Jenna whispered.

Both John and Lisa gave Glen a bewildered look.

"Jenna had a dream last night." Glen pointed to the bird bath in front of the hole in the stone wall. "She said Mommy told her to protect the birds, so she came out in the pouring rain and sat on the wall." He sipped his coffee and looked sternly at Jenna. "Something she'll never do again, right?"

Jenna nodded, her face rubbing against John's flannel shirt.

"What else did she say, honey?" Lisa asked.

"That's all I remember Grandma. I just remember that. And she looked so pretty,"

Lisa got up and rushed into the house. Glen was about to follow her when John called out to him. "Let her go, Glen. It's still so fresh, she needs time."

Glen watched Lisa slide the glass door shut, then sat down across from John and Jenna.

"I only have to go into the office for a few hours, John. Will you guys be okay watching Jenna?"

John nodded. "Not to worry. Everything will be fine."

Glen stared into the yard and rubbed his unshaven face. "I don't understand this, John. Who would make that hole and why? Or are we just making something out of nothing? Maybe it's a natural occurrence, a weak spot in the wall, and it's something that just happened. Should I let it go or call the police?"

"Have you spoken to the neighbors? Did they hear or see anything strange last night?" John asked, still rubbing Jenna's head.

"I called them this morning. Their son answered the phone and reminded me they've been on vacation for the past week... a cruise in the Bahamas."

"I think we met him once a few years ago. Did he hear anything or notice the hole?"

"No. He doesn't live there anymore, he lives in Boston. He's just keeping an eye on the house for them while they're gone. He was only there because he stopped by to check on things before going to work."

"What did he say about the wall?"

"Nothing. He hadn't seen it yet and was in a rush to get to his office. He said he'd check it out after work."

"Well, you might want to find out if he spent the night. When Jack used to watch our house, he liked to sleep in his old bed and eat us out of house and home." John laughed. "Until he became Boston's big shot advertising guru."

"I'll definitely check with him when he comes by later," Glen said.

"What's his name again, just in case he comes by before you get back from the office?"

"His name's Ted," Glen replied, "but everyone calls him Todd."

9

Jack held the remote, his thumb wavering above the play button. "The DVD is for Jenna's eyes only. No matter what, she should be the only one to see it. Preferably alone on her eighteenth birthday." Dana's words echoed in his ears, the sound of her voice as clear in his head as on the night she'd pleaded with him to protect the DVD.

He let his head fall onto the sofa pillows and closed his eyes.

Ten years? he thought. I couldn't even protect the DVD for ten days.

As he softly rubbed the play button, Jack realized he had no choice. He had to watch the DVD. It held information that might affect Jenna's future, and although he'd already failed Dana, viewing the DVD might help him salvage at least a piece of the promise he'd made.

He pressed the remote and crossed his arms, anticipating the first shot of Dana's face.

"Hi sweetheart." Dana leaned back in the Victorian chair positioned in the middle of her livingroom and looked directly into the camera lens. "I know this might be a little strange for you, but it's the only way I could think of to tell you some important things, including how much I love you."

Jack tightened his grip on the remote and let out a soft groan. Seeing Dana move and hearing her speak so soon after her death sent a tingle up the back of his neck. Her eyes were clear, her skin full of color and life. Jack figured she'd made the DVD at least six months before her death, during a time when she still looked healthy.

Goosebumps formed on Jack's upper arms. He'd expected to feel intense sadness, but he hadn't counted on this eerie feeling. The tears streaming down his face were a reaction to seeing his dead sister – missing her, distraught that she'd been cheated out of living her life and raising Jenna. But the strange eeriness he felt was more like the surreal sensation he'd only experienced in nightmares – confusion and fear mixed with the keen understanding that he was heading toward a destination he'd never anticipated.

Dana continued speaking, reminiscing through the events of their life together, holding Jenna's favorite stuffed animals up to the camera. "I'm sure you don't play with these anymore," she said, rubbing the fuzzy rabbit ears against her cheek, "but right now, these are your favorite toys, which means they're my favorite too." She went on, describing the day she and Glen had met, how, from the moment they married, both wished for a little girl as sweet and beautiful as Jenna.

Jack smiled, remembering his many conversations with Dana during her pregnancy. "I really don't care whether it's a boy or a girl," she once said, "as long as it's healthy and doesn't inherit Glen's genetic history of, you know, proboscises."

"Proboscises?" Jack asked. "What exactly is a proboscises?"

Dana laughed. "It's actually 'What ARE proboscises?' It's another word for honkers... schnozzes... beaks... trunks."

"I get it, Dana. Big noses! But Glen's nose isn't so big, he actually has a nice nose."

"Follow me," Dana said, clomping into the living-room, appearing as though she trailed two feet behind her oversized belly. "Don't tell Glen I showed you this. You promise?"

"I promise," Jack said, watching her pull a copy of Moby Dick from the overstuffed bookcase.

Dana opened the book, snatched a color photograph from the center and handed it to Jack. He studied the picture, holding it up to the sunlight shooting through the linen curtains. The photo displayed three men in their early twenties, each wearing a three-piece suit, and holding each other around the waist.

"Who the hell is this? They look like Larry, Mo and Curly wearing fake witch noses. This one looks –" Jack stopped talking. He drew the photo closer and opened his mouth, refusing to speak until the expletives passed his tongue and he found more decent words to utter. "I don't believe it! This is Glen?"

Dana nodded. "And his brothers," she replied, grabbing the photo and placing it back into the binding of the novel. "You can't ever let him know I showed you that. He'd kill me."

"Okay, I promise. But what happened? All of them have perfect noses now."

"Hello? It's called plastic surgery. They all worked during college, saving enough money to get their noses fixed. According to Glen, they set up their surgery appointments in the same order as their age. Frank went first, Glen went the next week, and Jason the week after that. The three of them sat around their apartment for weeks, not leaving until the bandages came off. Can you imagine?" Dana laughed, massaging her stomach with both hands. "This is the only picture he saved from the pre-beak era, as Glen calls it. I'm keeping it safe so we can show it to our child… once he or she is old enough to see such horror without screaming!"

Jack returned his attention to the DVD as Dana stood and walked toward the camera, leaving nothing to look at but an empty chair. The screen went black. A few seconds later the camera turned back on, showing a panorama of Dana's backyard. "And this, sweetheart, is where we have all our fun when the weather's nice," Dana said. The scene jumped as Dana made her way down the steps of the deck and walked toward the far end of the yard. There was a close-up of the swing set and then the sand box with a small red pail sitting in the center. "I don't know where the shovel is," Dana said softly, "but if I know you, Jenna, you're using it to build a mud castle on the side of the house."

The scene moved again as Dana walked through the blooming shrubs and plush, leafy bushes, exposing the stone wall that ran along the yard. Jack heard her set down the camera and he slid up to the edge of the sofa as she walked backward and pulled herself up so she was sitting on top of the wall. "I knew that birdbath would come in handy for something," Dana said. "Today, it's my cameraman."

Dana pulled her hair back and tucked it into the collar of her shirt. A serious expression swept over her face and she cleared her throat.

"Okay, we're going to get down to business now, Jenna. If you still remember, and I hope you do, back here is where we play some of our favorite games. In one of those games, I'd take coins and hide them inside this wall, giving you clues so you could find the coins and put them in your piggy bank. It's your absolute favorite. I'm not sure if it's because you like playing hide-and-seek or if you just inherited your Daddy's love of money!" She let her hands fall to her lap and rubbed her thighs. "Well, for the past ten years, I've been playing some hide and seek of my own. Before you were born, I had a job that paid a lot of money. After you were born, I quit my job, but was able to do freelance projects on the side. I invested that money and turned it into a lot more than when I started."

Jack felt his stomach clench. He knew Dana had done well during her short stint as a photographer, but he had no idea she'd earned enough to invest. He'd always thought of Dana and Glen as just getting by, never having the available funds to enjoy the luxuries of life. *Where is she going with this?*

"So, anyway," Dana continued, "for the past ten years I've built up a small fortune, a fortune your Daddy doesn't even know about." The look of guilt on her face was apparent, but she went on. "I didn't want to use it on an unsafe business venture. I wanted to make sure we had it in case of an emergency... or to send you to school... or if Daddy hit it big, we'd use it just to have fun!" She stared into the camera lens. "But then I found out I was sick," her voice quivered, "and I'd never be able to enjoy the money with you, so I decided to leave it for you." She pointed to the stones below her dangling feet.

"I thought about keeping it in the bank, to collect interest and keep it safe, but then I'd have to tell someone about it. The bank statements would come in the mail, fees would have to be paid, on and on and on. I wanted this to be my special gift to you on this special day. So I decided to hide it." She jumped down off the wall and walked toward the camera, grabbing it and focusing in on a slate-colored stone in the center of the wall. "It would be like we're playing our favorite game again, but this time there'd be a lot more than just nickels and dimes."

The view widened, but was still close enough to the gray stone to make out the strange markings on its surface. "This is the house Daddy grew up in. He said he'd never sell it and will always do whatever it takes to keep it. I know how much he loves this house and I truly believe he'd never let it go. That's why I know this is the safest place to hide your money." Jack watched Dana's index finger move into the shot and point to the single gray stone. "See this rock, honey? See the two holes and the large crack that makes it look like a smiley face? This is where you should start." The camera moved backward, showing a larger section of the wall. Dana moved her finger in a circular direction. "Last year, Daddy went away for a week on a business trip and you were in kindergarten. So I hollowed out a section of the wall, wrapped the money in plastic bags throughout this entire area, and sealed them up inside. It was a lot of work, but it was fun too. Just thinking of you breaking the wall and finding your surprise kept me going. I think I did a pretty good job. And the best thing is, this wall is safe because it's so well hidden and most people don't even know it's here. Except for you and I, of course."

Using the telephoto mechanism, Dana focused again on the stones to show three additional gray rocks with smiley faces, a total of four rocks forming a six-foot ellipse. "Within this circle, surrounded by these four stones, is my gift to you." She placed the camera on top of the stone wall, the shot only showing her face from the shoulders up. "Although I can't be with you as you turn into the beautiful person I know you'll become, at least I'll know I've given you something that will help you get through life." She pulled the hair out from inside her collar and let it spill onto her shoulders. "There's two hundred and fifty thousand dollars in this wall, Jenna. That's a quarter of a million dollars.

I'm telling you the amount so when it comes time for you to play the game and retrieve your money, you won't miss out on a single dime. I want to make sure you get everything you deserve."

Jack stood up, knees weak, thoughts spinning wildly inside his head. "A quarter of a million dollars," he whispered. "Holy shit!" His thoughts flew back to his conversation with Marc that morning and he started to feel sick. He realized Marc had viewed the DVD, or if Marc was telling the truth, then Cory had seen it the day before. Jack felt paralyzed, unsure who to pursue first. If Marc had seen the DVD, did he have the audacity to try and steal the money? Did Cory even know where Dana had lived? Had either of them shared this information with anyone else? All he knew was he needed to protect Jenna's money before anyone else got their hands on it.

He muted the volume on the television, ran to the telephone in the kitchen, and pressed the speed dial button marked Dana.

"Hello?" He immediately recognized his mother's voice.

"Mom? What are you doing there? Where's Glen?"

"Oh, nice to talk to you too, son!" she replied.

"Sorry, Mom, there's just something very important I need to speak with Glen about. Where is he?" Jack's anxiety was growing.

"He went to work. We're watching Jenna. What's wrong? When are we going to see you?"

Her quivering voice told Jack she'd been crying and he tried to calm himself down. She doesn't need this, he thought. He rubbed the back of his neck, wiping the sweat on his shirt.

"Nothing's wrong. I just wanted to ask Glen a question," said Jack, contemplating his next move. "Where's Dad?"

"He's in the back with Jenna, trying to figure out what happened to the wall. When do you think you'll —"

Jack fell backward onto the kitchen counter, holding onto its edge. "What do you mean 'what happened to the wall'?" he asked, unsure if he really wanted a response.

"It's strange," Lisa said. "You know the stone wall Dad and Glen built a few years ago?"

"Yes." Jack held his breath.

"Glen woke up this morning and found a gaping hole right in the middle of it. He thinks it was from last night's rain, but your father doesn't think so. Actually, I'm not sure what your father thinks, but he refuses to believe it was an act of God."

"There's no such thing," Jack said, "I'll be right over."

He hung up the phone before his mother asked any more questions.

Looking around his bedroom, Jack rolled his eyes: This room is messier than my life, he thought. A trail of dirty towels followed a path from the bathroom to the bed, where Marc had passed out the night before. Jack found his shoes lying in a pile beside the bed where he'd slipped them off once he'd assured himself Marc was well enough for him to close his eyes and get some sleep.

Bending over to grab his shoes, he noticed a small piece of paper beneath the dresser. On all fours, Jack crawled toward the dresser, realizing as he neared the paper that it was actually a business card with something written on the back. He was bewildered when he saw Mary Mulligan's telephone number scribbled in red pen. His confusion turned to surprise when he turned the card over: Cory Daniels, Executive Recruiter.

Cory was here! Marc had been telling the truth!

Jack tried to calm himself, realizing that although Marc was truthful with him, it didn't absolve him from his other actions. He still had plenty to make up for, but, since Marc had passed out after taking the pills, he obviously didn't break into the wall. Cory was the main suspect – and only Marc could help him locate Cory. Jack snapped up his shoes and headed into the living-room. After tying the laces, he took a deep breath, picked up the phone and dialed Marc's number. Marc answered the phone with a grunt.

"Marc, it's Jack. Listen, I believe you. I know Cory was here and it wasn't you who watched the DVD."

"Thank God, Jack. I wasn't sure if I'd ever find a way to prove it to you."

"Listen," Jack said, "something's happened and I need your help."

"Anything," Marc said without hesitation. "Anything."

"Can I pick you up in fifteen minutes? We need to go to Dana's house."

"Okay, that'll work. I just got out of the shower but I can definitely be ready in fifteen. I'll be waiting outside."

"Great," Jack said, "and did you eat something?"

"Yes, Jack. I ate something. Now just get over here."

Jack hung up the phone and tossed it onto the dining room chair. As he slipped on his jacket, a dozen thoughts ran through his head – the last of which focused on Marc, forgiveness and the possibility of rekindling their relationship.

"What am I, nuts?" he said aloud, searching for his keys. The guy is crazy! He tried to kill himself. He screwed me over and cost me my job. He's pretty much penniless. "He's a freakin' mess!"

As hard as Jack tried to control himself, he couldn't stop thinking about Marc: The intimate times when they shared personal thoughts; the endearing look in Marc's eyes when they'd discuss their future together; the softness of his skin; the sounds he'd make when…

First things first, the thought screamed in Jack's head. Solve the problems, then think about making yourself happy. As he approached the door, he turned around to see Dana staring at him from the television screen. With the volume muted, he couldn't make out what she was saying, but saw a tear crawling down her cheek, leaving a thin trail of mascara.

Trying to read her lips, Jack deciphered her final words before the screen went black: "I love you, Jenna."

The walkway was crowded with people relishing the final remnants of summer, breathing in the dissipating scent of the roses and tulips lining the paths along Boston Common Gardens. Mary and David hurried through the crowd, making their way to Charles Street, where several dozen people were enjoying late lunches and sunning themselves on a vast grassy area.

"Over there." Mary pointed to an empty bench. When they reached the bench, she pulled a handkerchief from her skirt pocket and wiped away chips of green paint.

"Always prepared," David said as he sat down, ignoring the green flakes.

Mary smiled. "Have to be." she said, "Keeps me on my toes."

David looked over the scene, catching glimpses of women with raised skirts, trying to tan their legs. Pulling his eyes away, he took off his sunglasses and peered at Mary. "So what's up?" he asked. "Why are we here?"

"I wanted to talk to you... away from the office. I have a few things to say and I didn't want anyone within earshot."

Now she had David's full attention. It wasn't like Mary to discuss business matters outside the J&M building – her office was her turf, the place where she felt most comfortable. "I'm ready." He placed one elbow on the back of the bench, rested his head on his closed fist and leaned closer.

"Well, first I'd like to apologize for the way I've acted over the Jack situation." She looked down at the handkerchief in her hands, pulling on silk-surged edges. "You were right. It took a lot of soul searching, but believe it or not, I actually heard what you were saying to me. I've been trying to get back at Max through Jack and it was the wrong thing to do. I know Jack is a good man and an asset to the company. I wanted to say I'm sorry."

David was surprised. He couldn't remember Mary seeing the error of her ways so quickly before. In all the years he'd known her, it was usually months before she'd admit to a mistake – especially one as large as this. Something must have happened.

"I accept, and thank you," he said. "Go on."

"Well, as crazy as this might seem, I think there might be some kind of set-up going on. I think Jack was... and I know this will sound like I'm quoting a TV show... but I think Jack was framed."

David tried to comprehend her words and motioned for her to continue.

"A little over a month ago, I received a call from an executive recruiter, Cory Daniels. He was very charming. You know, the kind of guy who knows all the right words, all the workable phrases. Anyway, he called a few months ago to check in and see if J&M could use his services. I told him we'd keep him in mind." Mary folded the handkerchief into a square and blotted her forehead. "He called me again a few days ago, right around the time the situation with Jack came to a head. And it was strange – the tone of his voice, the things he said. It all sounded like he knew what was going on. As though he knew Jack was on his way out and we'd need someone to take his place. But he was unaware of the fact that J&M promotes from within. It's our way. It's the only way our employees will…"

"Mary!" David grabbed her hand and squeezed it. "I know our policies. Now please, keep going."

"Sorry." She used the handkerchief again, this time to wipe her nose. "Well, I just thought the timing was too perfect, and the whole thing made me uneasy."

Feeling guilty about his outburst, David forced a laugh. "Mary, this sounds like an Agatha Christie novel."

"I know, David, but that's not all. There's a bigger mystery here. After Cory called a few days ago, I decided to do a quick background check on the person who told me about Jack's supposed lurid behavior." She paused and looked to each side. "Do you know Todd from the IT Department?"

David shook his head. "I should've known," he said. "The Mouth."

"Yes. Well, Todd's resume shows he worked at Stetson before J&M, and Cory got him that job."

"A strange coincidence maybe, but it doesn't prove anything."

"I'm not finished. Todd worked at Stetson up until the time Lance Talbot was thrown out. A week after that, Todd was working at J&M – courtesy of Cory Daniels."

Mary's conclusions started to seep in.

"So you think…"

"There's more, David." Now she was using the handkerchief to fan herself. "Jack's friend Marc… well, he was also at Stetson while Todd worked there, and he left right after the Talbot incident. Once again, getting placed at J&M – courtesy of Cory Daniels. When you and I discussed what happened to Lance, we were confident none of it was true, we thought he'd been framed, remember?"

David nodded, frowning at her.

"And now, with everything that's happened to Jack, and with the same people involved, well, something just doesn't feel right."

David glanced around the park, searching for something familiar, anything that would help ground his thoughts and offer a sense of security. He peered through the trees at the brownstone houses sitting along Beacon Street.

"Number twenty-four," he muttered.

Mary's brow furrowed, her head tilted in bewilderment.

"What?"

David pointed to the brownstones. "Third house from the end. Number twenty-four. That's where Marcia and I lived for ten years, during the long, arduous birth of J&M." He shook his head, remembering the sleepless nights and early morning pacing past the kitchen window, looking onto the Common grounds, most likely gazing at the location where he was now sitting. "I wanted an advertising agency, Mary. And now it's become a den of thieves and liars."

Mary put her hand on David's shoulder and gave it a slight squeeze.

"Don't even think that way, David. You've built a great business and do wonderful work. J&M is one of the top agencies in the city. This is just an aberration. Don't let it negate what you've done with the company. It's just a blip on the radar."

David wiped his top lip and whisked the moisture onto his pants. He felt a heaviness in his chest – a sadness stemming from people's raw disregard for others and the realization that he'd have to be the one to break the news to Jack. "That's what I told Jack before he left yesterday. 'Just a blip.' Now I realize why he was so upset."

"David, you can't let this get to you. It's like a cancer, except this form is curable. Once we get the information we need, we'll send the guilty parties packing and the company will be clean again. Free of disease."

"What else do you know about Todd or Marc? Any other background information?"

"Unfortunately, I only have access to employment records. Neither Todd nor Marc have any criminal charges, at least in their files. And wouldn't you know they're both out sick today?"

David looked at Mary, his eyes wild with rage.

"We have to figure out a way to prove their guilt," she said, "so we can get them out of J&M and maybe even sent to prison."

"That's if they're guilty, Mary. I don't want to cause an uproar in the company or hurt Jack even more, unless we're sure about the facts." He stood and reached for Mary's hand, helping her balance herself as she rose and wiped off the back of her skirt.

"Okay, David. I understand. And I'll think on it too. We've got to get rid of this disease as soon as possible. It's not good for the company."

Strolling along the path back to the J&M building, David and Mary walked in silence. David turned around to take one last look at the Commons. The grounds were almost empty, the vast green pasture appearing larger to him than ever before.

Peering up the slight hill to Number Twenty-four Beacon Street, he took a deep breath and blew the air through his pursed lips. A golden retriever chased a Frisbee and the autumn chill fluttered through the trees, a few leaves dancing along with the gentle wind. He had a sudden sense that the coming winter would be extremely cold – more frigid than the people of Boston had experienced in a very long time.

10

Marc sat in silence, watching the blur of trees as the car sped down the Mass Pike. He listened with half an ear as Jack told him about his promise to Dana, the DVD, and the hidden money. He heard the strain in Jack's voice, a raspy tension created by days of emotional distress and upheaval. Marc stared out the window, still unable to look at Jack, knowing he was the cause of his lover's pain. "I'm trusting you with this information, because I need you to help me find Cory. I hope you meant what you said... I mean, how you felt about me... and that you'll help me, without any more lies."

Marc restrained himself from reaching out and touching Jack's hand. He wondered how long it would take before Jack trusted him enough to smile at him again, to look into his eyes with the same warmth and lust he'd shown only a few days before.

"How I feel, Jack... not how I felt." Marc let out a sigh, leaving a circular pattern of fog on the glass. "This whole mess is my fault and I'm willing to do whatever it takes to make things right."

"Thank you," Jack said, pressing down on the gas pedal. The car jerked as it changed gears, helping them move past the awkward silence.

"I just can't believe Cory would do this," Marc said. "I know he's a smooth talker and a liar, but to tear down a stone wall and steal someone else's money? Who would do something like that?"

Jack didn't answer. He veered right, pulled off at the Natick exit, paid the toll, and headed down the ramp to the traffic light. The light was red and Jack tapped his fingers on the steering wheel. "I guess it was my time," he said.

Marc looked at him, confused. "What do you mean 'your time'?"

"My life was too perfect – great job, great boyfriend, money in the bank, respect throughout the industry. Why did I think it would last? It was my time for that inevitable wake-up call. Life can't be perfect. The shit had to hit the fan sooner or later. It just hit a little sooner than I expected."

Marc couldn't think of a thing to say, guilt overtaking his ability to find the right words. Weeks before he'd felt the same sense of life's possible perfection, like puzzle pieces fitting together, forming the picture of a life he'd always imagined. He knew it was close – he'd just been waiting to insert the final piece – Jack's invitation for him to move in and start their life together. If only he'd committed sooner, Marc thought, maybe things wouldn't have gotten to this point.

"Now I just have to get back on track," Jack continued. "Get life back to where it was." He put his hand on Marc's knee.

"I hope that's possible," Marc said, squeezing Jack's hand.

The light turned green and Jack made a left, following the signs to Route 30. Marc gazed out the car window and smiled at his reflection in the glass. Lifting his hand that had just held Jack's, he brought it to his face and took a deep breath. How strange, he wondered, to want someone so much, to be willing to drown in their scent or die for one last taste, and yet still betray them.

Through the mist of thoughts, images of his father exploded in his head, flashes of one of their last conversations – in the family-room, the smell of leftover meatloaf streaming in from the kitchen. Marc stared at the top of his father's head, the man seemingly unable to move his eyes from the television screen. The voice of Homer Simpson blared through the room, but his father managed to yell above the din.

"I want you to cut the shit," his father said, pulling on the short stomach hairs creeping out the bottom of his yellow-stained, undersized tee shirt. "Your mother says you've been a real pain in the ass. Treating your little brother like shit. Talking to her like she's your slave. Just cut the shit." Marc gazed at his father, wishing he'd raise his head and return the glance. Maybe it's better not to see the disdain in his eyes. "You're seventeen years old. Keep up this shit and you'll be out on the street. Got it?"

Marc scanned the room, fighting the urge to walk out the door for good. Flakes of paint clung to the ceiling, one small breeze and they'd be lying on the soiled, burnt orange shag carpet below their feet. Every chip on every overused, shabby piece of furniture caught his eye. Fighting his anger, he turned to the window, only to see a paint-stripped rain gutter hanging by a metal thread. He wanted to scream at the injustice. Why me? Why do I have to live like this? He looked at his father. Why did I get stuck with him? What am I doing here?

The rattle of pans coming from the kitchen stirred his thoughts, reminding him of his mother's loud whispers from the night before, pleading with his father to take the time to speak with their son. The sound of her voice, though muffled through the plywood bedroom door, sent a clear message: "You need to set him straight, I can't take it anymore." Still looking at the top of his father's head, Marc realized that if it weren't for her, his father would never have taken the time to start this alleged conversation.

Marc shrugged his shoulders, sticking his finger deep within one of the many holes dotting the sofa cushion. What scared him most was that he knew his father was right. His mother and brother were the only two people in the world he loved, and yet, he'd lash out at them for no reason at all. He couldn't understand his own behavior – one minute feeling intense passion for someone and the next wanting to hurt them in some way. Marc probed deeper into the sofa hole, fingering the foam that ripped beneath his nail.

He winced, reliving the slap he'd received a week before from his high school sweetheart, leaving a welt on his face that lasted through the night.

"I'm done with this, Marc!" Melissa had screamed, swelling tears falling from her olive eyes, leaving trails of mascara down her cheeks. "I can't take it anymore! One day you say you love me, the next day you treat me like shit. I deserve better than this!"

She stormed out of his room, passing his mother as she ran out the front door. He heard his mother call out to him and jumped up to slam the door shut before she had a chance to begin the interrogation.

Melissa's outburst had left Marc with an overwhelming sense of relief. He admitted to himself he'd been using her for the past two years to help him hide his true sexual identity. He loved her, yes, but not the way he loved the men he'd met in Glastonbury Park; strangers who didn't know his name, but understood how he needed to be touched and ravished in new and exciting ways. He considered Melissa his protector – the shiny coat of armor protecting him from the wrath and torment of the neighborhood –people, like his father, who he was certain would not accept his inclination. She'd been his unwitting assistant, asking for trust and compassion as her only form of payment. But those were two qualities Marc knew he couldn't offer.

Marc watched in disgust as his father struggled to lean over his own stomach, grabbed a cigar from the snack table, bit off the tip with his snuff-colored teeth, chewed it and then spit it out onto the floor beside him. He felt a flame rise from the pit of his abdomen and work its way into his chest.

"What's wrong with you?" his father asked, clouds of smoke surrounding his balding head. "You look sick or something."

Marc closed his eyes, determined not to say a word. But when he opened his eyes, his mouth opened too.

"I am sick." Marc put his index finger over his lips, forcing himself to keep his mouth shut.

His father crept his butt toward the edge of the chair, fanning the cloud of smoke with the TV Guide, squinting at Marc. "Sick from what?"

Marc held on as long as he could, but the battle between his brain and his mouth was over. His mouth proved to be the victor.

"From you!" he screamed, rising so quickly he fell back on the couch, forgetting he still had his finger stuck in the foam. By the time he disengaged his digit, his father was hovering above him.

"You little shit! What did you say?"

Marc rolled along the sofa cushions; the splash of hot air from his father's open, swinging hand whooshing against his left cheek. He continued to roll onto the floor until he lay about six feet from the raving maniac. From there he stood and looked directly into his father's eyes – the first he'd seen of them since the conversation started.

"I said you make me sick! This house makes me sick! This furniture makes me sick!" He waved his arm above his head. Now he was the raving maniac. "This dirty carpet makes me sick. Everything in this hell hole makes me sick."

Out of the corner of his eye, Marc saw movement in the hallway. His mother stood against the wall, wiping her hands on a dish towel, her face stricken with terror. His little brother Frankie, hiding beneath her apron, fingering the frayed edges.

"What's going on in here?" she asked, voice trembling. She looked at her husband. "Chuck, what's going on?"

Marc's father stuffed his cigar deep into his mouth and crossed his arms, letting them lean against his stomach.

"Seems your little boy don't like it here anymore, Marjorie. Says he's sick of it all. Sick of you, sick of me, sick of his little brother Frankie too." He raised his arms and let them fall in a circular motion like he was inviting all the angels in from the sky. "He's sick of it all, Marjorie. Sick of it all."

Marc heard the faint southern twang, a speech pattern his father resorted to whenever the anger went deep or he was preparing for a verbal assault. And by the malicious grin on his face, Marc knew his father wasn't nearly finished.

"Probably thinks he's too good for us too." he glanced at Marjorie, holding up his hand for her to stay silent before she even had the chance to speak. "And maybe he is." His sarcasm tightened the knots in Marc's stomach. "He's book smart, math smart and does lots of reading. Like those magazines you found in his room. Looks like he read those a lotta times, though there's a lot more pictures in those magazines than actual words."

Marc looked at his mother, who dropped her gaze to the floor. His mind was spinning: magazines… pictures… Could they have found his porno magazines? He'd hidden them so well in the back of his closet, behind…

His father's sudden guffaw made him shudder and he felt numbness in his neck. He swayed back and forth on his feet to keep his balance.

"Look at him, Marjorie. He didn't think we knew. I told you we should've said something and kicked him out then. But nooooo, 'He's our son', you said, 'He's our flesh and blood' you said. So I keep quiet about it and now look. We make him sick. Ain't that the best thing you ever heard in your life?"

The numbness spread throughout Marc's body, but, even so, he moved toward his room as though he was sleepwalking, hearing his father's screaming laughter, but not registering a single word. It was senseless chatter, hitting his eardrums but unable to cross the synaptic channels in his brain. As he walked past his mother, she gently placed her hand on his shoulder.

"It's okay, honey, it's not such a bad thing." The rest of her words, too, were blurry.

He walked to his closet, pulled out his suitcase and threw all his clothes in, hangers and all. Still in a daze, he carried the valise to the bathroom, tossed in his toothbrush, zipped up the bag and walked back into the living room.

"Honey," cried Marjorie stepping in front of him, "what are you doing? We don't want you to go. We love you." She wiped his face and he could feel her cool clamminess leave a trail on his cheek.

"Let him go, Marjorie. Let him see what it's like out there. He's had it too good here." His father chewed down hard on his cigar and spoke through his teeth. "Maybe he'll find a nice boyfriend to take care of him."

Marc looked at his father and didn't speak until their eyes locked.

"You make me sick," he said. "You've always made me sick. And you'll always make me sick." Marc was surprised by the low, even tone of his voice. It was as though someone else was speaking his words. "I'm going to make it big without your help and without your love." He glanced around the room. "I'm going to show you what it's like to live like a human being, not like an animal. You've forced your family to live in squalor because you've always been too lazy to get a real job. You're a selfish man and I will hate you forever."

He lifted the bag under his arm, stepped around his mother and headed toward the door.

"Don't you ever come back here!" his father yelled. "We don't want no fags in this house."

" Chuck! Marc! Stop this, please!" Marc heard the tears in her voice and in the sweeping groan that heaved from her throat as she ran to the door after him.

He didn't turn around – not for his mother's cries or the sound of the slamming door that sent shivers up his spine. What hurt most was not turning around to the tapping on the window of his little brother's tiny fingers.

"We're just here to get as much information as we can," Jack said, pulling into the driveway. "Don't mention anything about the money. For now, we have to keep it a secret."

Marc shook his head, trying to bring himself back into the moment.

"Got it," he said. "I can definitely do that."

Kneeling on the hardwood floor, Todd peeked out the master bedroom window into the backyard. His body was positioned well below the sill, keeping him hidden from view so he wouldn't risk capturing anyone's attention.

The house was empty except for the quiet hum of the hot water heater, the soothing sound that used to lull him to sleep as a child. He glanced at the eight-by-ten sterling silver frame sitting on the night table beside the bed and almost choked on his lollipop when he saw the photograph. Sitting on white sand with a backdrop of turquoise water, his father was positioned behind his new girlfriend, Mandy – a twenty-something buxom blonde who looked more like his granddaughter than his lover. His father's arms draped down her shoulders, his hands holding the inner crease of her elbows. They each held a wide smile, the whiteness of their teeth accentuating their tanned skin. The few hairs remaining on his father's comb-over stood at attention from either the tropical breeze or his father's own disbelief that he'd snagged a woman as hot as Mandy.

Frantically rolling the lollipop back and forth in his mouth, Todd grabbed the photograph and stared at it, shaking his head, recalling the photo of his mother that used to sit by the bedside, her smiling face revealing the true contentment she felt about her life, the inherent happiness that coursed through her veins up until the day his father decided she was too old for him. He never actually said it, of course.

He never told either of them, Todd or his mother, that she had aged ungraciously or that he couldn't bear another day of watching the skin droop beneath her arms or the veins in her legs bulge through her stockings. After thirty-five years of marriage, his words were few: he needed a change or he was going to die.

Todd threw the frame onto the bed, cursing his father, wishing he had died. Wishing it was his father, rather than his mother, who'd been sitting alone in a one-bedroom apartment when the chest pain threw her on the floor and left her to die.

"A heart attack," the paramedic said after Todd and his father arrived at the apartment. But Todd knew that wasn't the case. Bending over his mother's lifeless body, twirling her gray, brittle hair between his fingers, he looked up at his father, whose guilty expression assured Todd they were thinking the same thought: it wasn't a heart attack that killed her, it was a heart break.

"Bastard!" Todd whispered as he threw the saliva-soaked lollipop stick onto the silk pillows. He fell to his knees and continued peering at the group of people gathering in the backyard.

That morning, after answering Glen's phone call, he'd called in sick to J&M. Speaking to Glen stressed him out and he knew he'd do some kind of damage to J&M's computer system, and his job, if he went to work. Between Glen's call and the events of the previous night, his body was exhausted and his ability to concentrate on anything but the matter at hand was close to zero.

Todd wondered if Glen believed his story about stopping by to check on the house. He rubbed the top of his head, the soft stubble feeling rough against his chafed fingers, still sore from a night of splitting rock and scraping mortar with his fingernails.

"Holy shit!" he yelled, watching Marc and Jack walk across Glen's backyard to the wall. He straightened his back, trying to get a better view, but still hiding. "What the hell are they doing here?" Todd whispered as he backed away from the window, still on his knees. "What does he think he's doing?"

The blaring tone of his cell phone made him jump. He grabbed his chest, thinking the pain in his arm might be the first sign of a heart attack. He unhooked the phone from his belt, looked at the display and recognized Cory's number. Throwing the phone onto the bed, he let the phone ring. He could only handle one emergency at a time, and a call from Cory always meant a problem.

He walked into the bathroom, shunning the mirror, and paused in front of the sink to splash water on his face and head. Grabbing the face towel on the shower door, he wiped his face dry and threw the damp rag onto the toilet seat.

"I might as well get this over with," he muttered, realizing his only option was to join the group of spectators at the stone wall. Walking out of the room and across the carpeted landing, he took a deep breath, threw another lollipop in his mouth and rubbed his head until he hit the bottom step of the long staircase.

Before reaching the cobblestone pathway leading from the front of the house to the backyard, he stopped and turned around. After glancing up and down the street, he ran to the trunk of his Ford Escort and unlocked it. Beneath a mound of broken computer parts, empty MDVDonald's bags, and crumpled maps, lay a gym bag. He unzipped

166

the soil-stained bag and let out a sigh. Visible through the mud-covered plastic bags and fragments of dried cement, were the colors of money – beautiful hues of green and white he'd soon use to start his new life.

He slammed the trunk shut and wiped his hands on his pants, imagining himself cruising west on Interstate 80 in a Lexus convertible, music blasting, the hot sun warming his head. Todd gently patted his stomach, a surge of excitement almost making him wince. This is my time. I deserve this! He looked up at his father's house. Away from this shithole, away from that bastard. The words echoed in his head and the feelings they created gave him enough confidence to follow the stone path into the backyard. Once he convinced Jack and the rest of the group of his innocence, the only thing left to do was split the money with his accomplice, buy that Lexus, and head west.

Kneeling beside Jack, Marc sensed Jack's sadness as he rubbed his fingers along the inside of the gaping hole. He turned and looked up at Jenna whose small hands rested on her uncle's shoulders.

"That's a big hole, isn't it?" Marc asked her, breaking the uncomfortable silence that had surrounded the small group since he and Jack had arrived.

"Yes," replied Jenna, wrapping her arms around Jack's neck.

Marc turned his gaze to Lisa and smiled. She looked away, no change of expression or even the slightest attempt to return his smile. When he glanced at her husband standing beside her, John was peering over the wall at the stranger walking toward them.

"What the hell is he doing here?" Jack asked, still looking through the wall's opening.

"I think that's Todd," John said, "Glen asked me to talk to him and find out if –"

"I know who it is, Dad, I want to know what the hell he's doing here," Jack said, clenching his fists.

Marc twisted his head and saw Todd, both hands in his pockets, his gait slowing as he moved closer. He felt a tightening in his stomach and let out a sigh that caught Jack's attention.

Marc shrugged. "I have no idea, Jack. But I intend to find out." As he rose, Jack placed his hand on his shoulder.

"We'll both find out." Jack unclasped Jenna's hands from his neck and led her to his mother, forcing a smile. "Stay with Grandma for a minute, Jenna."

Lisa grabbed Jenna's hand and leaned forward. "What's going on, Jack?"

"I'll tell you about it later, Mom." Jack turned to his father. "Dad, could you take Mom and Jenna back to the deck? I need to talk to this guy for a minute."

"Jack, Glen asked me to talk with Todd about what he might have heard or seen. I think I should –"

"Dad," Jack interrupted, his patience wearing thin. "I'll take care of this. Please, go back to the house with Mom and Jenna."

John grabbed Jenna's other hand and the three of them walked to the deck, alternately swinging their heads around to catch a glimpse of Jack, Marc, and Todd.

Jack glared at Todd over the top of the wall. "What the hell are you doing here?"

Todd gave Marc a quick glance and then said, "Calm down, Jack." Todd pointed his thumb to the house behind him. "That's my father's house, you know that. He's away for a few weeks and I came by to check on it."

Marc noticed a small vein protruding from the right side of Jack's forehead. The tension in his stomach grew and he held his breath.

"I know," Jack said, "that wasn't my question. Why are you here now? Why aren't you at work?"

"I'm keeping an eye on the house. That's all. Glen called this morning to find out if I knew anything about what happened here. I told him I'd come over to talk about it. I decided to work from here today, so I could make sure that whoever did this to the wall wouldn't try to break in or something."

Jack glanced at his watch. "It's almost four, Todd. It took you all day to get your ass out here to find out what's going on?"

Marc watched Jack and Todd, his eyes moving from one to the other, anticipating an explosion. He was just about to speak when Todd moved closer and grasped the top of the wall.

"What the hell is your problem, Jack? This hole in the wall is as big a shock to me as it is to you. What are you getting at?"

"I don't trust you, asshole. I think you're involved in this somehow and you're hiding something. You have guilt written all over that pitiful face." Jack's voice was trembling and Marc sensed it was time to intervene.

"He knows," Marc said, looking at Todd with an expression he hoped would stop Todd from saying anything else. "I told him all about Cory's plan and our involvement." Marc glanced at Jack, then back to Todd. "That's why he thinks you're involved with this."

Todd took his hands from the wall and slid them back into his pockets. He dropped his head and focused on the rocks covering the grass.

"Involved in what?" Todd asked, slowly lifting his head, staring at Marc.

"The wall… this hole," Marc said. "Something was hidden in here, and now it's gone."

Todd took a few steps back and turned to Jack. "Okay, maybe I was involved with Cory, but I had nothing to do with this." He pointed to the hollowed-out section of wall. "It was probably Cory! It's just like him to do something like this."

"Oh, and it's not like you?" Jack leaned over and started to make his way through the hole.

"Jack, wait!" Marc grabbed the elbow of his shirt and pulled him back.

"Let go, Marc! I'm sick of this shit. I'm going to find out what he knows, even if I have to beat it out of him."

Marc wrapped his hand around Jack's arm and pulled him away from the wall, far enough so Todd couldn't hear him.

"Jack, I know Todd," Marc whispered. "If he's guilty, he's not going to tell you. As embarrassing as it is, he trusts me because of what I've done… to Lance Talbot and to you. Let me talk to him and find out what he knows. If he's guilty, I'll find out. Please trust me on this one. Remember, I said I'd do anything to make this up to you. Let me start with this."

Jack rubbed his hand along the back of his neck and rolled his eyes. "Okay, Marc," he said, staring into Marc's eyes, "I'm trusting you."

"I know," replied Marc, loosening his grip on Jack's arm, "And I appreciate it more than you know."

Marc awkwardly crawled through the hole and walked toward Todd, gesturing with his head for Todd to follow. As they neared the cobblestone path leading to the front of the house, Marc turned and gave Jack a reassuring wink. Jack didn't respond, he was pacing the length of the wall.

Once out of Jack's earshot, Todd stopped walking and turned to Marc. "What the hell were you thinking telling Jack about the plan? Are you out of your mind?"

Marc held his hand up to Todd's face. "Shut up, Todd. Keep it down." He looked at Jack, who stood at the other end of the yard. "I had to tell him. Trust me, it was the only way to handle the situation."

"Did you tell him about the money?" Todd asked, feverishly rubbing his head.

"No," Marc replied, kicking the chipped cobblestone with his sneaker.

"So what the hell are you doing with him anyway? I thought we were going to just split the cash and make a run for it."

"I went back to Jack's apartment early this morning to get my stuff. I'd left my keys and suitcase there and I wanted to –"

Todd pushed Marc's shoulder, causing him to stagger backward. "Are you kidding me? You have enough money to buy a new freakin' wardrobe! Hell, you have enough money to get anything you want. Why would you take the chance and go back there?"

Marc took a deep breath and looked at his stubble-headed accomplice, knowing the words he was about to utter would be wasted. "I'm giving the money back," Marc said softly. "I don't want to go through with it."

Todd held his hands up as though he were trying to fend off an attacking lunatic.

"You've got to be kidding me! Give it back? Why would you… how do you plan…" Todd shook his head. "What the hell is wrong with you?"

"I know you can't understand it, Todd, and I wouldn't expect you to. I'm not going to get into it with you. I've just had second thoughts and I'm going to figure out a way to get my half of the money back to him. You can do what you want with your half."

"You bet your ass I'll do what I want. I didn't scrape my hands raw to just give the money back. I'm going to use it any way I want. And the first thing I'm going to do is get the hell out of this town before Cory or anyone else tracks me down."

"That's fine. Do whatever you want." Marc looked at Jack, now standing on the deck with his family. "I'll call you later to set up a time to meet and split the money." Marc looked into Todd's eyes, waving his index finger less than an inch from his nose. "And don't even think about leaving with all of it. If you do, I'll tell everyone about it and we'll all track you down. And I promise, you won't make it out alive."

"Okay, okay." Todd laughed, turning away from Marc and walking toward his car. "I promise, I won't leave. Just call me by eight so we can make plans. I want to pack up and leave by tomorrow."

Marc ran to Todd and grabbed his arm. He pulled him backward and tightened his grip. "I'm serious, Todd, you leave with that money and you're done."

Todd pulled his arm and snapped it free from Marc's grip. He opened the car door and grabbed the keys from his pocket. "I told you, asshole, I won't leave. Just make sure you call me by eight tonight." He jingled his keys and smiled. "Calm down, we're in this together. Have I ever screwed you before?"

Marc stood in the driveway as Todd jumped into his car. The tires screeched as he backed out of the driveway and swung into the street, leaving a cloud of acrid exhaust in his wake. "That's what scares me," Marc whispered under his breath.

Walking back toward the wall, he racked his brain trying to figure out his next move. Telling Jack about stealing the money was out of the question. He knew it would destroy any remaining chance to repair their relationship.

His thoughts reached back to the events of the previous day: peeking out Jack's bedroom door, standing deathly still as Cory watched the DVD. Cory was already convinced he was out cold from the Valium – the pills he'd flushed down the toilet minutes before Cory arrived. As he spied the DVD, his plan to gain Jack's sympathy by feigning an overdose was quickly changing: there was money to be made – a lot of money. It could be his escape route from the drudgery of scraping pennies and living paycheck to paycheck, a way to contribute to a possible future with Jack – as long as he kept the source of his fortune hidden forever.

Once Dana pointed out where the money was hidden, Cory jumped up, shut off the television, and scooted out of the apartment. Covered only with a bed sheet, Marc scurried to the kitchen phone and dialed Todd's number.

"You want to meet at two o'clock… in the morning?" Todd yelled incredulously.

"Yes, it's the only time we'll be able to do this," Marc replied. "You want to get rich quick? You want to get out of this city? This is the way out. If you don't want to do it, tell me now."

There was a short pause and Marc listened impatiently to Todd's breathing.

"Okay, I'm in," Todd said, "but it's pouring out there and they're saying it's going to get worse."

Marc rolled his eyes and restrained himself from banging the phone on the kitchen counter. "Are you telling me you're scared of a little rain?"

More silence.

"Okay, two o'clock, my father's house. Just don't be late!"

The taxi ride from the T station seemed to take forever. The driving rain kept the cabby's speed under 50 mph and Marc was losing his patience. His heart had been hammering in his chest ever since Jack fell asleep and he snuck out of the bedroom. He was already five minutes late and forced himself to stay hopeful that Todd had the good sense to wait for him.

When the cab reached the house, Marc threw the money at the driver, slid across the seat, and out the door. He gave a sigh of relief, seeing Todd holding the screen door open for him. Marc ducked from the rain as he ran up the stone steps leading to the door. He passed Todd without acknowledgement, heading toward the back door.

"Hey, hold on, dude!" Todd yelled, closing the front door.

Marc turned around, beads of rain dripping from his face. When he took a closer look at Todd, he noticed his clothes were drenched and water dripped down his cheeks.

"Do you have everything? The chisel? The flashlights? The bags?" He paused for a second and squinted his eyes. "And why are you so wet?"

Todd smiled, wiping the moisture from his stubble. "Yeah, I have everything. And, actually, I started before you got here, just in case you didn't show."

Marc widened his eyes. Why did I trust him? "What the hell did you do that for? We're in this together! I'm the one who told you about it, for Christ's sake. What do you think I –"

"Hold on, Crazy Boy!" Todd raised his hands above his head, fending off Marc's anger. "There's still a lot of work to do. I just wanted to make sure this was going to work. And it does! The mortar breaks up easily, and, believe it or not, the rain is actually helping."

"Good," mumbled Marc, looking around for the tools.

"Everything's outside," Todd said, as he slid his coat on and pulled the hood over his head. "I'd say we have about two hours more to go."

With the rain soaking his hair, Marc leaned against the wall, flashes of Jack appearing out of nowhere. This is not the time, he said to himself, wiping the mixture of perspiration and rain from the back of his neck. This wasn't the time for guilt – it was an opportunity to start the life he'd always dreamed of. There was no way he'd let emotion stop him. He pulled the hood attached to his sweatshirt over his head and knotted the thin cord around his neck, suddenly thankful the blinds in Jack's bedroom had been closed when he'd left. The room had been void of any light, allowing him to sneak out without seeing the face of the one person he truly loved, and was about to betray, for the second time.

A warm breeze hit Marc's face as he walked toward the wall, playing out the script he was about to deliver. The faint scent of honeysuckle and dying foliage invoked an eerie feeling of déjà vu and he stopped his gait when he saw the snapshot of Jack and his family assembled on the deck. The image created a sudden yearning for a loving family of his own and he pictured himself beside Jack, talking and laughing with his parents and Jenna – not a stranger trying to make up for his sins, but part of a cohesive unit of people who depended on one another and provided the love and support he'd longed for since he could remember. Maybe, he thought, I can still have it.

As he leaned over and climbed through the opening in the wall, the warmth of the breeze turned frigid, sending a chill down his spine. He let out a soft groan that seemed to echo within the crumbling mortar and broken stone. Pushing himself through, his hands sunk into a pile of mud and gravel on the other side. Almost like quicksand, he thought, as he scrambled to his feet, wiped both hands on his jeans, and turned to look at the hole behind him. There was something inside – he felt it, sensed it – there was something in the shadow of the stones that tried to grab onto him.

"What the hell was that?" He wasn't sure if he asked the question of himself or the wall. Whichever the case, there was no response, only the sense of a ghostly presence. Still wiping his muddy hands on his pants, he backed away from the wall, running into Jack who'd come to meet him.

"What's wrong?" Jack asked, turning Marc around to face him. "You're white as a ghost."

Marc looked back at the opening and shook his head, determining the strange feelings he'd just experienced were all in his head and shouldn't be shared with anyone.

"Nothing, Nothing... I just slipped in the mud, that's all."

"So what did Todd say? Does he know anything?"

"He knows nothing," Marc replied, "but he did say Cory called yesterday afternoon and told him he had a way for both of them to get rich very quickly." Marc was amazed at how genuine the lie sounded, how the words rang with truth. He almost believed the story himself. "He actually made arrangements with Todd to meet over there," Marc pointed to Todd's father's house, "but called a little later to cancel. Something about his girlfriend being sick." Marc sensed Jack was buying the story and a wave of relief passed over him. "So we concluded that Cory must've come here in the middle of the night and taken the money. Why should he split it when he could have it all for himself?"

"What a son of a bitch," Jack said, turning around to glance at his family. He looked back at Marc. "How did you ever get involved with him, Marc?"

"Biggest mistake of my life," Marc replied, proud of himself for finally uttering some words of truth. "I definitely learned my lesson."

"Now what? How do we get the money back from Cory?"

"Leave that to me, Jack. I'll take care of it." Marc rubbed his hands together, trying to rid them of the mud that stuck to his fingers.

"No way, Marc. I want to get this guy. I want to see his face as I walk away with the money... after I kick his ass of course."

Marc smiled and ran his hand up and down Jack's arm. "I know,

Jack, but Cory's not going to meet with us if you're there. Todd's going to call him and set up a meeting for tonight. One way or another, we'll find out where the money is and get it from him."

"Where are you going to meet?"

"We're not sure yet. Maybe Cory's apartment. That's where he's probably hiding the money."

"Okay, we'll figure out the rest on the way home. I just need to find a way out of here without my family knowing what's going on."

Marc looked toward the deck and offered a smile, which he quickly wiped from his face when Jack's parents turned away. *Becoming a part of this family is going to be harder than I thought.* Jenna, who was picking dead leaves out of the terra cotta flower pots, looked at Marc and smiled. A surge of warmth pervaded his chest and he hoped she'd be his link into Jack's family.

"She's so sweet," Marc said, motioning his head toward Jenna.

"The sweetest," Jack replied, "and that's why we have to get her money back. Dana busted her butt to make sure Jenna was taken care of, and I'm going to make sure nothing else goes wrong." Marc looked back at the hole in the wall and shivered, recalling the cold wind he'd felt as he climbed through it. He still wasn't sure where the breeze came from or what caused it, but he sensed that if he didn't return the money, the unnatural iciness he'd felt for those few moments would stay with him for the rest of his life.

11

With his cell phone in one hand and a martini in the other, Cory paced the floor of his apartment, sensing betrayal with each step. He'd left multiple messages on Todd's voicemail, both at work and on his cell, and the past six hours without a response had transformed his frustration into anger.

He sipped down the last few drops of alcohol, placed the empty glass on the mahogany end table beside the sofa and walked to the narrow balcony extending the width of the living room. Leaving the sliding glass and screen doors open, he laid his cell phone on top of the waist-high cement wall and hesitantly peered over it, down fifteen flights of space. He'd always been proud of the view, often using it as an aphrodisiac for the women he'd bring home on the nights he was lucky enough to free himself from Janice's eagle grip. Leading them out to the balcony, he'd give them a few moments to savor the bird's-eye view of Cambridge and then press up against them from behind.

"I'll catch you if you fall," he'd whisper, gently pushing his hot breath into their ear, rubbing their arms and buttocks. He'd close his eyes, never allowing himself to gaze into the airy expanse. The height flooded him with the same queasiness and light-headedness he felt when he gazed out the window of an airplane. It wasn't the height that frightened him as much as the boundless void hanging between where he stood and the concrete walkway that crawled the manicured grounds so far below.

But tonight, anger pushed aside most of his fear, allowing him to savor the autumn colors of the precisely placed trees lining the path below. Still not Jack's view, he thought to himself, glaring at his cell phone, his envy rising like boiling oil. I want Jack's view!

Thinking about the DVD he'd watched the day before, Cory could almost taste that view. At first he considered stealing the money that night, but with Janice clinging to his every move and sheets of rain pouring down on the city, he decided to wait another day – counting on the fact that no one else knew about the hidden treasure. After more thought, he decided to involve Todd. Breaking down the wall would be difficult for one person and by offering Todd twenty percent of the riches, he'd have a willing assistant at his beck and call.

But Todd hadn't returned any of his calls and Cory was getting close to attempting the task alone. He glanced at his watch: 6:35.

"Six more hours," he said, walking back into the apartment, "and I'll do it myself."

The sliding screen door wasn't even fully closed when his cell phone rang. Cory tip-toed back outside – the sound jolting him back into reality, along with his fear of heights. He snatched the phone, jumped through the doorway, and ran into the living-room. The LED displayed Todd's number.

Flipping open the phone, he felt both anger and relief. "Where the hell have you been?"

"Things have been crazy at work," Todd replied. "I couldn't get back to you until now. Sorry."

"Sorry my ass!" Cory took a deep breath. He needed Todd's help and didn't want to push him away. "Okay, I'm outta line, I'm sorry. It's just that I found out about something that could make us both very rich and I need to talk with you about it."

"Oh, really?" Todd asked.

"Really. And the amazing thing is, it's sitting right behind your father's house." The silence made Cory think he'd lost the connection; he tilted the phone in search of better reception. "Did you hear me?"

"Yeah, sorry. You're kidding me. What are you talking about?"

"I'll tell you about it when I see you. Can you meet me at your father's house?"

"Okay. When?"

"How's eight o'clock?" Cory said, pulling the Ketel One bottle from the freezer.

"Perfect," Todd said, "I'll see you then."

Cory flipped shut his phone, scooped ice into the glass shaker and poured the vodka over the cubes. After lining his glass with a mist of vermouth, he emptied the contents of the shaker into the glass and slowly walked to the sofa, careful not to spill any of the liquid onto the newly stained wooden floors.

He sat on the sofa and leaned back. Scrunching his toes into the deep pile of the carpet, a wave of fear coursed over his skin. A flash of his father swinging from the prison's pipes hit him hard and he slid the lip of the glass back and forth along his chin. I will not get caught, he said to himself, forcing the words to replace the morbid image. I will not get caught.

This was the opportunity he'd been waiting for and he wasn't about to let it slip through his fingers. He swallowed a big sip of vodka and stared at the photo of Janice on the bookcase.

He lifted the glass as if making a toast. "And here's to you," he said,

"Good luck trying to track me down."

Marc sat on the edge of the bed, holding the phone tightly against his ear.

"Where's Jack?" asked Todd.

"In the shower," Marc replied, keeping an eye on the bathroom door, "We only have a few minutes, so let's make a plan."

"Cory's coming here, to my father's house, at eight o'clock to tell me about the hidden money. He has no clue we already have it."

"You idiot! We're supposed to meet at eight!"

"Calm down. We will meet at eight, just not here. By the time Cory gets to the house and figures out I'm not showing up, you'll have your money and I'll be on my way to freedom."

"Well, Jack thinks we're going to get the money from Cory and he wants to be there. He said –"

"No way!" Todd cut him off. "Jack can't be there. That won't work."

Marc scratched his head, slid his hand down the side of his face, and bit his nail. That's when it hit him: The perfect plan!

"I got it! Let's meet at Cory's place." Marc was delighted with his quick thinking. "Do you still have his key?"

"Yeah, somewhere."

"Well find it and make sure you're in his apartment by eight o'clock. When Jack and I get there, I'll tell him there's no way Cory will admit to anything with him there. I'll go in alone, we'll split the cash, and then go our separate ways."

"Are you really going to give him the money? That's just nuts! Don't you realize what you could do with that kind of cash?"

Marc leaned back against the headboard and smoothed his hand over Jack's pillow. He considered explaining his feelings to Todd, but knew he'd be wasting his breath.

"Yes. And yes," he said.

"And how will you explain the fact that you only have half the money?"

Marc heard the shower turn off and jumped to his feet. "Don't worry about that. I'll take care of it. I gotta go. Just make sure you're there by eight."

Marc hung up the phone just as Jack opened the bathroom door. A cloud of mist blew into the bedroom, and, when the fog cleared, Marc leaned backward, watching Jack tighten the towel around his waist and smooth back his wet hair, trying to see himself through the haze clinging to the giant mirror.

He felt an empty ache in the pit of his stomach, devouring the sight of Jack's muscular body – broad shoulders narrowing down a strong back to his waist, forming a perfect triangle, a form of statuesque perfection. Marc yearned for Jack's touch, remembering the intense passion they shared, the almost suffocating heat they generated every time they had sex.

"Hey!" Jack said, jolting Marc from his daze. "What's going on in there?" Jack pointed to Marc's head.

"Just thinking," Marc replied. "Did the shower help you feel any better?"

Jack fastened the towel around his waist and rubbed his hands together. "It helped, but I won't relax until we put Cory in his place and get the money back."

Marc looked away, gazing out the windows into the darkening sky. He couldn't wait either. He wanted this whole thing behind him and promised himself, as he felt the warmth of Jack's hand on his jeans, that he'd change his ways. After tonight, his days of deception were over – no more Cory, no more Todd, no more lies. From now on his life would be about truth and compassion toward the people he cared about. Turning his head, he looked deep into Jack's eyes and could feel the promise he just made to himself take root: no job or sum of money could take the place of the permeating wholeness he felt when Jack looked at him.

Jack knelt beside the bed and gently massaged Marc's thigh.

"You were right," Jack said, lacing his fingers with Marc's. "I am a control freak. It's something I've dealt with for—"

Marc squeezed his hand. "I'm sorry, Jack. I didn't mean what I said. I was mad and upset, I for—"

"No, Marc." Jack turned his head and laid his cheek on Marc's thighs. "It is all about control for me. And that's one of the reasons I loved being with you so much. You made me do things I wouldn't ordinarily do, try things I'd typically run away from. You added excitement to my life by taking me off the path I could control, the path I'd been on my whole life." Marc twirled his fingers through Jack's hair, feeling the warmth of his breath on his legs. "Everything was safe until I met you. Safe and controlled and… dull."

Marc heard Jack's voice quiver with emotion. He rubbed his head, fighting back his own tears.

"I've missed you," Jack said, leaning over to kiss Marc's forehead.

Marc didn't move. He inhaled deeply as Jack's smooth shaven face glided against his cheek, leaving a faint trail of moisture. Not wanting to risk spoiling the moment, Marc continued to sit motionless, barely breathing, not saying a word.

"We're going to get through this," Jack whispered, softly sweeping the wisps of hair hanging over Marc's eyes. "I really think we can make it… as long as we're always honest with each other. You just have to promise me you'll always tell me the truth."

Their faces were only inches apart and Marc welcomed Jack's breath into his lungs, the warm sweetness warming his chest, slowly dissolving and spreading throughout his body.

"I promise," Marc returned the whisper. "I promise forever."

When their lips met again, Marc closed his eyes, and, for the first time in his life, thanked God – for being alive and giving him a second chance.

Jack pulled the BMW into the visitors' parking lot, turned off the ignition and rubbed his hands together. The temperature had dropped almost thirty degrees since afternoon. It was the New England way of introducing winter with a soft blow, allowing Bostonians to get accustomed to the chill before the Canadian air masses pushed in and settled deep within their bones.

Looking up the side of the mammoth brick building, Jack saw lights from more than half the apartments, golden cubes of incandescence casting their glow into the darkening expanse of night. Standing firm against the frigid temperature, some tenants stood on their balconies, smoking cigarettes and talking on the phone, while others gazed mindlessly at the disappearing horizon.

The car was quiet except for the murmur of a young couple passing by, apparently arguing about the man's infidelity and the woman's lack of trust. In front of the car, a nineteenth-century-style lamppost sprayed an intense cast of white light on Marc's face, creating a ghostly lightness around him that made Jack cringe with dread. He tried to shake the feeling, but it wouldn't withdraw, it clung to him like a sticky sheath of melancholy until he pulled the keys from the ignition and slid them into his coat pocket.

"What floor does he live on?" Jack asked, breaking the silence that had followed them since starting their drive to Cory's apartment.

"It's a little hard to see from this angle, but it's on the fifteenth floor."

"You ready?" Jack rubbed his hand up and down the side of Marc's arm.

"I'm ready," Marc said hesitantly, "but I have one request."

"And what would that be?"

"You stay in the car."

Jack pushed his hand against the steering wheel, using it as leverage to twist his body and face Marc.

"You're kidding me, right?"

"No, I'm not." Marc looked around the half-empty lot and turned to Jack. "Think about it. We're not even sure he has the money in his apartment. And whether he does or doesn't, he's not going to tell me anything with you there. He trusts me." Marc smiled at his own words. "Well, he trusts me as much as he trusts anyone. Once he tells me what we need to know, you and I will get the money back."

Jack gazed out the fogged windshield and tried to focus his thoughts. He knew Marc was right; Cory would probably be intimidated by Jack's presence and they might lose any chance they had of finding the money. But this wasn't the way he'd imagined his encounter with Cory; he'd envisioned retrieving the information he needed and following it up with a punch to Cory's face. Thinking about it now, in the reality of the moment, he realized he'd have to postpone his fantasy and allow Marc to take the lead.

"You're right," Jack said. "But can you trust him? I mean, would he hurt you?"

Marc ran his hands through his hair and laughed, his breath steaming up the windshield, obliterating any possible view. "Cory might be a deceitful, self-consumed, lying thief, but I don't think he'd hurt a fly. As he's told me many times before, he's a lover, not a fighter."

"Your lover?" The words escaped Jack's mouth before he had a chance to restrain them.

Marc grabbed Jack's hand. "Absolutely not. The thought alone makes me sick."

"Good." Jack peered into Marc's eyes and grinned. "That makes me feel a little better."

Their hands still entwined, Marc rubbed the inside of Jack's palm with his thumb. "I'm going up now," he said. Using the sleeve of his jacket to wipe away the windshield's mist, he pointed to the building. "See the corner apartment on the far end with the light on?"

Jack scanned the giant edifice and counted the rows of apartments leading up to the roof. When he reached fifteen, he slid his eyes over to the far end of the building.

"Yes. I see it." Jack saw a shadow's movement and felt a twinge in his gut. "I think I just saw him!"

"Probably," Marc said, wiping the sweat from his forehead. "Now listen, when I have what I need and I'm ready to leave, I'll stand by the sliding door and raise both my hands above my head, okay?"

"Okay, but listen, I'm giving you twenty minutes. If I don't see you by the balcony door, or if you're not back in this car by then, I'm coming in."

"Jack, you have to give me more than –"

Jack tightened his grip around Marc's hand. "No! Twenty minutes, that's it. I just don't trust him, Marc, and you shouldn't either. If you can't get the money or any good information in twenty minutes, we'll just have to come up with another plan."

Marc opened the car door, stepped onto the pavement, and gently pushed the door closed. Leaning over, he peered through the window. Jack took the keys from his coat pocket, inserted the ignition key, and slid the window down with the press of a button. "I'll see you in twenty minutes… or less."

Marc leaned in further, his torso resting on the doorjamb. Jack tilted forward and caressed Marc's cheek, feeling the cool, damp skin beneath his warm palm. "Twenty minutes," he said, "or I'm coming up."

Marc took Jack's hand in his, pressed it harder against his cheek and then let it go, turning around to head toward the building. About to call out to him, Jack restrained himself, thoughts of Dana and Jenna steamrolling his swelling anxiety. He looked at the blue digits glowing from the dashboard clock: 8:00. He took a deep breath.

"Twenty minutes," he whispered, starting his countdown.

Jack didn't close the window until Marc disappeared behind the finely trimmed hedges, moving into the shadow of the towering edifice that stood like a behemoth against the black sky.

Marc smiled as he turned the doorknob, pleasantly surprised Todd had remembered to keep the door to Cory's apartment unlocked. This might be easier than I thought.

He closed the door behind him and strolled over to the sofa where Todd sat, feet up on the thick mahogany coffee table, beer in hand.

"Make yourself at home," Marc said, incredulous at Todd's shamelessness.

"Thanks, I will," Todd responded, lifting the bottle to his mouth.

Marc furrowed his brow when he saw the brown leather gloves Todd wore.

"What's with the gloves?"

Todd carefully placed the bottle on the table, in the precise spot where he'd already created a ring of moisture. "Just being cautious." He held his gloved hands in front of his face, twisting them around like a glove model in a fashion show. "Fingerprints. You never know."

Marc rolled his eyes. Typical Todd, he thought. "Whatever, Todd. Where's the money? Jack's waiting outside and I don't have much time."

Todd stood and walked to the balcony. He slid open both the glass and screen door, but didn't walk outside. Turning around to Marc, he grimaced. "I hid it," he said, looking to the floor.

Marc's eyes widened in disbelief. "What are you talking about?"

"I brought it with me, but I wanted to set things straight before I gave it to you."

Marc felt the heat of anger rise from his chest into his face. Todd had the upper hand and he knew he'd have to play his cards carefully.

"Okay," Marc said, "what is it you need to set straight?"

"What are you going to tell Jack about the other half of the money?"

With that question, Marc saw where the conversation was going. "I'm going to tell him that I couldn't get it, that Cory spent it on a new car or a house in Hawaii. I'll tell him half is better than none and we'll make it up somehow. Don't worry about it, Todd, I won't mention your name."

"I don't think giving your half of the money to Jack is a good idea," Todd said, fumbling with his gloved fingers.

Marc walked over to Todd, stopping close enough to feel his breath on his cheek. With his nose only inches from Todd's, he looked at his shaven head, the stubble sprouting like broom bristles.

"I don't give a shit what you think, Todd. Half the money is mine and I can do with it as I please."

Todd took a few steps back. Marc followed.

"That's what I mean!" Todd cried. "You could take this money and start a whole new life… without Jack." Todd turned away from Marc and looked out onto the balcony. "You could come out west with me… and… well…you never know…"

Marc shook his head. "Todd, that's not going to happen," he said, speaking to the back of Todd's head. "I mean, I'm flattered and everything, but…"

Todd stood motionless, still gazing out the doors into the invisible landscape. "You're like on this guilt trip and I don't get it. But that's your problem. My problem is that when Jack pressures you about the

190

money, I have no doubt you'll turn me in." He sauntered closer to the sliding doors and breathed in the cool air. "I came here hoping you'd reconsider giving the money to Jack."

"No," Marc said, realizing with that one word he'd probably destroyed his only chance of recovering Jack's money. He slowly walked around Todd and stood in front of him, the outside chill hitting the back of his neck. "Don't worry, Todd. We're partners, I won't turn you in. I promise."

Todd lifted his gaze from the floor and looked at Marc. He peered into his eyes, deliberately searched his face, and then locked into his eyes again. Leaning slightly forward, he closed his eyes and stretched his neck, his mouth slightly open, the moonlight glistening on his yellowed teeth. He reached out his hand and gently cupped Marc's crotch.

Marc tried to push him away and Todd pushed back, forcing Marc backwards onto the balcony. His waist hit the cement wall and he immediately turned to his side, looking down the endless space below him. A burst of perspiration exploded from his pores.

"I guess I'm just not good enough for you, huh?" Todd snarled.

"Todd, cut the shit!" Marc's fear caused his voice to falter. "I almost fell, for Christ's sake! You could've killed me!" He tried to gain his composure as he moved away from the wall, stopping before he reached Todd. "Enough already. Just give me the money. I give you my word that I won't involve you. That's the best I can do."

Holding his gloved hand up to Marc, Todd shook his head as he rolled his eyes. "Stay right there," he said.

Marc put his hands in his jacket pockets, trying to warm his icy fingers. He thought about leaning over the wall and placing both hands over his head to notify Jack everything was okay, but the close call with plunging to his death paralyzed him. He could barely move and his only thought was to get the money and once again be on solid ground. Leaning on one leg, he snuck a look into the apartment and saw Todd walking out of Cory's bedroom with a black gym bag. He held it over his shoulder, a wild grin covering his face as he walked toward the balcony.

"You want the money, Marc?" Todd asked, letting the bag drop from his shoulder and dangle from his hand, almost touching the floor. With the motion of a pendulum, Todd swayed the bag, using every muscle in his arm – first in front of him toward Marc, then behind him, back inside the apartment. After two more swings, he gained enough momentum to bring the bag above his head. He opened his gloved hand and let it go. "Here, take the God damn money!"

Instinctively, Marc lunged upward, pulling his hands from his pockets, reaching backward for the bag of money flying above his head. As if time had frozen, the bag seemed to hover above him, and, for an instant, the tips of his fingers scraped the canvas fabric, imploring him to follow in its path over the cement wall. And he did – first his torso and then his legs, floating over his head as his cheek scraped against the outside of the balcony wall. He reached out, extending his hands, kicking his legs, trying to grab onto something, anything, but nothing surrounded him but empty space. As he looked up into the black space between the billions of stars, he thought he heard a scream.

Was that me? A strange calm seized him. His arms still flailed and his legs kicked, but the movement was purely instinctive, his mind too consumed to think about survival. He had only two thoughts: When would he hit the ground, and had he been a good enough person to one day meet Jack in heaven?

Jack started the engine and turned on the heater, the temperature too cold to ignore. He quickly moved his glance from Cory's apartment to the dashboard clock – ten minutes had passed and he was starting to get antsy. He looked back up to the balcony and shook his head, still aghast at his situation. He never imagined he'd be in the midst of a real-life drama; a set of circumstances playing out like a sordid news story he'd read in the Sunday morning paper; a crazy turn of events that happened to someone else, living in a small town, somewhere half way across the county.

But this was his drama. His sister had died; his lover had deceived him; his niece was out a quarter of a million dollars she didn't even know about. And now here he was, sitting in his car, trembling from the cold, alone and trying to make sense of it all. He banged his open hand on top of the steering wheel and forced himself to stop trying to think about signs he'd missed or things he could've done differently. This is where I am. This is what's happening. Deal with the past tomorrow.

The silence of the car broke with the ringing of his cell phone.

"Hello?" he said, without looking at the caller ID.

"Hey, Jack, it's David. Are you okay?"

Jack smiled and took a deep breath. "Okay?" he said. "I guess it's all how you look at it." For a split second he thought about telling David what was going on, but decided against it, figuring he'd fill him in once it was over. "Anyway, yes, I'm fine. I'm just in the middle of something. Can I get back to you?"

"Sure, no problem. I just wanted to tell you something Mary and I discovered today, but we can discuss it tomorrow."

"Mary?" Jack raised his eyebrows. "What's she up to?"

"Actually, Jack, she's come around. She's been doing some investigative work, on your behalf, and she came up with some good stuff."

Jack kept his eyes on Cory's balcony – nothing. He looked at the clock. Marc had five minutes left. He had some time and was too curious to hang up now. "David, I'm waiting for someone, but I have about five minutes. So, go ahead, tell me what my friend Mary found out."

"We don't have any hard evidence, yet, but it appears there's something going on between Marc, Todd, and this guy Cory Daniels – an executive recruiter. It seems before he placed both Marc and Todd at J&M, he placed them at Stetson – just about the time Lance Talbot was booted out on those fake kiddie porn charges."

Jack exhaled loudly, nodding his head. "Old news, David. I already know about it. And you're going to tell me Cory placed Marc and Todd at J&M to get me thrown out, right?" Jack heard David stutter on the other end of the phone. "Am I right?"

"Yes, that's what we're thinking," David answered, "but how…? I mean, I know you and Marc have a relationship… and I was hoping his deception wasn't true… I just wanted to make you aware of what we were thinking… just in case."

"Thank you, David. I appreciate it and I'm still trying to get to the bottom of it. Marc and I are working things out and –"

Jack stopped talking as he caught a glimpse of movement on Cory's balcony. The figure looked like Marc, but he was too far away to know for sure and the fifteenth floor was a long way up. He turned off the engine, opened the car door, and leaned against it, trying to get a better view.

"Jack? Are you there? Jack?"

Jack heard David's voice coming from his cell phone. "Sorry, David, I have to go. I'll call you back."

"Is everything okay? Jack, I –"

Jack snapped his phone shut, slammed the car door, and walked toward the hedges. Standing on his toes he peered over the eight-foot high natural fencing and squinted his eyes. Marc leaned against the balcony wall and, for an instant, seemed to look right at Jack. He felt his heart skip a beat as he saw Marc talking to someone standing by the patio doors. From where Jack stood, he could only see a shadow, so he made his way closer to the building to try and get a first hand look at Cory.

Still gazing upward, he saw what looked like a gym bag swinging out the sliding balcony doors and instantly knew that the bag held the money. His anger intensified, picturing the faceless thief stuffing Jenna's money into a bag, thoughtless of the fact he'd stolen such a big part of a little girl's future.

Jack moved off the stone pathway, continuing toward the building but moving further out to get a full shot of the balcony. Suddenly his legs felt like lead, paralyzed by the sight of the bag taking flight over Marc's head and across the busy street into the forested wetlands.

But that wasn't what made him scream – it was the vision of Marc's limbs thrashing as he fell fifteen flights, not making a sound until he crashed onto the pavement five feet from where Jack stood.

12

"Here's an aspirin," the man said, holding a small white tablet inches from Jack's face, "It's extra strength."

Jack lifted his hand to grab the pill, wincing at the pale crimson, dried bloodstains on his fingers. He didn't know how long he'd cradled Marc's head in his hands, caressing his face, rubbing his twisted arms, wishing that a gentle touch and a silent prayer could bring him back. Now, sitting on the vinyl sofa in the main lobby of the apartment building, he couldn't remember how he'd gotten there. The only thing he knew for sure was his head pounded and the invisible vise squeezing his temples wouldn't loosen its grip. He wiped his hand on the towel sitting on his lap, snatched the pill from the man's hand, and tossed it into his mouth.

"Would you like some water?" the man asked with a gentle kindness. Jack shook his head and swallowed hard. He felt the tablet slowly make its way down his throat, scraping against the walls of his pharynx. He swallowed again. "I guess not."

The man slid a small black, leather-bound book from the inside pocket of his suit jacket, flipped it open, and grabbed the pen from behind his ear. "Okay, Mr. Fontaine, let's talk about what happened." His voice was soft, with a raspy edge, like a smoker who wasn't yet ready to admit he was hooked. How does he know my name?

Jack pulled his stare from the small notebook and scanned the man's face; a hint of genuine compassion shone through his unshaven beard and sallow complexion. His hair was slicked back, exposing large green eyes surrounded by a furrowed brow that didn't match his sympathetic demeanor. His features reminded Jack of a slightly older version of Marc: a strong, handsome face outlined with clearly defined cheekbones and a vague indication of preppiness. This is what Marc would've looked like if he didn't, if he wasn't, if...

"Chief!" A short, stocky man in a police uniform rushed through the front door. "They want to take the body now, okay?"

Without looking up from his small black book, the chief answered. "Yeah, fine." He sat down next to Jack on the sofa, and, with an exhausted sigh, extended his arm along the back of the cushion. "Mr. Fontaine, as I said, my name's Larry Doonan and I'm the Assistant Chief in charge of this case. I'll make this as easy as possible for you." He looked Jack squarely in the eyes. "Now, can you tell me how you knew the deceased?"

The deceased! The hammering in Jack's head grew steadily, matching the rhythm of his heartbeat, so loud and distinct, he heard the blood pulsing in his ears. Outside the glass doors leading out to the front walkway, two men in white uniforms slid a stretcher into an ambulance, the body beneath the bloodstained sheet completely covered, motionless, held secure with thick, black restraints. Twirling red and yellow lights atop the ambulance reflected against the windows, creating a blinding glare that made Jack's head spin. He dropped his face into his hands.

"He was my lover," Jack mumbled through the spaces between his fingers.

"I see." Doonan slid his extended arm back to his side and shifted in his seat. "Now you said you don't live here, so tell me what you were doing here."

For a split second, Jack wondered if he should call someone. Doonan was repeating things he'd supposedly said, things he couldn't remember saying. He looked at the mahogany grandfather clock standing against the far wall by the elevator. It was 9:15. Almost an hour had passed since he'd seen Marc walk out onto the balcony, an hour that had gotten by him without the faintest glimpse of memory. He considered calling his father. Then thought about calling David, then his lawyer. I didn't do anything wrong, he thought. He could feel his lucidity gradually return and made the decision to tell Doonan every detail of what occurred – everything except for the bag of money he'd seen flying over Marc's head, now sitting somewhere in the woodlands less than thirty yards away.

When Jack finished, he looked at Doonan who'd been nodding and writing throughout his account. "I don't know if he was pushed or if he tripped and fell. All I know is if you find Cory or Todd, you'll know exactly what happened."

The lobby buzzed with activity – policemen scurried about, traveling up and down the elevator, stopping everyone entering or exiting the building. Jack leaned back into the sofa and slid his hands under the towel, hiding the pale reddish stains.

"We didn't find anyone in the apartment, Jack, but the door was open." Doonan scribbled in his book and tapped the end of his gold-plated pen against his teeth. "And you honestly didn't see who Marc was speaking to?"

"No," Jack said, exasperated. "I told you. The angle was bad. That's why I walked along the path – to get a better view. All I know is he expected to meet Todd here and they were going to talk with Cory. The next thing I know, Marc came onto the balcony and then…" Jack rubbed his hands together beneath the towel.

Doonan placed a hand on Jack's shoulder and squeezed it. "I got it, Jack. I think I have all I need. I have a feeling that once we find Daniels and this Todd person, we'll make sense out of everything." Doonan paused and slid his hand from Jack's shoulder. "Here's my last question: Two hundred and fifty grand is a lot of money. What do you think happened to it?"

Jack closed his eyes, imagining the bag of money lying atop a pile of soggy leaves; in a puddle of muddy sediment; slowly sinking to the bottom of a murky pond swarming with mosquitoes. He'd need help finding the bag, but knew Doonan wasn't the one to ask.

"I have no idea," Jack said, "and right now I don't really care."

Doonan stood, slipped the book back into the jacket pocket of his suit, and held out his hand to help Jack stand. Jack didn't accept his help, a small grunt escaping his lips as he stood.

"Is there someone I can call to come get you? I don't think you should drive."

Jack threw the bloody towel onto the couch. He fingered around his pants pockets for his keys, a sense of relief running through him as he felt the familiar edge of his keychain – so far, the one thing he knew hadn't changed during the last hour and a half of his life.

A commotion at the side door, an entrance to which only apartment dwellers had access, caught their attention. A team of police officers surrounded two men who'd just entered the building. The stocky officer from before rushed over to Doonan, the beak of his cap now pointing up to the ceiling.

"It's Daniels," he whispered in Doonan's ear, "and his friend Todd."

Jack heard the names and felt wild rage in the pit of his stomach. Before he could surge forward, Doonan grabbed his arms.

"No, Jack, we'll take care of this. I think you should just go home and I'll call you in the morning."

Jack glared at Cory until their eyes met. Cory's expression of recognition smacked Jack like a blast of arctic air and he continued to push against Doonan's pressing hands. He shot his gaze from Cory to Todd, who looked everywhere but at Jack.

"Jack!" Doonan raised his voice. "Go home, please!"

Jack stopped pushing and dropped back onto the sofa, his eyes still locked with Cory's. "I'm not going anywhere until I find out what happened."

Doonan turned to Cory and Todd, then to the stocky officer who stood waiting for his next command.

"Bring them upstairs," Doonan said. "Cory in the master bedroom, Todd in the living-room. I don't want them together."

Three police officers escorted them to the elevators, with Doonan trailing a few feet behind. Jack didn't take his eyes off Cory until the elevator door was completely closed. He watched the numbers above the car alternately light up, stopping at fifteen, staying lit until an elderly woman in a plaid overcoat shuffled to the elevator and pushed the up button. The handles of a white, plastic shopping bag hung around her wrist and she rummaged through it with her other hand. When she found what she'd been looking for, she glanced at Jack and offered a smile. She has no clue, he thought. Just another night of quiet solitude, sipping tea and watching TV.

He turned away, silently wishing he could be sitting beside her.

The elevator sluggishly pulled itself up to Cory's apartment, the low groan of stretching cables interrupting the strained quiet. Without lifting his head, Todd moved his eyes from the broad back of the officer in front of him over to Cory, standing at the opposite end of the car, squished in the corner closest to the elevator doors. Cory didn't return his glance; his eyes were closed, lids quivering. Todd figured he was using this time to review the story they'd contrived. He looked to the floor at the polished black shoes of the officer, letting his eyes creep up to the gun and the handcuffs hanging from the black leather belt. He felt his insides start to shake, the sight of the holstered weapon a harsh reminder of reality. They were the same tremors he'd been fighting when he made the decision to call Cory from the rest area he found along the Mass Pike.

He'd wrapped himself in a thin flannel blanket he found in the trunk and crouched in the backseat of his car. He hadn't stopped trembling since he ran from the apartment building into the evening chill; shivers ran through him as they used to many years before during his frequent childhood bouts with high fevers. But this time his mother was not around to lay a cool cloth on his forehead or soothe him with a lullaby. He was on his own, haunted by Marc's terrified expression as he twisted and fell from the balcony; the guttural croak he'd made as his face smacked the cement wall; and the eerie quiet that followed until a crackling thud jolted Todd from his stupor.

At that moment, as he stood by the balcony doors, an intense understanding of what just happened pierced his stomach – forcing the beer he'd enjoyed only moments before up his esophagus and out his mouth, a clear spray of liquid dotting the balcony wall. His head spun from disbelief, panic, and the futile denial of what he'd witnessed. Overwhelmed by the instinct to flee, he ran out the apartment door, down fifteen flights of stairs, through the employees' entrance, and directly into the building's back parking lot where he'd left his car.

Minutes later he was merging onto the Mass Pike, using every ounce of energy to stay within the white lines and maintain the speed limit. He pulled into the first rest area he saw and steered the car toward the back of the McDonald's, away from the pale yellow light of the golden arches. He quickly reconsidered, fearful a patrolling police car might take notice of an occupied vehicle sitting in the darkness. He swerved the car around and steered into the middle row of parked cars, between a brown Lexus SUV and a Ford van, hoping he'd feel safe enough to plan his next move.

Crunched up in the backseat of his car, he still couldn't focus. He pulled his hands from beneath the blanket and punched the sides of his head. "Think!" he yelled, the sound of his voice bouncing off the windows, sending an intense vibration through his ears and down the sides of his neck. "Think! Think!"

He brought his knees closer to his chest, clasping his icy fingers in front of his shins. Resting his chin on his knees, he felt the heat of his breath warming his cold legs. Options raced through his head, colliding with an obstacle at every turn. His father was inaccessible, floating around the Bahamas on a cruise ship, most likely enjoying his fifth meal of the day with his trophy of a girlfriend. He couldn't go to the police, they were looking for a killer and he feared they'd lock him up without giving him an opportunity to vindicate himself. Cory was his only hope, and he silently prayed that offering him half the money would be enough.

When he saw Cory's Jaguar enter the parking lot, Todd leaned over into the front seat and flashed his lights. Cory took the space directly in front of him, his brilliant headlights illuminating the car's interior. Todd shielded his eyes and pulled himself over the console and into the driver's seat, the blanket still draped over his shoulders.

Cory opened the passenger side door and sat down, slamming the door shut. "Okay, asshole, I'm waiting for an explanation. I've been waiting over an hour for you." Cory crossed his arms and leaned his back against the door.

"Bad shit went down tonight, Cory." Todd watched a couple walk by, digging in their bag, hungrily shoving fries into their mouths. "And I don't know what to do."

"Well, you can start by explaining yourself."

Todd turned to Cory, his shivers worsening. "Marc and I took the money from the wall last night," Todd blurted, trying to gauge Cory's reaction. "I was at my father's house today and Marc and Jack were there, in the yard. Jack confronted me... we yelled at each other... he almost hit me..."

Cory squirmed in his seat. "Make some sense, Todd. You're telling me shit I don't need to know. I saw the hole in the wall and figured it was you or Marc. I'm not stupid, you know. Now get to the point. And stop shaking already, you're making me nervous."

"Okay. Okay. Now don't get pissed, but we blamed you for taking the money and said that –"

Cory shot Todd a malicious glance. "That's it. I'm done!" he yelled, before pulling the handle of the passenger door and placing his right foot on the pavement.

Todd grabbed his arm, trying to pull him back. "Wait! There's more."

Half out of the car, Cory turned to Todd. "You expect me to help you after you screwed me like this? You must be out of your mind."

"Marc's dead," he uttered.

Cory slid back inside the car and closed the door.

"We were in your apartment and Marc wanted his half of the money to give back to Jack. I got pissed and threw the bag of money over the balcony. Marc jumped up to grab it and…just…fell over the wall."

"Holy shit," Cory whispered, rubbing his chin. "So now they think I was involved. God damn it, Todd! Now we're both screwed."

Todd let go of Cory's arm, slipping his hand back beneath the blanket. "I'm sorry Cory, I really am. I screwed up. But you have an alibi – you were at my father's house waiting for me. I swear, if you make me a part of your alibi, I'll give you half the money."

Cory looked at Todd and laughed. "Half the money? You ARE nuts! I won't save your ass for less than two hundred grand. You screwed me, Todd, and you're going to pay for it."

The money was the least of Todd's concerns. He yearned for freedom from a possible prison term; freedom from the sick feeling in his gut; freedom from the sound of Marc's body smashing the ground. "Whatever you want, Cory. Take all the freakin' money. I don't care. I just want to get out of this."

Cory looked out his window. "Did anyone see you?"

"I don't think so. I stayed far enough away from the balcony so Jack couldn't see me and –"

"What! What was Jack doing there?"

Todd pushed his back up against the driver's side door, trying to distance himself from Cory's wrath. "Jack drove Marc to your building, but he stayed downstairs."

"Did he know you were meeting Marc there?"

"I think so. I mean, Marc told him we were going to get the money from you." Todd shook his head as though the movement might help focus his thoughts. "But I'm not sure. I think so."

"Well, which is it?" Cory screamed, "You think so? Or you're not sure?" He turned to look out the window. "God, could you be any more lame?"

"Give me a break!" Todd yelled back. "I'm confused. It's been a crazy night and I'm just trying to get my thoughts together." He closed his eyes and pressed his fingers against their lids, trying to remember his conversation with Marc. "I'm not a hundred percent sure, but I think he told Jack I was going to be there."

Cory slapped his knee and blew a loud breath, fogging up his side of the windshield. "Okay, let me get this straight. Right now, Jack thinks I stole the money. Marc told him you and he were going to meet at my apartment to supposedly get the money from me. Is that right?"

Todd nodded. "Yeah."

"Are you sure he didn't see you?"

"There's no way." Todd said. "I even checked the view from

downstairs before I went up to your apartment. It's too high and the angle sucks."

"At least I know I have privacy." Cory smirked, thinking back on his adulterous adventures. "Are you sure no one else saw you?"

"The hallway and stairwell were empty when I ran away," Todd said, a warm ray of hope settling down his shivers. "I jumped in my car and came right here."

"You'd better hope no one saw you," Cory said, warming his hands beneath his thighs. "Where's the money?"

"Half of it is sitting in the forest across the street from your apartment."

Cory let out a deep sigh. "And the other half?"

"Well hidden," Todd muttered.

"Well hidden where?" Cory's anger welled in his throat.

"It's far away. Very far away. You help me with this and I'll tell you. I swear, I'll give you the whole freaking payload. Just get me out of this, please."

Cory lifted his wrist up to the moonlight, twisting his arm to see his watch, a smug expression on his face. "Okay, here's what we'll do. If I know Marc, he never told Jack he stole the money, which means Jack still thinks I have it. He and the cops, who have probably infested my building by now, can search my apartment, my car, my office, even my bank accounts and see that I don't have it. And I was with Janice all last night, so I have an alibi."

Todd crossed his arms and leaned forward. "That's fine for you. What about me?"

"Hold on a second, "Cory shouted, rolling his eyes, "one thing at a time. Now, I'll admit to watching the DVD and that I considered stealing the money. We'll tell them I asked you to meet me at your father's house, but didn't tell you why – something about a big payoff. This way, we can place you at his house tonight, with me. Then we'll say that when I told you about my plan to steal the money, you brought me into the yard and showed me someone had already taken it. That puts both of us in the clear."

"Okay," Todd said, blowing warm breath into his hands. "It's a little confusing, but I think it'll work. There's only one thing – if we go with the story that neither of us took the money, then who did take it?" Through the windshield, Cory gazed at the stars with a subtle grin. Todd knew it was his sick way of referring to Marc. "Oh," was all Todd could say.

"If we stick to the story, we should be okay. Do you have it down?"

Todd nodded. "Yes. I'll have it straight in my head by the time we get to your building. I'll just keep going over it in my mind until I get it right."

And he did just that. Standing in the elevator, Todd brushed up on the string of events Cory had developed into a pretty solid alibi, revising a few details as the elevator crept toward the fifteenth floor. When the doors parted, the officer in front grabbed Todd's arm. They followed the din of a dispatcher's crackling voice, emanating from a distant police walkie-talkie, until they reached Cory's apartment.

Out of the corner of his eye, Todd caught a glimpse of a canvas gym bag sitting on the dining room table. His insides grinned. It was almost an exact duplicate of the bag now sitting across the street, except the canvas was clean and a nametag with Cory's personal information hung from one of its handles – just the way he'd hidden it in the closet seconds before Marc arrived.

"I'm confused," Doonan said as he leaned back into the upholstered recliner. He swiveled the chair and looked out the window, then swiveled back to face Todd. He pulled the wooden handle jutting out from the side of the chair, lifting the footrest so his feet were level with his waist. A quick scan of the bedroom had offered him insight into Cory's sense of taste, personality, and his deep bond with bachelorhood. A black lacquered bed filled most of the room, a few faint scratches on the railed headboard denoting past conquests. Matching nightstands sat on both sides of the bed, each holding a straight-lined, contemporary steel lamp, their soft light reflecting off the caramel colored faux painted walls – walls that were completely bare except for a large, unframed mirror above the slim dresser positioned in front of the bed. Doonan sank deeper into the chair. Stark was the only word that came to his mind.

Todd sat on the edge of the bed, his legs dangling off the thick mattress, his dirty sneakers barely skimming the floor. "You were supposed to meet Marc here, and yet you met Cory at your father's house. Why wouldn't you just come here and wait with Marc until Cory came home, so you could both speak with him together as you'd planned?"

Todd stared at his hands, picking at his fingernails, refusing to look at Doonan. "I thought Cory would give me some of the money... you know... being it was my father's house and everything."

"Is he that nice a guy?" Doonan asked.

"What?" Todd stopped picking his fingers and looked directly at the wall in front of him.

"Is Cory so generous a person that he'd share the money with you? I mean, if he went through all the trouble to break through the wall himself, in the middle of a thunderstorm, why would he give you any money?" Doonan pushed his heels against the footrest, returning the recliner to its closed position. He leaned closer to Todd.

"I don't know," Todd whispered under his breath, "I just thought he would. And I know he really didn't trust Marc, so I figured it was better if I spoke with him by myself."

Doonan rose from the chair, stood in front of Todd, and let out a sigh. "Then what happened?"

"When I got there, Cory started telling me about the DVD and the money. At first it was like he had no idea the money was already gone. So I brought him outside to show him the wall. He seemed pissed."

"What did he say?" Doonan asked, scribbling in his book.

"He blamed Marc. He said that if I didn't take it and he didn't take it, it must've been Marc. He said Marc was bullshitting all of us and we should come back here to see if Marc even showed up."

"Did you believe him?" Doonan paced the floor, around the bed, past the closed door. He glanced at the officer standing against the far wall and continued his interrogation. "Well, did you believe him?" he asked, crouching in front of Todd.

"I got all confused." Todd looked up and Doonan finally saw his eyes. By this time they were filled with water, a perfectly formed droplet glistening down his cheek. Too perfect, Doonan thought. "I didn't believe him at first. Marc was so convincing. But the more Cory spoke, the more sense it made. Especially when he talked me into coming here to see if Marc actually showed up."

"Well, he did show up," Doonan said.

Todd once again stared at his fingers. "I know. The officer downstairs told me he was dead. Do you know what happened?"

Doonan didn't respond. He simply looked down at his pad, flipping the pages, pretending to read his notes. He sensed pieces of truth in Todd's story, but also detected fragments of lies, in his story and his body language. Someone had been with Marc in Cory's apartment; he just needed to find out whom.

"You know it was an accident," Doonan blurted, sitting beside Todd. "Jack was outside. He saw the whole thing. He also said it didn't look like Marc was pushed. It was more like he tripped." Doonan allowed a few seconds of silence to pass between them. "So whoever was with him is running from us for no good reason."

Todd wiped a tear with the back of his hand, replying only with a deep sigh.

"By the way," Doonan started, "we found half the money."

Todd looked Doonan straight on. "Where?"

"In there," he pointed to Cory's bedroom closet, "stashed behind a pile of shoe boxes."

"Damn him!" Todd yelled, furiously shaking his head. "I don't know who to believe anymore."

Doonan flipped shut his notepad and rubbed the soft leather against the grain of his shadowy beard. Join the crowd, he thought as he nodded to the officer to keep his post. He walked out of the bedroom and gently closed the door behind him, hoping the next suspect would be his last.

13

Except for a large rock leaning against the wooden railing, the flight of stairs leading to Jenna's room was empty. The entire house was so profoundly quiet that for a moment Jack thought he'd gone deaf. He snapped his fingers to make certain he could still hear. The click echoed up the stairs, almost visible as it curved around the bend into the pitch black of the hallway.

With each step up the staircase, a dim, fiery-colored glow fell before him, helping light the way like an usher's flashlight in a darkened theater. He followed the orange beam to the top of the stairs, turned the corner, and stopped in front of Jenna's room. The door was closed, but sparks of bright blue incandescence peeked through the narrow slit at the bottom, illuminating the tips of Jack's toes. He realized he was barefoot and turned to look for his shoes. Seeing nothing but blackness, he grabbed the corner molding and leaned back to peer down the stairs. In the shadowy light, he saw his muddy sneakers beside the solitary rock, their laces hanging through the railing and over the side of the steps.

Using the molding as leverage, he pulled himself back, planted his feet firmly on the shag runner covering the hallway floor, and stared at the pale blue light outlining Jenna's door. He stretched his fingers to touch the small, circular knob, surprised at how cold it felt. With one turn he opened the door and felt his heart skip a beat.

Dana and Marc sat on Jenna's bed, holding hands, both looking at Jack with an expression of pure remorse. Fear tore through his body and he tried to scream, but only a throaty groan escaped his lips. He brought one hand to his face, rubbing his lips and tongue with his fingers, attempting to physically pull the paralysis from his mouth.

"Dana!" His lips could barely move. "Marc!" he tried to shout, the vibration of his muffled voice buzzing through the fingers that still held his tongue.

Neither Dana nor Marc made a sound. Together, they slowly fell backward onto the bed and looked toward the ceiling, still holding hands. Jack called out to them again, but there was still no response. He wanted to move toward them, but his feet were like lead. And they were cold, their frigid chill slowly spreading through his entire body. He hugged himself as the coldness turned to fear and confusion, sweeping through him like a polar wind with tiny fragments of razor-sharp ice specks penetrating his clothes and piercing his skin. Unsure whether to turn and run or stay where he was, Jack froze – shaking, crying, waiting.

The sound began as a distant rattle, gradually increasing to a loud crackling. The walls began to crack, a blizzard of paint and plaster chips flying past his face. Dana and Marc rose from the bed and with their feet never touching the ground, they glided across the room, disappearing into the splintered walls. Falling to his knees, Jack screamed as the voices of his dead lover and sister called his name in a unified chant.

"Jack! Jack!" Now only one voice and one hand touched his shoulder "Wake up!"

He opened his eyes and shut them again, blinded by the intense spotlights recessed in the ceiling. He quickly realized he was still in the lobby of Cory's apartment building and must've fallen asleep after calling David.

"Jack, what the hell's going on here?" David crouched beside him, a Red Sox cap concealing his slept-on hair.

Jack wiped the sleep from his eyes and shook his head, trying to throw off the remnants of his nightmare. He pulled himself up, relieved to see David's familiar face.

"Hi David," he said, holding back a yawn. By the dazed look in David's eyes, Jack realized his call must've woken up the Macrae household. "I'm sorry to bother you so late, but I didn't know who else to call. I didn't want to upset my parents and I…"

David sat on the couch and placed his hand on Jack's knee.

"Don't worry about it, Jack. Just tell me what's happening."

"Okay. But it's a long story."

He recounted the events of the evening, and when he was done he leaned back on the arm of the sofa. "Now I'm just waiting for Doonan to tell me what he found out from Cory and Todd," he said. "And then, tomorrow, I'm going to find the bag that's sitting across the street somewhere."

Scratching his head, David reclined against the opposite arm of the couch and slid his hand down his face. "Wow," he sighed. "This is unbelievable, Jack. I just can't imagine –"

Jack stiffened, sat straight up and leaned toward David. "There's one other thing you should know. I didn't tell Doonan about the bag across the street. I can't chance them taking it into custody and holding Jenna's money forever." He ran his fingers through his hair. "Or some dirty cop stealing it and blaming it on evidence tampering. It belongs to my niece and I made a promise to Dana. A promise I have to keep."

"I totally understand, Jack. And I'll help you look for it." David glanced around the room, making sure no one could hear their conversation. "But you should really tell Glen about this, and probably your parents too. They should know what's going on and I'm sure they can help."

"I will." Jack took a deep breath. "I just want to get tonight over with and then I'll call them in the morning."

David unclipped a cell phone from his belt and flipped it open. Jack looked at his watch. "Who are you calling? It's almost eleven?"

David smiled. "My wife. I'm telling her to get the guest bedroom ready. You're staying with us tonight."

"No, David, I can't. There's too much going on and –"

"No two ways about it, Jack," David interrupted, continuing to push the phone buttons. "I can't let you go home by yourself after all this."

Jack was unexpectedly relieved. He couldn't imagine returning to his apartment, trying to sleep in the bed where he and Marc had shared their last earthly touch, their final affirmations of love, trust and passion.

"But what about J&M?"

"Tomorrow's Saturday, Jack. Time to relax." They both smiled, realizing the contradiction of his words.

"I don't even know what day it is anymore."

"That's why you're coming home with me. We'll get things straightened out, don't worry."

As David spoke with his wife, Jack heard the soft ring of the elevator, signaling the car had reached the lobby. The doors slid open and Doonan stared straight at him, notebook in hand, jotting down notes from his conversation with Cory.

Cory anchored himself on the sofa as Doonan commanded the officers and forensic team to leave the apartment and wait in the hallway.

"I'll just be a few minutes here," he said. Before closing the door, he peered through the opening. "And keep the noise down out there. People are trying to sleep."

He strolled to the sofa across from Cory and sat down, rubbing his palm against the cushion beside him. "Nice place," Doonan smiled. "Did you decorate it yourself?"

Cory couldn't tell if Doonan's comment was genuine, but he had no choice but to play along. "Thanks." he said, watching Doonan eye his notepad. "Yes, I decorated it myself."

Doonan smiled again. "Okay, let's get down to it. And before we begin, I want you to know if you tell me the truth and help with this investigation, I promise you won't end up like your father."

Cory felt his body tense and stretched his arm along the sofa cushion in an attempt to stay composed. "How'd you know about that?"

Doonan turned the pages of his pad. "How did you know Marc Whittaker?"

"I'm an executive recruiter. I helped him get a job, and then we became friends."

Doonan nodded and made some notes in his book. "Why don't you tell me where you were tonight and what you know about all this?"

Cory glanced at the bedroom door, wondering if Todd had stuck to their story. He glanced back at Doonan, who waited patiently for a response.

"Okay, yesterday I found out about the money –"

"What money?" Doonan interrupted.

"Jack's money. Well, his sister's money. She hid it in the wall behind Todd's father's house and –"

"How did you find out about it?" Doonan asked, scratching his five o'clock shadow with his notepad.

"I was supposed to meet Marc at Jack's apartment to help him move some stuff out. When I got there, the door was open. I walked in and found Marc unconscious on the bed. There was an empty bottle of Valium on the floor and I figured he overdosed."

"Did you call 911?"

"No. He was breathing okay, so I decided to leave and let Jack take care of it." He looked down at his feet, realizing how thoughtless his actions must sound. "I probably should've called someone, but really, I was sure he'd be okay."

"The money!" Doonan demanded.

"On my way out of Jack's apartment, I noticed a DVD sitting on the table. I don't know why, but I stopped and watched it. Jack's sister was on the DVD, talking to her daughter, telling her about money she hid in the stone wall." Cory shifted on the sofa, feeling perspiration from his armpits trickle down his sides. "And I admit it – I thought about stealing the money."

Doonan looked around the room and shrugged his shoulders. "Seems like you make a pretty good living. Why would you have to steal a dead woman's money? Or should I say, her child's money?"

"There's always room for more," Cory muttered, "But it was wrong and I could kick myself in the ass for even thinking about it." Doonan motioned for him to continue. "At first I figured I'd steal the money myself, last night. But when the rainstorm hit, I decided to wait until tonight. So I called Todd and met him at his father's house. When I got there, Todd showed me the hole in the wall and said someone had already taken the money. That's where we were tonight… when this whole thing went down."

Doonan stood, sauntered into the kitchen and grabbed a bottle of Poland Spring from the refrigerator. "Mind if I have some?" he asked, holding the bottle in mid-air.

"No, go ahead."

"Would you like one?"

Cory shook his head.

Doonan slowly returned to Cory and stood behind him. He gulped some water and swept the coolness of the bottle across his forehead. "So, let's see. You leave an unconscious man, who might be on the brink of death from an overdose, lying in an apartment without calling for help. You then pry into a stranger's business by watching his DVD and rummaging through who knows what else. And then you decide to take money that's not rightfully yours, but find out you've gotten there too late. Do I have it right?"

Cory cringed. Doonan's account hit a tender nerve and his mind went into a tailspin: he'd already followed in his father's footsteps. He pictured himself tightening the noose around his own neck, a hangman's rope made from the ragged tatters of a fellow inmate's denim shirt.

At first he barely recognized the emotion, but he gradually felt the faintly familiar tugging of fear. "Yes, that's right," he muttered.

"Did you see Marc at all today?"

"No."

"What time did you leave the apartment tonight to meet with Todd?"

"Around six-thirty."

"Did you lock the door when you left?"

"Yes," Cory started to get nervous. Doonan's questions were like a barrage of bullets, coming too fast, not giving him time to think.

"How did he get in?"

"Who?"

"Marc."

"I think he had a key," Cory said.

"You gave Marc a key?"

"Yes, I think so. Like I said, we were friends."

"Do you give all your friends keys to your apartment?"

"No, just some."

"Does Todd have a key?"

"I think so." Cory thought again. "No, I'm wrong. I didn't give Todd a key. I don't trust him enough." He shifted nervously on the sofa.

Walking behind Cory, Doonan finished the last of the water in one gulp and wiped his mouth on his sleeve.

"Why don't you trust him?" Doonan leaned on the back of the couch, looking down at the back of Cory's head.

"I just don't, not with my personal stuff."

"But you trusted Marc?"

"Yes,"

"But why would you give him a key?"

"I thought I'd be nice. He pretty much lived in a dump and I told him he was welcome if he ever wanted to crash here or something. I felt bad for him."

Doonan leaned further over Cory's head.

"So bad that you left him to die?"

Cory turned and looked up. "I told you, he was breathing fine. He wasn't going to die."

Doonan walked to the dining room table and ran his hands over the outside of the canvas gym bag. "And where did this come from?"

Cory squinted, trying to focus on the bag. He'd seen it when he first entered the apartment, but thought it belonged to a cop or a member of the forensic team. His heart was racing.

"I thought it was yours," he replied. "What is it?"

Doonan lifted the bag a few inches from the table and let it drop. "You don't know what's in here?"

Cory shook his head.

"It's filled with money. A hundred and twenty five thousand dollars to be exact."

"Where'd you find that?"

"In your bedroom closet," Doonan said smugly.

"That son of a bitch!" Cory said, smacking his head.

"Who's a son of a bitch?"

Cory felt his heart skip a beat. He'd let his emotions break free and now he'd have to explain his comment. Who hid the money in his apartment? Was it Marc? Was Todd trying to frame him? He couldn't organize his thoughts quickly enough.

"Who's a son of a bitch, Cory?" Doonan repeated.

"I think I need to call my lawyer," he sputtered.

"Why is that, Cory? Like I said before, just tell me what happened. If you weren't here tonight, then there's nothing to worry about, right?"

Cory leaned over and held his head in his hands. "I need a lawyer."

"Todd didn't need a lawyer," Doonan said, making his way around the sofa to sit beside Cory. "Why would you need one?"

"Todd's too stupid to call a lawyer."

Doonan fanned his notebook a few inches from his face. "He seems pretty smart to me," Doonan teased, "and I guess he thinks he's innocent, so he doesn't feel the need to bring a lawyer into this."

"Believe me, he's not as smart as you think. Now I'd like to call my lawyer."

Doonan let out a sigh. "Are you sure, Cory? I promise you, it'll only complicate things."

"Yes, I'm sure."

Doonan stood, strolled to the door and turned to glance at Cory.

"I'm sure," Cory repeated.

Doonan opened the door, whispered something to one of the policemen standing in the hallway, and disappeared. As the policeman walked in, Cory turned to the bedroom door and shook his head.

"Todd, you son of a bitch," he whispered, grabbing the cordless phone from the sofa table and dialing. "You son of a bitch!"

Doonan looked at the man standing next to Jack, and, after careful examination held out his hand. "Larry Doonan, Assistant Chief of Police."

David grabbed his hand and shook it hard. "David Macrae."

Jack shuffled closer to Doonan. "Well, what did you find out? Which one of them was with Marc?"

Doonan kept his eyes on David. "We should talk in private, Jack."

"It's okay," Jack said. "David's a close friend. I told him everything."

Doonan collapsed into the cushions of the armless chair sitting across from the sofa and gestured for Jack and David to sit.

"So which of those losers was in the apartment with Marc?" Jack asked.

Doonan tapped the pen on his knee. "If it were that easy you wouldn't need me, would you?"

Jack let out a sigh. He felt the exhaustion pervading his bones, the events of the day starting to take root in every breath he took. "What do you mean?"

"I mean, it's the typical noncompliance scenario. Both Cory and Todd have their own story, complete with an alibi and a shade of truth."

Jack pulled himself to the edge of the sofa and clasped his hands. "One of those creeps was with Marc tonight," Jack said, the tone of his voice causing Doonan to stir in his chair. "Take them into custody. Beat it out of them if you have to! They can't get away with this!"

"Jack, no one's getting away with anything," Doonan said. "It's just going to take a little longer than we'd like."

"Are you going to take them down to the station and throw them in jail or something?" David asked.

Doonan smirked and shook his head. "It doesn't work that way, not in a case like this. I have nothing to bring them in on. But believe me, these guys are amateurs. I guarantee within the next forty-eight hours each one's story will get closer to the truth until I have enough to figure out exactly what happened. Right now they don't trust each other, which is the first step to getting what we need. We'll keep a close eye on them, but we'll also stand back a bit and let them fall into their own trap. You have to trust me on this." Jack turned to David, who sat on the arm of the sofa, nodding in agreement.

"Remember, Jack," David said, "Todd is known as The Mouth because he can't keep anything to himself. He'll screw up, one way or another. Don't worry."

Doonan shifted in his seat. "Another thing, Jack. I need to see that DVD."

"Why?"

Doonan looked Jack directly in the eyes. "To help verify your story and get the money thing straightened out."

Jack shot up, his arms hanging in mid-air. "My story?" he screamed, "You think I was involved in this? You've got to be kidding me!"

Doonan rose, positioning his face only inches from Jack's. For a few seconds they locked eyes until Jack turned to David.

"Please, Jack," Doonan said, "it's protocol. We have to take all evidence into account."

With David's nod, Jack turned back to Doonan and dropped his arms in surrender. "Fine. I'll bring it to you tomorrow"

Doonan flipped his notepad closed. "That's great. The precinct's on East Central. You know where that is?" Doonan asked, slipping the pen into the inside pocket of his suit jacket.

"Yes, I know where it is." Jack sighed. "Now what do you mean by 'get the money thing straightened out'?"

"We found a bag of money in Cory's apartment." Doonan continued before Jack had the chance to erupt. "There's about a hundred and twenty five thousand dollars in it. That's only half the amount you said was hidden in the wall."

Jack thought back to the bag that flew above Marc's head into the shadows across the street. "Where's the other half?"

"That's a good question." Doonan glanced at David, then back to Jack. "Think about it, and if you come up with any ideas let me know when you drop off the DVD tomorrow."

Jack grabbed Doonan's arm as he started to walk away. "Chief Doonan, that's Jenna's money. Please don't let anything happen to it."

"Don't worry, Jack. It goes in the safe tonight. I'll personally make sure no one touches it. Now get some rest and I'll see you in the morning."

As Doonan walked away, Jack grabbed David by the sleeve of his jacket.

"The other half of Jenna's money is sitting across the street somewhere, David. I have to get it before someone else does."

"Jack, let's wait until tomorrow. No one's going to go after it tonight. It's dark and there are too many cops around." He zipped his jacket and pulled a ring full of keys from his pocket. "And do you really think that Cory or Todd is stupid enough to snoop around so close to a crime scene where they're suspects in an investigation?"

Jack stayed quiet, allowing his silence to answer David's question.

Switching off the police radio, Doonan lowered the window and pulled the unmarked car alongside the group of teenagers sitting beneath the yellow streetlight that marked the intersection of Archer and Trumbull. Bits of gravel crackled beneath the tires; the faint echo of crickets enshrouding the still night air – summer's death obvious with every chirp.

As he neared the group, he saw the fiery trail of a burning cigarette fly across the yard behind them into a dense cluster of bush. The tallest of the three boys walked to the car and crouched beside Doonan's window, leaning his shoulder against the door once the cruiser reached a full stop.

"Hi, Chief," the boy said, the ripe scent of tobacco wafting into the car, "what's cooking?"

"What's cooking, Danny, are the hydrangeas you just tossed that cigarette into. Do you think the Carltons want to smell your burning cancer stick while they're trying to sleep?"

Danny turned toward the huddled group behind him to see the three girls laughing, their mouths covered by their hands. The other two boys gazed up the street as though waiting for a bus that had never arrived.

"No, sorry," replied Danny.

"And what are you and your friends doing out here so late? It's almost one o'clock in the morning."

"It's Friday, Chief. Well, actually, it's Saturday. There's no school. It's called a weekend."

Doonan laughed. "I know what it's called, but it's still late to be hanging out here. Look around you." Doonan pointed up and down the street. "The houses are dark which means people are trying to sleep. I don't think they want to hear you and your friends yelling and giggling all night. It's time to go home."

"Man, I thought you were cool," Danny moaned, looking at Doonan through a curtain of bangs that almost reached the bridge of his nose. "I guess you're not." He pushed himself away from the car and started back to the group like a dog reprimanded by its brutal owner.

Danny was a good kid, Doonan knew that, but past experience told him that if given too much rope Danny would hang himself. He'd done it many times before: getting into trouble in order to gain the respect of his peers and the attention of his parents. His last charge for shoplifting at the Walmart almost landed him in the detention center until Doonan stepped in, using his clout to get Danny off with the promise never to enter the megastore again. And now, with the winter months approaching, Doonan feared Danny's boredom might spark a recurrence.

Doonan snapped his fingers.

"Danny, come here," he commanded, immediately realizing his tone resembled that of Danny's overbearing father, a man who Doonan suspected was the source of his son's behavior. "Please," he added.

Danny hesitantly returned to the car and bent over, his head blocking Doonan's view of the others who were now silent, apparently waiting for the outcome of Danny's run-in with the cops.

"I'm sorry, it's been a long day," he started, "it's just that for some reason, because I live on this block, people think I'm the mayor. They come to me for everything: too much noise… illegally parked cars… even potholes. I'm just trying to keep you out of trouble and my doorbell from ringing. I have enough going on, okay?"

Danny let out a sigh. "These people are real conservative pains in the ass, huh?"

"Not all, just some." Doonan scratched his head, opting to keep the rest of his opinions to himself. "Now keep it down and stay out of trouble, I'm counting on you." He rubbed Danny's stringy hair, at the same time pushing him back toward his friends.

Danny gave him a thumbs-up and Doonan returned the gesture, raising his window and stepping softly on the gas pedal. In front of him, the street was empty except for the foggy beams of light streaming down from the streetlamps. He looked in the rearview mirror to see Danny lighting a fresh cigarette, his friends offering high-fives as they danced the dance of victory. Doonan knew that by the time the sun rose, his doorbell would be ringing.

He pulled the car into the driveway of the modestly-sized colonial and shut off the engine, silently berating himself for forgetting to turn a light on before he'd left that morning. He slouched into the driver's seat, staring through the windshield into the blackness of the night sky. Entering the dark, lonely house was the last thing he wanted to do and the sergeant's invitation to "meet the guys" at O'Hara's Pub started to intrigue him. He'd originally declined the invitation, as he always did, determined to maintain a professional relationship with his coworkers. Doonan knew that once the beers started flowing, so would the questions about his personal life: Why aren't you married, Chief? Got a girl? When was the last time you were on a date? Is it true you're into guys? He couldn't risk getting cornered, especially tonight. He had to keep his head clear for the Whittaker case, and for Jack Fontaine – the grief-stricken lover whose chiseled features had danced behind his thoughts on his drive home.

Keep it professional... Don't get involved. The words resounded in his head like a broken record – an annoying but appropriate warning not to repeat the mistake he'd made two years earlier, the day after the papers touted him as Massachusetts' youngest deputy chief ever to be promoted to assistant chief. At thirty-one, he'd already shot up the ranks and proven himself to be what the current Chief of Police called, "a cut above the rest."

With the skin on his back still vibrating from a day of congratulatory slaps, he walked out the precinct doors into the parking lot and headed toward his RX7, looking forward to a special dinner with his parents, younger sister and her twin boys who he'd heard had been celebrating their birthday for the past three days.

Out of the corner of his eye he saw a figure standing by the chain-linked fence surrounding the lot. He slid his sunglasses down to the tip of his nose to see better, immediately recognizing the young man now waving by the locked gate. It was the older brother of Derek Lichert, the sixteen-year-old kid he'd picked up for selling marijuana three weeks earlier. After a heart-to-heart with the boy, during which Derek wept until he choked, promising he'd never deal with drugs again, Doonan called in some of his IOUs to help keep the kid from getting locked up.

He'd first seen Derek's brother when he stormed into Doonan's office, summoned by his mother to pick up his little brother. There had only been a quick nod and an ingenuous thanks, but Doonan remembered being taken by the man's striking good looks: a head of thick, wavy blond hair curving its way around the face of what could've been a Calvin Klein model. His strikingly grey eyes, which Doonan caught for only an instant, were penetrating, seeming to look into him rather than at him; his body, slim, but taut, was easy to gauge through the tight black tee shirt and even tighter Levis. The man turned his gaze toward Derek, grabbed him by the collar and pushed him out the door, leaving Doonan silently begging for another glimpse.

And now he had it. As Doonan strolled closer to the fence, the man searched his eyes for a place to engage his stare. Doonan slid his glasses back up his nose and hung his fingers on the linked fence, like a prisoner dreaming of freedom, spending his days staring over the barbed wire, singing to the sun.

"Remember me?" the man said, his voice as inviting as his eyes, "Steven Lichert, Derek's brother."

Doonan nodded, attempting to tame the pounding in his chest.

"I never had the chance to say thank you," he said, grabbing the links directly above Doonan's fingers. "I know it's been awhile, but I wanted to say thanks."

"You're wel—" the words caught in his throat. He laughed, attempting to ease the awkwardness he'd just inflicted on himself. "You're welcome."

"I also wanted to congratulate you on your promotion." He paused and pulled a folded page from the community paper from his back pocket. "You're on the front page."

Doonan felt the heat rise to his face. "I saw it," he said. "That photo sucks. I hate it."

"I don't. Actually, I think you look great." Steven looked to the sidewalk and scraped the tip of his sneaker along the rocky surface. Doonan wished he'd raise his head, Look at me again… show me that face. As though a genie had gotten wind of his request, Steven lifted his face and smiled with the whitest of teeth, as perfect as the face that held them. "You know, I live about a mile and a half from here. I had to leave my car at the shop and I was wondering…"

He knew he shouldn't, but he couldn't help himself. "You need a ride?" Doonan asked.

"If it wouldn't be a problem, I'd really appreciate it. It's only two minutes away."

Doonan looked at his watch. He had two hours before meeting the family for dinner and could think of no better way to spend it than with Steven Lichert, even if it was for only two minutes.

"No problem at all." Doonan clicked his remote to unlock his car doors. "Stay right there. I'll open the gate and pick you up."

After the gate slid open, Steven opened the passenger side door and practically jumped in.

"Seat belt," commanded Doonan, almost under his breath.

"I know," Steven laughed, "it's the law."

From the second Doonan heard the click of the seatbelt buckle, he felt uneasy – something wasn't right. It was something that came from deep within, an unknown space located somewhere between his gut and solar plexus that knew exactly when to send a warning signal to his brain. It was a feeling that had helped keep him alive through his nightly shifts on the streets. It's only two minutes away…

When they reached the apartment complex, Steven pointed to an empty parking space way in the back and Doonan pulled in. He turned in his seat and looked at Steven, almost mesmerized by the way the setting sun turned the color of his eyes a dark slate. With the engine still running, Doonan reached out his hand.

"Nice to see you again," he said.

Steven's hand passed right by Doonan's toward the ignition. He gave the key a slight twist and turned off the engine.

"Wanna come up?" Steven slid his hand down the steering wheel and onto Doonan's leg. Less than two seconds later, Doonan's zipper was down with Steven's hand slithering inside.

Doonan heard his warning signal blare against the background noise of his yearning, an urge that ravaged his insides with each touch of Steven's hand. Fighting the burning desire, he opened his eyes and pulled Steven's fingers from inside his briefs.

"Whoa there, pal!" Doonan lifted Steven's hand, holding it in mid-air unsure what to do with it. Although this kind of situation had been a fantasy of his for more years than he could remember, he knew he couldn't risk his reputation, or his morals, on something so meaningless. "What's this all about?"

Steven used his eyes as bait, trying to lure Doonan in with the promise of fulfilling his every need and desire. "Let's go upstairs." His voice was now a whisper, the heat of sex causing his shallow breaths to sound irregular and jerky.

"I don't do that," Doonan replied, placing Steven's hand gently onto his Levis, "and why me?"

Steven sat up and blew hard, pushing his back against the leather seat, staring blankly out the windshield.

"What's wrong with you, dude? I see the way you look at me. Why not just go for it?"

Doonan asked himself the same question. "It's just not me. That's all."

Steven sighed. "Cops, shit, you're all the same." Doonan smiled, not knowing what else to do. "Okay, I understand. But while we're here, can you do me a favor?"

Shit, here it comes.

"What is it?" asked Doonan.

"Derek's in trouble again. Marijuana. They picked him up in the city last night. He needs your help."

Doonan looked down and lifted his zipper. Shaking his head, he cursed himself for not seeing this sooner.

"Now I get it," Doonan said. "You blow me and I save your brother's ass." Steven Lichert was stoic, responding by looking out the passenger-side window. Doonan rolled his eyes, embarrassed for them both. "Sorry, can't do it. Your brother promised me he'd stay clean. That's why I helped him out the last time." Turning his head to look out the window, he saw his reflected eyes staring back at him. He thought twice about not helping Derek, but knew Derek had to pay the price for what he'd done – it was the only way he was going to learn. He pulled his bottom lip with his top teeth and forced out a breath. "I kept my promise, he didn't keep his."

Doonan could feel Lichert looking at the back of his head, waiting for him to turn around. When he did, Doonan noticed the dark slate of Steven's eyes had paled, a sort of wickedness surrounding his irises.

"How about this for promises, Larry Doonan?" Lichert grabbed the news clipping from his back pocket. "You don't help Derek and I promise that the same reporter who wrote this article about you will receive a phone call claiming that the new assistant chief of police picks up guys in the streets and forces them to blow him."

Doonan felt like he'd been kicked in the gut, his day of celebration quickly turning into a cop's worst nightmare. The thoughts spun around his head so fast he started to feel dizzy. His stomach seethed with anger, at himself for letting things get this far and at the amazing beauty who had turned into a hideous creature right before his eyes. He took a deep breath to focus his mind and, as usual, it worked.

He began to laugh, slapping his knee with his open hand.

"You think this is funny?" asked Lichert, Doonan's indifference obviously making him angry.

"No," Doonan replied, "what I think is funny is the look you'll have on your face when three undercover cops find five grams of crack in your apartment." He stopped laughing and took out his notepad, turning to the last page, pretending to calculate numbers.

"What are you talking about? I don't have –" Steven stopped mid-sentence. The light bulb had illuminated, he knew where Doonan was heading.

"Let's see," Doonan continued his phony calculations, "possession of five grams of a controlled narcotic substance, in this case, crack. That translates into 500 grams of powder cocaine." He continued to mumble, "divided by three, multiplied by…"

"I get it." Steven sighed.

Doonan flipped the pad closed and looked directly into Lichert's eyes. "That's a minimum of five years in a state prison. Locked up, behind bars." He scanned Lichert up and down. "And with a body like that, I'll be able to hear you begging for mercy from wherever you end up."

"I said I get it!" Lichert said, getting out of the car and slamming the door.

"Hey!" screamed Doonan, pressing the button and lowering the passenger side window. He waited for Lichert to stoop down and look at him. "I hope you get it, asswipe. And if I ever see your face again, it'll be ten grams. Now beat it!"

As Doonan raised the window, Lichert threw the crumpled up news clipping into the car, hitting Doonan on the right side of the head. "And you're right, the picture does suck!"

Doonan watched him walk away and slam the screen door behind him. He lifted himself slightly off his seat and glanced in the rearview mirror.

"I look better in person," he whispered to himself.

Keep it professional… Don't get involved. This time he said it aloud, wondering how intensely the loneliness would hit once he entered the dark house. He reconsidered taking a crack at O'Hara's, but instead pulled the key from the ignition and opened the car door, images of Jack Fontaine still with him. But this time there was no warning signal, nothing inside telling him to back off or be cautious. This time, he felt a sense of calmness with an edge of excitement. He turned away from the ranting in his head and surrendered to the thought, the possibility that one day someone, someone like Jack Fontaine, would be waiting for him in this house — with the lights on.

14

The chrome-orange glow of the rising sun enveloped Jack's apartment, casting odd shadows along the walls and floor. Glen stood by the windows, his body a silhouette against the backdrop of the open sky, his stooped shoulders undulating like a dinghy floating upon the swell of the ocean.

Jack turned off the VCR and looked at David standing in the kitchen, drinking from a bottle of filtered water. He'd left the living-room when the DVD began to play, in an effort, Jack supposed, to give Glen a sense of privacy.

"Glen," Jack said softly, "are you okay?"

After a few moments, Glen cleared his throat and turned around. With a look of embarrassment, he used his sleeve to wipe the tears from his face. "I'm fine," he replied, his voice shaking with emotion. "It's just hard to watch."

Jack nodded. "I know," he whispered.

"The worst part is, she didn't trust me to take care of the money she left for Jenna. I don't understand it." Glen looked to the floor and shook his head. "Did she think I was a total screw-up?"

Jack stood and walked to Glen, slowing his pace so he'd have more time to think of a soothing response. He remembered his conversation with Dana, her reluctance to give Glen responsibility for the money, concerned with his forgetfulness and flightiness. He put a hand on Glen's shoulder.

"I don't think that was it." Jack said softly. "I think she wanted to mend the rift between she and I. By trusting me with this information, she was saying she wanted me to be a part of Jenna's life."

As Glen lifted his gaze from the floor, a tear dangled from his lower lid. "Do you think so? Because I'd hate to think she didn't trust me." Jack put his arms around Glen, embracing him tightly. "I know so," he whispered in his ear.

David walked down the three steps leading from the kitchen to the living-room and sat on the arm of the sofa. "What now?" he asked as the two men slowly separated. "What's our next move?"

"The next move," Jack said, rubbing his hands together, "is to get the DVD to Doonan and then find the bag of money."

"What about your parents?" asked Glen. "Don't you think they should know what's going on?"

Jack pulled the DVD from the player and walked over to his coat hanging from the back of the dining room chair. Flinging it over his shoulder, he turned to Glen and winked. "Once we have the money and life is almost back to normal, I'll tell them everything. I just don't want them worrying about things they can't control."

"Well, they know something's up," Glen said, donning his jacket. "Especially since I asked them to come over at five o'clock on a Saturday morning to watch Jenna."

"What did you tell them?"

"I said we had a big deal going down at work and I needed to get things together for a Monday morning presentation."

Jack opened the door, allowing the two men to walk past him into the hallway. "Did they buy it?"

"For now," Glen said.

"Well 'for now' is good enough," Jack muttered. He slid his key into the lock and turned it until he heard the faint click of the bolt. "let's just hope we have some good news for them later."

He joined Glen and David by the elevator, nervously banging his keys on his leg as the three of them waited for the car to arrive.

"More importantly," Glen said, "Let's hope we have a good story to tell Jenna when she turns eighteen."

"I didn't expect you to be here so early on a Saturday." Jack placed the DVD on Doonan's desk.

Doonan looked up from the clutter of papers and smiled. He stood, extending his arm to shake Jack's hand. Jack gripped his hand firmly and smiled back, noticing the chief's clean-shaven face and recently gelled hair. Sunlight passing through the vertical blinds lit up his face – accentuating the solid cheekbones, elongated jaw line, and the negligible depression in his chin, once again reminding him of Marc. Even the eyes – deep, dark, and searching.

"In this line of work, a Saturday could be a Tuesday, a Sunday, or a Thursday. It's pretty much a blur." Doonan held his white, coffee-stained mug up to Jack. "Would you like some coffee?"

The din of walkie-talkies and laughter from another room stirred Jack from his stare and he unclasped his hand from Doonan's. "No thanks," he said, glancing around the room. His gaze stopped at the giant whiteboard covering the entire right side wall of the office. Different colors of erasable marker filled the cells of a barely visible grid - names, dates, and notes were scrawled across the surface. In red marker, on the top row of the grid, he saw the name Whittaker. He moved his eyes across the row and recognized his own name, as well as Cory's and Todd's. A yellow post-it dangled from Todd's name. Jack squinted, trying to read the chicken scratch.

"You won't get much from that," Doonan said, rising from his chair. He pushed back the engraved wood nameplate and leaned against the desk. "I write them in code… my code… only phrases I can understand." He swallowed a swig of coffee and set the mug down on the edge of his desk.

Doonan was less than two feet from Jack; the closeness creating a slight uneasiness that made him wonder if he should stay put or take a few steps back. He decided to stand his ground.

Doonan crossed his arms and looked at Jack, searching his face. "I want you to know something." After a moment's hesitation, he continued. "I believe your story and honestly don't consider you a suspect. I'm going to watch the DVD so I can put the details in my report. That way, when we return your money, no one will ask any questions. Everything will be black and white."

Jack wanted to reach out and hug the chief. Although they'd only met the night before, the circumstances made him feel as though they'd known each other a lot longer. Instead, he straightened his arms by his sides and clenched his fists.

"I appreciate that, Chief, I really do." He glanced back to the whiteboard. "Anything happen since last night?"

Doonan checked his watch. "Well, we did get in touch with Marc's parents last night and right now they're probably on their way to the Medical Examiner's office to pick him up. Would you like to meet them there?"

Jack shook his head. "No. I've never met them, and from what I know about them, I'd rather keep it that way."

Scratching his chin, Doonan raised his eyebrows. "How long were you and Marc together?"

"About six months." Jack said, knowing what Doonan's next question would be. "Marc didn't really talk to his parents. That's why I never met them." He felt as though a peach pit had lodged in his throat. He swallowed hard, trying to push it down. He envisioned Marc's funeral attended by family and friends, people Marc hadn't spoken to in years. Jack wondered if he should find out when the service was being held or where they'd bury Marc, but he quickly dismissed the thought. He'd have his own ceremony, just him and Marc, in a place where he could tell Marc how he truly felt and how much he'd miss him.

"The report showed no signs of foul play," Doonan added. "No contusions or injuries caused by a struggle. As you said, it appears he either tripped or fell backwards."

Jack closed his eyes, remembering the thin stream of blood flowing from the corner of Marc's mouth.

"I still don't understand how that happened. You said you couldn't see the person in the apartment, which means the other guy wasn't close enough to push him. The drug tests were clean, so it's not like he was stoned or drunk. I just don't get it."

Jack stared back at him and shrugged.

"Other than that, I have nothing new to report," Doonan said. "We're keeping a close eye on Cory and Todd. I'll pay them a visit later today just to keep up the pressure and see if they've had enough time to think things over. You know, ask them if they've decided to add a little truth to their stories. I really hope to have this all settled by the end of the day." Doonan turned to the window, stretching his neck to get a better view of Jack's car. "Who's in your Beamer?"

"David, my boss. You met him last night. And my brother-in-law Glen."

"What are you guys up to so early?"

About to reply, Jack stopped himself. Although Doonan's tone was that of a curious friend, an acquaintance who might want to join them for a casual breakfast or a ride to the hardware store, Jack's inner voice screamed to him: Remember, he's a cop. Be careful what you say.

"There's a lot going on," Jack responded. "And we couldn't sleep. We're going out for breakfast, that's all."

Doonan nodded and turned to Jack, his eyes still scanning Jack's face. Jack forced a smile and reached out his hand, hoping he'd escape without any more questioning. As they shook hands, Jack had the strange impression Doonan didn't want to let go.

"Are you sure you told me everything, Jack? I just have this sense that you're hiding something."

Surprised, Jack could only nod his head. He looked into Doonan's eyes and caught an expression displaying more than just the need to solve a murder and casually slide into the next case. Doonan softened his grip around Jack's hand, but continued to hold on.

"Chief," a voice yelled from the next room, "there's a call on line eight!"

Doonan pulled his hand from Jack's, rose from the edge of his desk, and looked toward the empty doorway. Once again he turned into the tough cop.

Jack's forced smile turned into a real one. "You think I'm hiding something? I could say the same about you."

Without responding, Doonan marched behind his desk and pressed one of the blinking red lights on his phone. His reddened face answered Jack's question. He picked up the phone, glanced at Jack, and gave him a slight wave.

Jack returned the wave and left the office, but paused in front of the precinct doors and considered going back to discuss what just occurred between the two of them. He decided against it, realizing there was still too much to do, and no matter how much Doonan reminded him of Marc, he wasn't Marc.

He pushed open the glass doors and took a deep breath. The cool, autumn air penetrated his lungs and as he glanced toward his car, he couldn't help but laugh. David and Glen each held their fishing boots up to the window, shaking them in an effort to hurry Jack along.

For the first time since he discovered the money had been stolen, Jack felt a weak sense of exuberance: the possibility he'd soon have Jenna's money back and would be able to fulfill his promise to Dana. A promise, only hours before, he feared he'd never be able to keep.

Thin streams of sunlight filtered through the trees, helping light the muck beneath their feet. Jack looked above the giant maples into a sky filled with thickening gray clouds. The slight breeze that greeted them when they climbed over the fence into the forest had turned into a cold wind, pulling leaves from the trees and swirling them through the air. Jack turned to Glen and David, who were still trying to adjust to the large rubber boots protecting their feet.

"It's more like a marsh in here than a forest. What's with all the mud?" David asked.

"There's a lot of wetlands around here," Glen replied with the authority of a city planner. "That's why I thought we'd need the boots."

David turned to Jack with surprise. "I didn't know Glen was a land engineer," he chuckled. Jack shrugged his shoulders, struggling to pull his boots over his pants.

"I'm not," Glen said. "When we were kids, this used to be a park. On weekends my family would come here for picnics. There were other families too. It was a lot of fun." He looked at the monstrous building across the street, his smile turning into a scowl. "Until they started to develop the area. Now, as you can see, it's just muddy, overgrown woodlands."

He looked at David who appeared to be battling his boots. "I might be too old for this," David said. "I can barely pull my feet out of the mud."

Jack laughed, zipping his jacket. "Don't worry, David. You'll get used to it." He continued to scan the area. "I just hope the bag didn't get caught in one of these trees."

"No way," Glen said. "The force of the throw, combined with the weight of all that money, wouldn't allow it to get caught."

Jack and David turned to Glen, both struck by the shrewdness of his statement.

"Oh, he's a physicist too!" David joked.

"Just logic," Glen retorted. "I'm hoping the bag isn't at the bottom of a sink hole covered by mud and leaves."

Jack pointed through the trees to the giant building across the street.

"Okay, Mr. Physicist." Jack used his finger to help Glen find Cory's apartment. "Count fifteen floors up and then find the corner apartment. That's where the bag was thrown from." He arced his hand across the sky of trees until it was even with his line of sight. "Where would it land?"

With his gloved hand, Glen rubbed his chin and twisted his head. "I said logic, not clairvoyance. Your guess is as good as mine." He pointed to an area approximately fifteen yards from where they stood. "But I'm thinking it might end up somewhere around there. I suggest we start by that tree stump and then spread out in different directions."

Jack looked at David, who was still trying to pull his feet from the muck beneath them. "Can you do it?"

David slipped on his gloves and rubbed his hands together. He lifted his feet and walked toward the stump, each step more of an effort than the last. "I think I can," he uttered, trying to pick up his pace, "I think I can."

Glen patted his back. "Come on Little Engine that Could. I know you can do it."

Jack stood ankle-deep in a pool of dark, viscous liquid. He lifted his left foot and watched the ooze fall from his boot, thankful he'd remembered the boots stored in the back of his bedroom closet. He looked at his watch. Almost an hour had passed since they started their hunt, and the search area had become so expansive, Glen and David were no longer in view. The wind had picked up, creating an eerie howl as it moved through the massive maples. The sky was completely silver-gray, and, for a moment, Jack imagined he heard a familiar voice in the breeze. He looked to the side, then behind. A ghostly chill ran through him, the odd sound reminding him of the eerie voices from his nightmare. He closed his eyes and shook his head, trying to push away the fear. When he opened them again, the voice was gone. Except for the monstrous trees and scurrying sounds from a roaming squirrel, he was alone.

He continued trudging through the mire, humming a tuneless sonata in an attempt to fill the quiet. Branches crackled ahead and he stopped to listen, gazing into the endless wall of trees. Within seconds, he heard the sound again – this time from a thicket about twenty yards to his left. He started to call out, but something stopped him. Fear? Panic? He wasn't sure and he didn't care. On automatic pilot his legs crept forward, each step burning his thigh muscles as he pulled the boots from the mud.

As the rustling sound grew louder, Jack slowed until he saw the outline of a figure standing beside a large rock. Tree limbs enveloped the area in deep shadow, making it difficult to make sense of what he saw. He squinted, and, at the same time, the figure moved. An unexpected ray of sunlight hit the egg-shaped head. For a second Jack froze, his heart beating like a hammer against his ribcage. He squinted his eyes tighter to make certain the sight before him wasn't his imagination. When he saw the head jolt upward and the eyes stare directly at him, his sense of reality clicked in. He wasn't dreaming or imagining anything. Todd stood less than ten yards in front of him, beside a waist-high boulder on which sat a pair of gloves, a long-handled ditch spade, and a black gym bag.

Rage bubbled in the pit of Jack's stomach and he rushed through the mud toward Todd. Screaming as fiery pain tore through his legs, he kept his rhythm, increasing his speed with each step. Like a heat-seeking missile, his eyes locked on the target, ready to destroy, allowing nothing to stand in his way. His animal-like howls pierced the silence, releasing the emotions he'd suppressed for so long. And, although the sound of his own voice troubled him, he knew in a way it helped propel him closer to his mark.

As Jack closed in on Todd, he saw fear in the other man's face – the wide, searching eyes looking for an escape. Todd turned to run and then stopped, one leg hanging in mid-air, when he saw Glen approach from the other direction. Now only a few feet from Todd, Jack knew this was his chance to catch his prey. With a guttural scream he lunged at Todd, knocking him down into the mire.

He gripped Todd's neck with both hands as fleeting visions of Marc's falling body pierced his mind. The pain in his heart collided with an intense loathing for Todd's shameless deception, and he tightened his fingers around Todd's throat. Todd writhed beneath him, his yellow teeth dotted with mud, desperately turning his head from side to side.

He mouthed, "It was an accident!" Pieces of dirt caught in his mouth and he coughed. "It was an accident!" he croaked. Jack squeezed his legs around Todd's waist, pinning his arms, and then loosened the grip on his neck. Todd spit dirt and tried to raise himself on his elbows, but Jack pushed him backward, forcing his head back into the mud. "He wanted to give the money back to you! I got pissed and tossed it over the balcony!"

Jack tightened his grip, feeling Todd's windpipe under his fingers. "What are you talking about, asshole? Marc didn't have the money!"

Todd struggled to free his arms from Jack's legs. Jack squeezed them harder, but loosened his hold on Todd's neck enough for him to speak.

"We took the money! Marc and me! We broke through the wall and stole it!" Todd tried to catch his breath, the tiny fragments of rock lining his lips and slipping into his mouth. He turned his head to the side and spit. "Then he wanted to give it back."

Jack's head reeled. Was Todd telling the truth? Had Marc stolen the money? Had Marc really known where the money was all the time? "You lying sack of shit!" He pushed Todd's head into the mire. "You killed him and now you're blaming him! You no good son of a bitch!"

"Jack! Stop! You're going to kill him!" Glen ran toward them. "Let him go!"

Jack tightened his grip; Glen's voice was only a muffled hum blending with the wind. Pushing Todd's head against the wet ground, he caught sight of a fist-sized rock about a foot away. With one hand still clutching Todd, Jack seized the rock and held it in the air, wondering if Todd's head would crack like an egg.

The bang was like a clap of thunder, an explosion that echoed through the trees, sending birds into flight and forest-dwelling creatures scurrying deep into their hiding places. Jack dropped the rock and looked up. Glen stood above him, his eyes wild with fear. Jack saw Doonan trudging toward them, his arm above his head; the gun in his hand still facing the sky. Two officers ran ahead of him, handcuffs clinking against their thick leather belts. Jack turned to the motionless body beneath him, released his fingers, and pulled himself to his feet. Glen crouched beside Todd and grabbed his waist, twisting and pulling, trying to position him on all fours. He hit Todd on the back in an effort to loosen whatever might be obstructing his breathing. "I hope you didn't kill him," Glen said, smacking Todd with increased force.

A few seconds later, when Todd started to cough, Glen fell backward, blowing out a sigh of relief. "Thank God," he whispered.

Doonan stood beside the boulder, examining the shovel, gloves and the gym bag filled with money. He looked down at his shoes, invisible under a layer of mud that also covered the bottom third of his designer pants. He shook his head and glared at Jack. "Didn't I tell you we had it covered?"

Jack tried to wipe the grunge from his hands onto his pants and quickly realized it was hopeless; the mud just smeared from one spot to another. "Yeah, you told me," he muttered, eyeing the bag.

Doonan turned to the two policemen and pointed to Todd, who was cursing through his bloody drool. "Take him in. And clean him up before he gets in your car. He's a mess."

Jack heard sloshing sounds behind him and turned to see David slogging through the trail he'd made while trying to catch Todd.

"What happened?" David leaned forward, breathing hard, and glanced at the policemen who were dragging Todd away. "Was that Todd?"

"Yes," Doonan said. "And before we discuss this any further, I have questions for Jack – in private."

In unison, David and Glen headed back through the mud in the direction of Jack's car. Before Doonan could speak, Jack held up his hand.

"Don't say it!" Jack started, his voice hoarse from screaming. "Yes, I knew the bag of money was somewhere around here." Jack took a deep breath. "I was watching Marc on the balcony last night, trying to see who he was talking to. All of a sudden I saw the bag fly over his head. I couldn't tell who threw it or where it came from. I just saw him reach out and try to grab it. Then he fell backwards over the wall." Jack ran his muddied fingers through his hair and shook his head like a dog shaking rain from its coat.

Doonan wiped the spray from his face. "Did I hear Todd say Marc was with him when he stole the money?"

"Yes, that's what you heard, but I don't buy it. I can't believe Marc would do that to me."

Doonan grabbed Jack's arm, positioning himself so they stood face to face. "But he also said Marc wanted to give the money back to you. If that's true, then Marc had second thoughts about what he'd done."

Jack shook his arm from Doonan's grip. "No way! Marc overdosed on Valium the night the money was stolen. He was completely passed out."

"Did you see him take the pills?" asked Doonan, reaching for his notebook.

"No, but when I came home I saw the empty pill bottle on the floor and Marc heaving over the toilet."

Doonan was silent for a few seconds. "Did you stay up all night to take care of him or did you fall asleep?"

Jack looked to the ground, trying to pull the memories from the far corners of his mind. "I fell asleep."

Doonan flipped through the pages of his book, stopping when he reached a section of his notes that was of apparent interest. "Last night you told me the morning after Marc took the pills, you woke up alone in bed. When you walked into the living-room, Marc was getting ready to leave."

Jack nodded.

"Was he getting ready to leave, or had he just returned?"

Jack's legs wobbled as he remembered the mud stains on Marc's sweatshirt, the flecks of perspiration on his face as he sat across the table. "He couldn't eat. He was sick to his stomach from vomiting all night."

"Maybe he couldn't eat because he'd already eaten." Doonan said softly, "Or maybe the guilt was making him sick."

Jack thought back to the conversation with Marc. "Why do you think you're such a bad person?" he'd asked. "Because I'm a loser," Marc had responded. Still, he couldn't believe Marc could act that well. "You should have proof before you start making accusations." He glowered at Doonan.

"I intend to. But I want you to be prepared in case we find something that implicates Marc."

Jack turned away, realizing the wind had stopped, its eerie howl replaced by silence. Glen and David waited a hundred yards away, leaning against the hood of his car. "I suppose you're going to take that bag of money with you?" he asked.

"Yes, I have to take it. But I'll have it back to you by tomorrow, Monday the latest." Doonan smiled and slipped on his sunglasses. "I'll bring it to you myself."

Jack spun around and sloshed toward his car, looking forward to walking on solid ground. At this point his left boot was missing. It must've slipped off during his struggle with Todd. He thought about turning around to retrieve it, but kept walking, imagining a scene ten years from now in which he and Jenna searched through the marshy grounds together, in search of the famous boot Uncle Jack left behind the day he recovered her fortune. But lost his faith in love.

15

Jenna perched herself atop the stone wall, her legs dangling, heels banging rhythmically against the rocks. Her grandmother sat beside her and squeezed her hand.

"Stop, Jenna," she insisted, "you'll ruin your shoes doing that."

Jenna looked down at Jack as he ran his thumb along the curve of two stones, smoothing the mortar that held them together. Feeling her stare, Jack gazed back, cupping his hand in front of his eyes to shield them from the blaring sun.

"Not only will you ruin your shoes," he said, "but the banging is about to drive us nuts!" Looking to Glen for a nod of agreement, Jack couldn't hold back his laughter – smudges of mud, like smears of eye grease used by athletes to reflect the sun, arced beneath Glen's squinting orbs. "Too sunny for you, Glen?"

Glen turned to Jack with a bewildered expression.

"Daddy," Jenna yelled, "your face is a mess! You're all dirty."

Glen wiped his face with the back of his hand and looked at John, who was completely stain-free, meticulously positioning a misshaped rock into the wall.

"Don't look at him." Jack laughed. "He's a professional. He doesn't get dirty."

The echo of distant church bells rang through the yard, and, as the twelfth chime dissipated into the air, Lisa jumped from the wall as though a five o'clock whistle had blown. "C'mon, Jenna," she said, "time for lunch."

"Who's that?" Jenna asked, one hand on her grandmother's shoulder, the other pointing to the metal gate between the front and back yards. "Who's that man?"

They all looked toward the stranger, a tall, slim figure leaning against the fence as though uncertain of his welcome. Recognizing his solid form, Jack stood, wiped both hands on his pants and motioned for Doonan to join them.

"It's a friend," Jack said as he walked to meet the chief.

After shaking hands, Doonan took a step back and examined Jack's soiled face and clothing. "Why is it that you're always covered in dirt?"

"Hmmm, a cop with a sense of humor. I didn't know you were allowed to have one."

"I found it this morning," said Doonan, removing his sunglasses and looking into Jack's eyes.

Jack nodded in approval at the cop's blue, tight-fitting tee shirt and faded jeans. "A sense of humor and civilian clothes. Is this really you?"

Doonan laughed. "Well, you said you were repairing the wall and I thought I'd stop by and help." He looked to the wall and saw only a small hole remaining. "But it looks like I'm too late."

Jack turned to the wall, then back to Doonan. "Yeah, you're late on a number of counts. You said I'd have Jenna's money back almost a week ago."

Doonan pointed his thumb behind him, in the direction of his car parked in the driveway. "I know. That's another reason I'm here. The money's in the car, along with the DVD."

Jack glanced over Doonan's shoulder, relief flooding through him.

"I had to cut through a lot of red tape, you know."

"I'm sure, and I appreciate it. Thanks for leaving it in the car. We're still hoping to keep this whole thing from Jenna. If she saw the bags, she wouldn't let up until she knew exactly what was in them."

Doonan peered behind Jack toward the four faces staring at them. "Is that her?"

Jack nodded. "Yes, why don't you come meet her?" He started to lead Doonan toward the wall, but the policeman gently grasped his arm.

"Before I meet her, can I ask you a question?"

"Sure."

"Are you still refusing to consider pressing charges against Cory and Todd? They're rotten, no good thieves. I can pin enough charges on them to put them away for a few years at least."

"No." Jack shook his head. "I really want to put this whole thing behind me." He looked deep into the teal green of Doonan's eyes. "And in a way, Marc's just as responsible as Cory and Todd. I don't want to drag his name through the courts and papers. And I really don't want to relive everything that's happened. It's not worth it. We have Jenna's money and that's all that matters."

Doonan crossed his arms and shook his head. "If that's the way you want it, you're the boss. But I really think —"

Jack held up his hand and smiled. "Look Chief, they both lost their jobs, and their faces and names were splashed all over the local news. They've become outcasts, and from what I've heard, they'll both be moving far away. I have my family and my job. Right now, that's enough for me."

"So what happens next?"

"Well, we've opened a beneficiary account in Jenna's name – an account we all have access to. Tomorrow, Glen and I will deposit the money in the bank and place the DVD in a safe deposit box." Jack looked toward the wall and gently shook his head. "Something I wish Dana had done in the first place."

"Speaking of which, the DVD was amazing," Doonan said, smiling and waving at a gawking Jenna. "She really loved that little girl. And the fact that she put you in charge of the DVD means she loved you just as much."

Jack studied Doonan's face. The expression he held made Jack feel safe somehow, as if the stranger before him had an inherent understanding of who he was and what he wanted from life. Doonan's eyes shone with so much integrity and unbounded compassion that Jack forced himself to look away. It's still too soon, he thought.

"One day I'll have to tell you the whole story, Chief."

Doonan pointed to the wall. "Well, it looks like things are beginning to get back to normal. The wall is just about fixed, the money's where it should be, and like you said, you have your job and your family. Seems like you have everything under control."

Jack flinched, thinking back to the fight he'd had with Marc the night after Dana's funeral. "It's all about control," Marc had said, "you always need to have everything in perfect order. Life just isn't that way."

Jack slid his hands into his pockets, tilting his head up toward the cloudless sky.

"Maybe that's not such a good thing," he said, returning his gaze to

Doonan's.

Doonan bit down on his lip, obviously trying to figure out the implication of Jack's statement.

Jack scratched his thighs from inside his pockets. "I mean, maybe being in control isn't all it's cracked up to be. There are too many things that can change in an instant, things we can't plan for. And if I keep trying to prepare for them, I won't be living a life. I've been in control for twenty-eight years and look where it's gotten me." Jack laughed at Doonan's baffled expression. "Look who I'm trying to explain this to – a cop, the epitome of preparedness."

Doonan ran both hands through his hair and offered Jack a flurried smile. "I guess you have a lot to teach me."

"I'm just learning myself." Jack chuckled. "But as soon as I get it down, we can begin your lessons."

"Well, can you start now by calling me Larry?"

Jack closed his eyes, pretending to ponder the request. "Uh, actually, I think I like Chief better." He looked at his family, then back to Doonan. "C'mon and join us for lunch."

Doonan slipped his sunglasses on. "Thanks, Jack, but I don't think so. I have too much to do."

"What? Go to the precinct and write some more code?" Jack asked.

Doonan smiled. "I just feel a little… strange. Helping out with the wall is okay, but sitting with your family and having lunch? I feel out of place."

Jack grabbed his arm and gave it a slight tug. "C'mon, Jenna's never met a cop. I'm sure once she gets to know you, she'll love you."

"But will everyone else?" Doonan asked, hiding behind the dark glasses.

"Give them some time," Jack replied, knowing what Doonan meant. "It's all about giving them time."

The scent of burning wood wafting through the yard flooded Jack with memories of past winters, long ago seasons filled with snow and sleighs, when life was nothing more than building snowmen and igloos. He felt an intense yearning to return to that time, to start again and do things differently, creating an existence that fit his expectation of what life should be.

"Daddy's making a fire," Jenna said, "I know it's not that cold, but I asked him to do it anyway. We could all sit around the fireplace and cuddle."

On his knees, Jack turned from the wall and stroked the soft wisps of hair that didn't quite make it into her ponytail. For a fleeting moment, the shape of her large, blue eyes and round, angelic face brought back flashes of Dana – the childhood games they'd play together, secret clubs, seashell hunts when they'd spend hours searching for just the right shells to put in their goldfish bowl. At night, unable to sleep from sunburns and anticipation, they'd sneak into the kitchen and huddle above the table of shells, meticulously designing their fish's new home.

He swallowed his emotion, not wanting to upset Jenna. "Where's Gram and Gramp?" he asked, scraping chunks of dried cement from the stone he'd just placed in the wall.

"They went with the chief to get dinner."

"Oh, so the chief is having dinner with us?" Jack asked, quickly realizing she wouldn't understand his sarcastic tone.

"Uh huh, because I invited him," she said with pride. "I like him! He's nice and he looks strong too."

Jack shook his head and smiled at her. "To be young again," he said, holding her face in his hand.

"There's still a small hole, Uncle Jack," Jenna said, pointing to the wall.

"I know sweetie, but we're out of stones." Jack glanced upward at the darkening sky. "It's getting late. I'll have to come back tomorrow and we'll dig one up that's just the right size."

Jenna grabbed his hand, pulling him toward the house.

"Where are we going?"

"You'll see, just come on!"

Jack followed, trying to shake the dirt off his clothes as they hurried across the yard and onto the deck. Jenna pulled him through the kitchen and into the living-room where she stopped to catch her breath.

"There," she said, pointing to the staircase.

Jack looked to the stairs. His body froze when he saw a large stone leaning on the railing, halfway up the stairs, in the same spot it had been in his dream. He put his hand over his heart and took a deep breath. "Where did that come from?" he asked, unable to find his full voice.

"I brought it in last week, but it was so heavy I couldn't make it up the stairs all the way, so I left it there. I think it looks nice. It's my lucky stone."

Jack walked warily to the stairs, slowly climbing each step. He almost expected to hear the same noises he'd heard in his nightmare –

the screams, the eerie hum – but, except for the sound of Jenna's breathing and the crackling of burning logs, the house was quiet.

He grabbed the stone with both hands and turned it upside down and side to side. You're being paranoid. Let it go. "This will fit perfectly into the hole. Now we can close it up for good. Do you want to help me put it in or…"

When he looked up, Jenna was gone, the pitter-patter of her footsteps already tapping across the kitchen floor.

Dusk was settling in and Jack turned on the spotlights as he walked out the sliding glass door onto the deck. He could see Jenna through the bushes, standing by the wall, her arms crossed, each foot alternately kicking the stones. "Okay," he said, holding the rock over his head, "I want you to put this last one in."

Jenna jumped up and down with excitement. "What do I do? What do I do?"

Jack dropped the stone on the ground and slid the masonry glove onto his hand. He scooped wet mortar from the canister, plopped it into the opening and spread it evenly over the surrounding rock.

"I'll put it in," he said, lifting the stone, "and you'll put the finishing touches on it, okay?"

"Okay," Jenna whispered, standing like a soldier awaiting her next order.

As he positioned the stone, he felt a gentle breeze hit his face – a cool, wisp-like flow of air from the hole. He crouched down to investigate the opening and saw a trace of movement, an almost invisible stream of fog wafting about, seeping through the shadows of stone.

Jack turned to Jenna who squatted beside him with anticipation. "Did you see that?" he whispered.

"See what?" she asked, placing her hand on Jack's shoulder and leaning over to get a better view. Jack turned back to show her, but the movement had stopped. The fog was gone.

"See what?" Jenna leaned harder on Jack's shoulder, trying to see something that wasn't there.

Jack shook his head. "Nothing, it must've been my imagination. I'm just a little tired, I guess." He tried to forget what he'd seen, but the hair standing on the back of his neck said something different.

He twisted and turned the stone into the opening until it was positioned just right. Filling his hand with another scoop of mortar, he leaned over the wall and smeared the dripping cement onto the other side of the stone and into the gaps before smoothing it with the tips of his fingers.

"Now it's your turn," Jack said, sliding the other masonry glove onto Jenna's tiny hand. He daubed mortar deep into the remaining crevices. "Now use your glove to smooth it out."

Together, they patted and flattened the mortar, smoothing it down until the patch resembled the rest of the wall.

"There!" Jack pulled the glove from Jenna's hand, tossed it onto the ground, and dropped his beside hers. "We're all done."

Jenna smacked her hands together. "We're done!" she yelled, almost tripping as she ran up the deck steps and into the arms of her grandfather. "We're done!"

Jack turned and delicately rubbed his fingers along the wall. He thought about Dana – imagining her in the house, setting plates on the dining room table, asking Jenna for the third time to wash her hands. He held back the tears, realizing he'd never see his sister again.

Backing away from the stone wall, Jack's shadow, cast by the spotlights behind him, lengthened along the ground with each step he took. The wall was once again solid; the hole only visible in the memories of those who knew. He watched in silence as a second shadow appeared beside his, a flowing darkness that made him question the reality of the moment. When he felt a hand fall softly on his shoulder, he let out a deep sigh of relief and closed his eyes, wondering if Doonan would have enough mortar to fill the hole in his heart.

A Word From Rob

I hope you enjoyed reading "In the Shadow of Stone" as much as I enjoyed writing it! I'd love to hear your thoughts about the book, the characters and anything else you liked (or didn't)!

You can always write an Amazon review or contact me anytime at Rob@AuthorRobKaufman.com

Also, if you liked "In the Shadow of Stone", I'm sure you'll enjoy reading my other books. Learn more about them at Amazon by using the links below…

The Perfect Ending
A Broken Reality
One Last Lie

ALTERED
(Justin Wright Series – Book 1)

Thanks again for reading "In the Shadow of Stone"!

To receive emails about my new books, events and news, sign up for my mailing list at www.AuthorRobKaufman.com.

9 781096 302186